# Waking the Echoes of Fate

A. Elliott

ISBN 979-8-9985026-6-8

Cover design by J.N. Ignacio

*For Justin,*
*without whom this book would not have been written.*

*Thank you for the way you love me loudly,*
*For your unwavering belief in everything I do,*
*And for always being my home.*

*In the hands of forgotten daughters,*

*a hidden truth is kept.*

*When the bloodline thins to one,*

*the roots of fate are met.*

*The end will soon begin,*

*foretold in ash and creed.*

*A key shaped in shadow will wake,*

*and she who bears it will bleed.*

Prologue

Trust no one. Those were the last words my mother ever spoke to me.

At the age of seven, I sat on the floor next to my mother's bed as she lost herself to delusions, sweat rolling off her skin. On the day of her death, she placed a small stone in my hand. Its color was that of frost, and despite it being held in her warm hands, it was cold to the touch. The stone contained what looked like many runes once carved into its surface, no longer legible. I kept that stone, always hidden in my pocket, because it was the last thing she'd given me.

Weeks after her death, I woke to a wrinkled face looking down at me, long white hair pulled into a braid. The owner, a woman whom I'd never met before, grabbed my hand and tried to pull me from my bed.

"Come, Child," she whispered. "And bring the key."

A chill shot through me, but I gave in to her efforts, something compelling me to follow. Dressed in only my linen nightdress, I trailed behind her as she deftly made her way through my home and into the night air.

We entered the forest and walked for what felt like forever, though it couldn't have been more than an hour. My feet ached with every stab of a twig or cut from a rock. Of course, I hadn't thought to put on shoes.

After some time, we arrived at a small fire, where a cloaked figure was waiting, watching. My heart hammered in my chest as their gaze locked with mine, the fire illuminating a face covered in black symbols.

"She has the key?" the figure asked.

The woman stared down at me before saying, "The stone, Child."

A moment passed before I realized what they could've meant, and I pulled my mother's stone from my small dress pocket. I reached out to give it to the figure, but they recoiled at my offering.

"I cannot touch it. This ceremony belongs to you," they said with a shake of their head. "Keep it in your hand."

The fire crackled as something was thrown into it, and sounds I'd never heard before left the figure's lips. My head became laden, and my vision started to spin as the smoke from the fire thickened.

The elderly woman left my side and knelt in the dirt, raising her head to the figure. Before I realized what was happening, fire glinted off a blade as it was dragged across her neck. She fell to the ground, and the sound of her breath fighting against the rise of blood escaping her body began to haunt me. I looked down, afraid to see whatever would happen next.

Instead, I focused on the blood as it ran across the ground and reached for me. My eyes closed just before it touched my skin, but I couldn't hide from the metallic smell that filled my nose or the sticky warmth that coated my feet, mixing with the dirt already caked there. My earlier regret of forgetting my shoes felt childish, as if the blood not being able to touch my skin would've been enough to save me.

I felt the presence of the figure standing in front of me even before opening my eyes. Shaking, I looked up.

"You, Child, are the key bearer. The gods will be watching you, now that they know you hold it. You must guard it. The cost of this secret is great, and the payment is always in blood," they said. Then, they reached up and slit their own throat. For so long, I thought they meant their blood, and I couldn't have been more wrong.

For a long time, I stood where they left me, unsure of what to do next. I wished that someone would come for me, to take me home. But when I finally gave up on the notation that my father would somehow know to find me, I opened my eyes, swallowing hard at what lay before me. Turning, I started back the way I thought we'd come. I hadn't made it far when a woman on a dark horse entered my path.

"Hello, Little One... The Norns were not kind when they wove your fate." She watched me for a moment, but if she noticed the blood covering my body or the tremors crashing through me, her melodic voice gave nothing away. "The Aesir have given you too great a task for one your age, content to sit back and watch..." She paused, seeming to go far away in thought, before her face contorted, something rippling through her. "I will do what they will not. The Night has a gift for you, Child. It will be for you to decide if you will hone it."

The woman slid down from her horse, taking a few steps forward. She bent down, reaching out to me, but it was velvet shadows that caressed my skin. Then, she was gone. I don't know how I made it back to my bed that night, but I do know I dreamt of the gods.

The sagas tell of how the gods belonged to another world, worshiped and revered by the people they created. The full truth of what happened is not known, but it is said that one day a new god surfaced, much younger than the twelve. As love for him grew, the people began to lose faith in the Aesir. This eventually led to their death in that world and the creation of this one.

The Aesir still loved their children, so they created us in the light of those that followed them before, giving us their languages and customs, as well as the freedom to make our own. But our gods are vengeful, and the one thing they did before abandoning that world to the young god was lock their trickster with him, for they believed him to be responsible for this new god surfacing. Now, the path through Yggdrasil is blocked; the only means of opening it, lost long ago.

# Chapter One

If this had been anything but a sword fight, I wouldn't be disarmed, lying in the dirt on my ass. But here I am, waiting for the breath to return to my body. A broad hand blocks the blue sky above me; I place mine inside of it as it lifts me.

"You have to work on your balance, or this is going to keep happening," Erik says.

"You've been saying this for years. At some point, we have to accept swords aren't my thing." I place the practice sword back with the others before heading toward the table of water.

"You're great with a bow, but you won't always have the

distance. You have to learn to use a sword."

The glare I shoot his way is enough to make him stop talking. Erik and I have been training together since childhood, and I know the speech he's about to give me word for word. *A sword provides the greatest reach; daggers are no match against a swordsman. While you might be fast, you could never win in hand-to-hand combat against a man. Once he grabs you, you'll be overpowered.* I have heard it a thousand times. And although I'd been training almost my entire life, I had never needed to use any of it. My father forced me to start training with my brother and Erik sometime before my tenth name-day, but Hagen stopped training with me years ago. I think I only keep up with it to hold onto some form of normalcy in my life.

"Fine, I'll leave it alone—for now." His hands push his light brown hair, damp with sweat, away from his face. His expression changes, face softening, as he takes me in.

"Will I be seeing you tonight?"

I hate catching him looking at me like I set the sun in his sky. He must realize I don't look at him the same way.

"You saw me last night, and a few nights before that."

"But I want to see you every night." Erik steps closer to me, wrapping his arm around my waist and pulling me toward him.

Thankfully, the training grounds are empty this late in the

evening. Someone seeing us is the last thing I need.

"I told you this had to stay casual." I push out of his grasp, giving him a pointed look.

"Fine, I *casually* want to see you every night. I don't know what you're so worried about. It's not like the village doesn't expect us to end up together."

"No one expects that. Besides, I'm sure Hagen needs you for something this evening."

He and my brother have been friends as long as I can remember. When Hagen took over as Jarl of Thurisa after our father's death, Erik was appointed as his general. As for me, I exist here, mostly. Some days it feels as though I'm more wraith than person. I help where I'm needed, stay out of the way when I'm not.

I know sleeping with my brother's closest friend is wrong, but he's beautiful, and I was lonely when I finally gave in. His feelings have been clear for a few years, but I pretend I don't notice. I hoped I'd been clear that we would never be anything, but the longer things go on, the more the line blurs. Regardless, tonight I plan to usher in my name-day at home, alone, with a book.

"Oh, that reminds me, Hagen asked to speak with you after training,"

Great.

We find my brother where he usually is, in a small office at the back of our Great Hall. He sits at an old desk in the center of the room, the smell of books and parchment greeting us before Hagen can be bothered to. His desk, like the walls, is stacked with books and cluttered with paper.

Like me, he has our mother's features, dark hair and green eyes, though his have the start of crinkles in the corners. He's tall like our father, but slighter than he was. It's strange to think that he and I are all that's left of what was once a family. Are adults without parents still considered orphans, or is that title only reserved for children?

Hagen is unwed, which is unwise given that we have no other siblings. Not that our village is all that grand, but Hagen has done a great job strengthening our position as a trading port in the last few years. This has brought added wealth to Thurisa's citizens, but if something were to happen to him,

I'm not sure how they would feel about me as his heir.

The first leader of Thurisa, a distant ancestor of my father's, was a woman. She is known for being a great leader; sagas are still told of her to this day, though Thurisa has not been led by a woman since.

"Ah Thyrvi, I have something I was hoping we could discuss before your Name-Day," he says, looking up with a smile and gesturing to a chair across from him. "Erik, since you're already here, you might as well stay."

Shuffling through the layers of correspondence, he pulls out a piece of parchment, the seal already broken. "I have received an interesting proposition from Kenaz. It seems our growth over the last few years has captured the attention of King Langavin. He is offering a partnership that would open the door to many opportunities for Thurisa, as well as bring us under his protection."

I don't know much about the king, or Kenaz itself for that matter, aside from it being the largest city, located multiple days to the Northeast of us. It is likely that many merchants pass through here on their way to Kenaz or receive shipments in Thurisa that eventually make their way to the city. The king, once a jarl, gained his crown at a young age and is responsible for uniting many villages under his rule, effectively putting a stop to inner island raids. Raids between villages are almost nonexistent these days, other than the last one. In theory, raids from the sea could still happen, but many of the port villages have closed, having moved inward a long time ago. Thurisa is the only functioning port, though some people do build homes along the coast.

"Looks like we'll have two reasons to celebrate tomorrow!" Erik says, giving my brother a joyful smile, Hagen doesn't return.

But there's obviously more to it than what he's chosen to lead with; there always is with my brother.

"What's the catch?" I ask, less enthused. Hagen looks down for a moment before continuing to speak.

"We'll owe fealty to the king, provide aid in the defense of other villages, as they will for us, should it come to it. A few smaller political matters... and he requests your hand in marriage to his second son."

There it is. The reason he's having a real conversation with me as opposed to a few polite words in passing. When his eyes meet mine, I can see he's braced for a reaction.

Erik stands. "No!"

If I could kill someone with just a look, I'm not sure which of them I'd choose first.

Hagen keeps his eyes locked with mine, ignoring Erik's outburst as if he'd been waiting for it.

He knew.

My stomach sinks. How long has he known about Erik and

me? The realization is more concerning than the potential of an arranged marriage.

"Listen, I've always known my marriage would be one to benefit Thurisa, and if King Langavin had a daughter, I would take your place," Hagen says before taking a long breath. "Father wished for you to be able to marry for love, and if you tell me you've been fucking my best friend for the better part of a year because you love him, then you have my blessing. Is that what you two are telling me?"

I can only imagine the sight of my jaw hitting the ground as those words left his mouth. Okay, I'd kill him first.

If this was some kind of payback, I walked into this room woefully unprepared.

I don't love Erik. I don't need to examine my feelings to know that. I haven't actually thought about marrying anyone, but even if I did, it wouldn't be him.

The issue of marriage was going to come up at some point. I guess I hoped I was going to avoid it, given everything else. Taking a long breath, I feel Erik's eyes on me as Hagen raises his eyebrow, as if prompting me to respond. I slightly shake my head no, and I hear wood hitting the ground before I can look Erik's way. In his haste to leave the room, he knocked over his chair, slamming the door behind him.

"You didn't have to do that! We could have had this discussion alone," I say, letting my annoyance spill into my tone.

"Maybe, but he deserved it for even allowing a relationship between you two. Did he really think I wouldn't notice? His feelings have always been obvious, but him no longer fucking every woman that travels through Thurisa was a dead giveaway." Hagen leans back in his chair, head braced in his hand as if he's already sick of dealing with this.

"I'm the one who chose to hide it."

"Oh, I know, dear sister. He would've shouted it from the rooftops had you allowed it."

I stand needing to move and walk over to the bottle of dark liquor he keeps stocked, pouring us each a drink. It's obviously going to be a long evening. Handing him a glass, I lean against a bookshelf.

"What about the offer, Thyrvi? I know you're bored here. This would raise our status. You could get out of Thurisa, have a fresh start, see new things, and do new things. You might even learn to like the guy. If you don't, and the whole thing is unbearable, you'd still have the option to annul at the Winter Solstice." He pauses, looking around the room with a sigh. "I'll be arranging my own marriage after this as well."

Is this the point we have reached in life? Long gone are the dreams of love, the magic and fairy tales over. Now we're letting our futures be dictated by practicality and a solid offer? Trading one monotony for another. Our parents would be so proud. Hand-fasting is more of a trial, but once the Winter Solstice arrives, you can either end things or proclaim your marriage to the gods. Which means no one gets married from November through March. I'd be cutting it close in October.

"When you say it like that, it sounds so romantic," I joke, taking a long drink from my cup and letting the burn overpower my shock for a moment. "How long ago did you receive this offer?"

"Just yesterday evening. I wanted to think things over before I brought it to you."

"And when do I need to give you an answer?" I ask.

"A messenger hand-delivered it. They're waiting in the village for your response."

"What do you know about my potential husband?" I ask, realizing there's another person in this situation as well.

"Admittedly, not much. Theorin, the first son, has a bit of a wild reputation. The second son, Gaelen, less is known of. I believe he travels often, something you might enjoy."

The truth is, Hagen isn't wrong. I'm bored out of my mind, and I don't have a future here. The village has mostly moved on, but it's a reminder of the past and everything that happened.

"And what's in it for you?"

"This would benefit Thurisa. That's always my goal. It's true, it would come with a political rise and additional connections, but that can only help us further grow."

I'm sure there's more to it that he isn't telling me. Hagen never does anything without maximizing the gain.

"And just how far are you wanting to grow, *dear brother?*" His eyes, always calculating, lock with mine, but he doesn't answer the question. A chill makes its way up my spine, and I know I can't push the issue anymore. I know if I do, I'll find that I didn't actually have a choice in this matter to begin with. I'm going to agree anyway, it makes the most sense for our village. So, there's no point in destroying my sense of autonomy tonight. I take a deep breath, holding it in for a second before exhaling.

"Fine, I'll do it." Pushing off the wall of books, I walk out of the room. I don't think many people in the village will be saddened by my departure; most will likely be indifferent, but this is my family's legacy. My father loved this village deeply, and if I can help protect it and allow it to grow, it's an easy choice.

## Chapter Two

As the sun rises on my Name-Day, it's hard not to think of my parents. They should be here, enjoying the celebration with everyone else. They had truly loved each other, and my father was so different after my mother's death. I don't think they would approve of what I've agreed to do, but I know there's no backing out now. Hagen's satisfied face at my acceptance revealed he'd wanted this far more than I realized.

I catch myself twisting my bracelet. My mother's stone, now wrapped in leather and secured to my wrist. No one has sought or even mentioned it since that night. I never told anyone about it, or that night, and who would believe me if I did? To me, it's just something that was hers, a comfort on the worst days.

Gathering myself, I finish pulling my hair back, tying it into a single braid, and wrapping it in a bun. Its dark contrast with my skin really brings out the circles under my eyes. I stayed up later than I should have, contemplating my conversation with Hagen. When I finally fell asleep, the dreams began.

I often dream of the goddess—the melody of her voice, the soft caress of her shadows. A few years passed before I pieced together that the woman I met that night was the goddess Nott, older than the Aesir, but spoken little about. Some dreams are more memory; I can always tell those apart because of the blood. Other times, she rides Hrimfaxi across the sky or comes to me holding an owl. She always repeats the same things she said that night.

Every time but one. *The Tree*. Mentioned once and never again.

Shaking my head as if to clear it, I change into a linen shirt and a pair of leggings, heading outside. I inhale the fresh air and close my eyes as the sun warms my face. Before I can open them again, a hand wraps around my arm.

Of course, it's Erik.

"Let me go," I say, pulling my arm out of his grasp.

"You don't have to do this! We can marry—Hell, we can leave! Anywhere you want."

The desperation in his voice catches me off guard as I take in his appearance. I thought I didn't sleep well last night, but looking at Erik, I'm not sure he slept at all. His hair is disheveled, the stubble on his face longer than I've ever seen it. Actually, he's still in yesterday's clothes. This is my fault. Where did I go wrong? Aside from the night I started it to begin with. I never should have allowed things to continue for so long.

"I can talk to him! We can figure this out." He gestures to the building where my brother likely still resides. People walking by start to turn, noticing the scene taking place.

"I'm sorry you're upset. Nothing about how last night went is ideal. But I was clear this was never going anywhere." I try to keep my tone down to avoid attracting more attention.

"You're not an idiot, Thyrvi, you know I care about you. I thought us being together in secret was your strange process of accepting that we're meant to be together."

"I'm sorry if I gave you the wrong impression, but I've always been clear that we were never going to be anything more than physical. I was never looking for anything serious."

"Nothing serious? You just agreed to marry a man you've never met." His tone changes from a desperate plea to something harsher.

"That's different, and you know it. Now, if you'll excuse me, I have someplace to be."

I don't. I never do. He likely knows that, too. Still, I have to walk away before this turns into something we'll both regret.

It's not as if being married to Erik would be terrible. He would treat me well, and he already knows his way around my body. Still, I can't resign him, or myself, to a life of watching him love me, knowing I'll never reciprocate it. I knew sleeping with him the first time was a mistake, but I needed someone. I assumed the novelty would wear off, and he'd move on to someone new, as he always has. I didn't realize I was going to lose the only friendship I still have left.

I make my way down the road toward the Branton's bakery, my favorite place for pastries. After the morning rush, Earie starts working on recipes for the next day. I know she'll let me help her and give me a place to hide from Erik.

I've known the Brantons my whole life. Earie always knows when I need a task and when I want to be left alone. She was my mother's best friend, and the only person I have left who tells me stories of her. I don't want to talk today, though. There's been enough of that. I just need something to occupy my mind in the one place that still feels like home.

At this hour, the village is already filled with merchants making their way to the docks, carts being pulled by horses with goods being shipped out or brought in. When my grandparents and parents were around, Thurisa wasn't always this busy. It was just those who lived here. Even more so after my mother's death, my father becoming more concerned with outsiders, and potential raids. With his precautions and the village strengthening its militia, most of it stopped. With many inner island villages united under Kenaz, I don't think the others wanted to take the risk. The raid that killed my father was the first in years. We haven't had another since.

Our militia trains each morning with Erik. Though most of the men have jobs and roles in the village, they all have shifts on the gates and, most importantly, the docks. All boats wishing to make port in Thurisa must be searched and properly taxed. People mumble about missing the "old days", but the truth is, everyone here has significantly prospered from Hagen's choices.

That's why I'll continue to do whatever it takes, whatever Hagen asks of me. I might not like it, or him, most of the time, but I know him, and whatever he's doing will help the village, even if it benefits him. Agreeing is the least I can do.

## Chapter Three

"Would you like to discuss whatever it is you're taking out on that dough?" Earie asks.

I've been here for the better part of the day, though we haven't spoken much. I don't know how I feel about everything enough to explain it to another person, and she's usually not one to press things until I'm ready.

"No... I don't know." Sighing, I shake my head. "Hagen has a plan, as usual. I just wasn't prepared for it."

"Ah. Yes, since your brother was young, he has always had some grand idea or another. But that doesn't mean you have to let him pull you into it."

"I'll be fine. I'm just processing everything."

"If you're sure … But I'll be here when you're ready to talk about it. For now, I think you have a party to get ready for."

I look out the window to find the evening has already arrived. I say goodbye, rushing out of the door and into the filling streets. Looking down, I realize I'm covered in flour. I'll have to be a bit late then. People, mostly locals, are making their way to the great hall, but those here for the port are welcome to attend as well. It's not that they're all coming to celebrate my Name-Day. No one misses the events held in the great hall, and most importantly, free ale.

After making it back to my room, I quickly wash the flour out of my hair and comb through it, leaving the curls to fall loosely around my shoulders. Standing in front of my wardrobe, looking at the practical dresses and abundance of tunics and leggings, I settle on a blue dress, fitted in the bodice, with a square cut neckline. The skirt falls loosely, and I grab a pair of comfortable brown flats that will make dancing easier.

I've heard the style is more elaborate in busier towns like Kenaz. Our seamstress shop has beautiful and delicate fabrics, but Brynja usually creates dresses with those to sell to shops in other towns. There's no need for them in Thurisa.

The hall has filled by the time I arrive; everyone starting to drink and welcome each other. Many of them won't be standing by the end of the night.

Scanning the room, I see Hagen speaking with someone I haven't seen before, and he hands them a folded parchment. The messenger from Kenaz, I would assume, casually holding the paper that will change my life forever as though it's nothing. But if he's here, maybe I could use this to my advantage. Surely someone from Kenaz would have more information about my "betrothed".

I grab a drink, watching as the man retreats to a table off to the side, currently occupied by two other men.

"Thyrvi!" Hagen shouts, pulling my attention from the messengers' table, gesturing for me to come to the front of the hall.

Wincing, my newly obtained cup of ale and I make our way toward him. At least we can get this part over with early.

"My dearest sister! Today is her twenty-fifth Name-Day, and

the reason we celebrate!"

Cheers sound through the hall, everyone glad of the reason to drink.

"I'm also pleased to announce that she's received an offer of marriage that's going to bring great growth to Thurisa! So, in her honor, let's drink!"

Congratulations echo through the hall, and I feel the bile reaching up my throat at his words. People start to move in my direction, to be cordial, as if they don't ignore my existence most days. I should've realized he'd announce it tonight. The more people he tells, the less chance I have of backing out. I down my ale before I can vomit on all of the people pushing in towards me, using my empty cup as an excuse for escape.

I look for Erik in the crowd, but I don't see him. It's for the best he missed the announcement, but a pang of sadness hits me at the thought he'd skip my name-day. I might not want to marry him, but I'm realizing I did come to depend on his constant presence.

I take my time before making my way over to the messenger's table. The more time they have to drink, the better. I dance with Len Branton first, my father's friend and general, before Hagen appointed Erik to the position. He often trains with me, not trusting Erik to supervise my training alone.

A few of the older men from the village ask too, being polite. The men my age here avoid me, once due to my childhood, but they quickly overcame that around puberty. No, now it's likely because of Erik.

After enough time has passed for everyone to have had a few rounds of ale, the visiting men from the docks find their courage. This used to be my favorite part of the evening, all of us drunk enough to drop our inhibitions but not yet sloppy. The musicians read the room, picking up the pace as everyone cheers, and more people make their way onto the dance floor.

I've been keeping my eye on the table with the messenger from Kenaz. Noticing when two of his companions stand, walking away, cups in hand. Seeing my chance, I grab another drink and make my way over, quickly taking one of the newly opened seats. The conversation immediately stops, and the remaining two men look at me, seemingly unsure of what to do next.

"Hi, I'm Thyrvi," I say, looking at my target. A smirk of amusement crosses his face.

He isn't what you would expect from a messenger, more a bear of a man, really. His dirty blond hair is pulled into a bun at the nape of his neck, and his full beard makes him seem more like a warrior than someone who goes around arranging marriages. If I had to guess, he is in his mid-thirties.

"I saw the jarl's announcement. We wanted to wish you a

happy Name-Day, but you seemed occupied."

He gestures between himself and the other man as he says we. I smile politely at his companion before turning back.

"And what is your name? I assume you're from Kenaz?"

"You assume correctly. My name is Bjark. What is it that I can do for you? Brother force you into this, so you're hoping to find a way out?"

Well, that was direct.

"Um, no, I agreed to the arrangement." I take a large drink of my ale before continuing. "My brother didn't have much information about my would-be husband. I was hoping you could enlighten me."

A low chuckle reverberates through Bjark's body.

"I don't know the prince as well as my friend here does. I'm sure he'd be glad to fill you in." He stands, slapping the other man's shoulders. "I'd better go see that Soren and Rorik haven't found themselves in any trouble."

I watch as he walks away. I can't believe how quickly he got out of this.

Inhaling deeply, once, before I turn to look at the other man, actually noticing him this time. His dark hair is kept shorter than Bjark's, but still long enough for some pieces to fall forward into his eyes. Eyes that are pools of dark slate. His beard is full, but kept closer to his face.

I watch as his lips form a smirk. He clears his throat before he pushes the hair back out of his face. Clearly, he noticed I was staring. I close my eyes for a moment. None of this is going as planned. Not that I have a real plan. Drinking less would've probably been a good starting point.

"So, Thyrvi." He says my name slowly, as if testing how it feels in his mouth. "What is it you would like to know?"

His eyes land on my hair, which I can only imagine is a tangle of curls and sweat after dancing.

"Anything, just what kind of person he is, mostly. Hagen mentioned that he travels."

"Yes. He travels a lot for the king. He's never in Kenaz for very long."

"I would often be alone then?" I ask, not intending to say it out loud, but the words tumble out of my mouth at this point.

Amusement is evident on his face. "I doubt that."

"Are you close with him then?"

"Closer than many."

"Then what kind of person is he? What things does he enjoy?"

The smirk returns to his face, and he takes a large drink of his ale.

"I'll make you a deal. Dance with me, and I'll answer your questions," he says, nodding toward the dance floor.

"I don't even know you."

"That didn't stop you when you danced with those other men. It's your Name-Day, you're supposed to be having fun!"

"I am having fun, and dancing with them was different."

"How so?" He stands, offering his hand for me to take.

"Well, I get the impression you're trying to distract me, and they weren't."

"They were trying to distract you, just from the voice inside your head telling you not to sleep with them tonight," he says with a laugh.

"What's your name?"

"If you come dance with me, maybe I'll tell you."

I stare at him before downing the rest of my ale, and wondering how I lost control so quickly. Before I know it, my hand is in his, and a smile is spreading across his face. He is probably the most beautiful man I've ever seen.

After several dances, my dress is plastered to my body, and I need more ale. He finds us full cups and gestures to the door. Outside, I pause, appreciating the chilled air hitting my skin. It's refreshing after being in the hall, packed with people.

"How is it that you're turning twenty-five today and yet unwed?" he asks.

It's not unheard of, but I admit it's uncommon, and slightly frowned upon for one to still be unwed, given my family's political role. I'm lucky Hagen never pushed the issue sooner.

"My father loved my mother. They grew up together in the

village and fell in love as teens. She died when I was seven, but I remember how they were with each other, the stories they would tell of the times before my brother and I came. He was never the same after her death and hoped my brother and I would marry for love," I say, looking up at the night sky. "He died a few years ago. My brother has plans and ambitions, so I should've known this was coming."

He raises an eyebrow. "You said you agreed to the marriage?"

"I did agree, but I didn't know we were at this point. It's not something I would've sought out. It's a political move for my brother, but he's done a lot for the village, and in his own way, has helped everyone here." I pause to take a breath. "To be honest with you, I want to leave. I don't have a real role, and there certainly isn't anyone here I would want to spend my life with. So, I'm looking at this as my way of helping."

A thought immediately comes to mind. I'm so stupid for not thinking of it sooner.

"Oh gods. He isn't in love with someone, is he? Someone he already hoped to marry? Was he forced into this?"

Marrying someone while they love someone else would be just as bad as marrying someone I could never love, but who loved me. The sound of his amusement pulls me from my panicked thoughts.

"No, I don't know that he's ever been in love."

34

"Oh. Yeah, me either. What about you? Married?" I ask.

"No, it's never really been a focus of mine, and I don't stay in one place for very long."

"I've always wanted to travel and see the world, meet new people, and read new books. I've never left Thurisa, though."

"You will soon."

His hand reaches out and touches the curl that has fallen in my face, sliding it between his fingers. I don't know why, but the act makes my stomach flip, and I suck in my lower lip. His eyes fixate on my mouth.

"I hope you had a nice Name-Day, Thyrvi," he says, drawing out my name again.

I feel a pang of disappointment as he lets go of that curl. For a second, I thought he was going to kiss me, which is a ridiculous thought given the reason we're here. I've likely had too much ale, and since these aren't sailors leaving in the morning, I can't afford the trouble this will get me in.

"You didn't tell me your name or answer my questions." I realize I'm trying to prevent the night from ending, and it isn't subtle.

"My name is Eldrin, and if I tell you everything you want to know now, you won't have a reason to find me tomorrow. Goodnight, Thyrvi." He winks and offers a mocking bow before turning and walking away.

## Chapter Four

I didn't think to ask about timing last night, but knowing how soon I'm expected to leave would be helpful. I can't leave Thurisa without resolving the situation with Erik, which is why I find myself standing in the training yard instead of finding food to cure this morning's hangover.

The yard is filled with the clashing of swords, the twang of bow strings being released, and the sound of the usual chatter from those training or standing around. But there is no sign of Erik. Strange as I have never known him to miss practice.

I head towards the town square, hoping to catch him as he

passes through, but the sweet aroma of bread and sugar captures my attention, and my stomach.

"Thyrvi, I was hoping you would stop in today," Earie says from behind the counter. Her dark hair is pulled back into a bun, but the curls starting to gray around her temples are breaking free. She's in her fifties now, the proof beginning to show on her face, though I think it complements her beauty.

"Is that so?" I ask with a smile.

"I heard the announcement last night, but you seemed to be having a nice time, so I didn't want to interrupt." I know she's waiting to see if I'll choose to elaborate, but as much as I love her, I won't. Not yet, at least.

"Yes, Hagen couldn't wait to announce it."

"I'd be honored if you'd let me make your dress."

A look comes over her face that tells me she's thinking of my mother.

"It's really nice of you to offer, but I know how busy you are with the bakery."

It would take up so much of her time, and I would feel guilty.

"Were your mother still with us, she and I would be doing it together. Let me do this for her," she says firmly, knowing I won't protest after that.

"Fine, but only if you let me help here if you need it," I say. "And we're making Hagen pay for the fabric."

We both laugh and agree to the deal. Before leaving, I purchase a pastry with baked sweet cheese and make my way to a bench outside.

Not seconds after taking my first bite, I hear my name being yelled from behind me. I turn to find Saoirse, Earie's daughter, making a beeline in my direction. Our families have a long-standing friendship, and I love her parents, so I see her in passing all the time. That said, she hasn't directly sought me out in years.

"I need to speak with you," she says.

I can only imagine the confusion written on my face, mid-bite of pastry. I quickly chew, not savoring any of it as I had hoped to do.

"About what?" I ask, just as uncouth as I'm feeling right now.

"I wish to come with you when you leave." She pulls her mass of red hair away from her face. The only thing she got from her father.

"But you hate me." I all but choke out my response.

"I don't hate you. We're adults now, I think we can leave the past where it belongs," she says before exhaling. "Besides, you can't go to Kenaz alone, and I need out of here."

"I most certainly can, and will, go alone." Annoyed with her response, I glance back at my pastry. "I see you multiple times per week, and we act as though the other doesn't exist. You can't just decide you're leaving with me and expect me to go along with it."

"Look, this is stupid, but if you need to hear me say it, fine. When we were younger, I had feelings for Erik. I was jealous of his feelings for you, and I hated how you would ignore him. By the time I was mature enough to realize the situation for what it was, it was too late to go back. I was stubborn, and it was easier just to leave things the way they were than admit the truth."

"Wow. You must really want to leave to admit that." I turn back to face her when she laughs.

"That's an understatement. There isn't anything left for me here."

I realize then that she's referring to her husband. He died in the same battle as my father, and suddenly, this conversation makes so much more sense. They got married after our friendship had already ended, so I don't know much about it. They weren't married long, but every time I saw her, she looked happy.

Admittedly, I don't know how she took his death, too busy with my own grief, but I can imagine. Especially since she's standing here asking this of me now.

"I guess it wouldn't be awful to know someone there. Will your parents be upset?"

"No, I already told them. Besides, they love you, so they're worried about you leaving."

I nod, not really knowing how to respond to that.

"And your solution is to come with me, giving them another thing to worry about?"

"My father doesn't worry about my ability to use a sword," she says, giving me a pointed look. "They will worry, but they will feel better if we're together. Besides, they understand why I need to leave."

"Alright. I'll figure it out," I say, wondering if I should tell Bjark or if Eldrin can handle this. It's not as though I've ever hated her. I didn't understand what happened at the time. I'm still not sure I do. I always assumed that being my friend became too much. Being so young was hard enough without having a friend whom people feared.

"So... how'd Erik take the news?" she asks with a grin.

We jumped from speaking ten words a year to gossiping pretty quickly. I guess it's not that surprising when Saoirse knows everything that happens in the village.

"Not well, he was pretty mad at me. I was hoping to talk to him this morning and clear the air."

I can see the remnants of our old friendship scratching their way to the surface, but having this conversation with her doesn't completely feel natural yet.

"That's unlikely. He was pretty drunk last night. I heard he made a bit of a scene. He's probably sleeping it off. Or he's too embarrassed to show his face. Besides, you don't owe him anything; he knew what you were willing to give. He chose his path anyway."

"Maybe. Did you see what happened?"

"Not maybe, you know I'm right. And no, Erik hadn't even shown up yet when I left. I have my sources, though."

She always has.

"I need to get back and help mother, but come find me when you have more details about our adventure out of here!"

Perhaps she's right. At least, I probably don't need to be standing out here waiting for him. It's then that I notice one of the men from Eldrin and Bjark's table entering Ula's tavern. They must be staying there. It's popular with travelers, mostly merchants. There's another tavern closer to the docks, but it's usually filled with sailors. It's the best option for a night out if you want a smaller chance of village locals spotting you.

I entered the tavern before I even realized I was walking toward it. It's almost empty, which makes sense given the hour. I find Ula behind the counter, preparing for the day. She's a sturdy, no-nonsense type of woman. The kind of person who does well running a tavern, as people tend not to question her authority. But she's also incredibly friendly.

"Good morning," I say with a smile.

She turns and looks at me, suspicion on her face. The only

time she sees me in this tavern while the sun is out is if I'm trying to sneak out of a room upstairs. And even then, we both pretend it didn't happen. Of course, it's been a while since I've done that.

"If I asked which room the man with the short dark hair is staying in, would you tell me?"

"And would this have anything to do with you two dancing in the hall?" she asks, cocking her eyebrow.

"No, nothing like that. I need some information about my departure that he forgot to fill me in on last night."

She gives me an all-knowing look before telling me he's staying upstairs, second room on the left. I thank her before quickly making my escape out of this awkward situation. Reaching the top of the stairs, I take a few steps before I'm standing in front of his door. I hesitate, suddenly unsure as the force that pushed me this far winks out. Realizing it's going to seem even stranger if I get caught standing here, I finally knock.

"Rorik, I said I would be there in a minute," someone that sounds like Eldrin says from the other side of the door.

Not knowing how to respond, I knock again. After a shuffling sound, the door opens. The shuffling was clearly him putting on pants while walking to the door, where he now stands shirtless.

My eyes travel up his body, starting at the top of his pants, where hair is reaching toward his navel. I make my way up to the muscles filling out his chest and finally land on his face. He has that smirk again, but he also looks just as surprised as I am.

"Hello, Love, I wasn't expecting you," Eldrin says.

My body warming at his words.

"Can you put a shirt on?" I ask, rolling my eyes.

He lingers for a moment before moving out of the doorway. His room is empty. There's a bag in the corner from which he pulls a shirt, and some papers are scattered on a small table. His bed is messy, as though he had just gotten out of it.

That heat returns as I look away, embarrassed, seeing his bed feels too private. The most noticeable aspect of his room was that it smelled overwhelmingly like him—the smell of amber becoming familiar after smelling it mixed with his sweat last night.

"To what exactly do I owe this visit?" he asks, turning to me now that he has found a shirt.

"I was hoping you might know when the betrothal ceremony would take place?" I ask. "Also, I need to bring someone with me when I leave."

He raises an eyebrow. "If you were hoping to bring the drunk from last night, I don't think that's going to work out."

Confused, I ask, "What?"

"When Bjark returned last night, he mentioned a man who

was pining over you. Seems to be upset over the coming nuptials. Heard he was removed from the hall. I thought you said you weren't in a relationship?"

He must be talking about Erik. Gods, how much of a scene did he cause last night?

"I said I'd never been in love, and that I wouldn't spend my life with anyone here. Not that there's never been anyone. Erik is a friend I grew up with. He has feelings for me, and I guess I took advantage of that." I shouldn't have to share any of this with a stranger. "I don't think I owe you an explanation for that."

His face softens. "You don't, I'm sorry."

"You have a habit of responding to my questions with your own, and then only you get answers."

He laughs before looking at me with a smile. "Sorry, it's an occupational habit. A message was sent yesterday. The betrothal will happen in a few days, and then we'll all leave a day or two later."

"Gaelen can get here from Kenaz that quickly?" I ask.

"He isn't in Kenaz; he was on orders from the king when this was set into motion."

"So, he will be here soon, then?" My stomach starts to sink before the words can leave my mouth.

I knew I was going to have to meet him at some point, but having this conversation is making everything that much more real.

"Calm down, you have time," he says, obviously noticing my panic. "But since I'm going to be here a while longer, care to show me around?"

It's not as if I have anywhere to be. I obviously won't be training with Erik today.

"I guess I could fit a tour into my ever-demanding schedule. What do you want to see?"

"Everything," he says, still smiling.

Outside the tavern, the sunlight is blinding compared to the dark interior.

"I assume you know your way around the town square?" I ask.

"Yes, I can find the Great Hall as well, as well as that amazing bakery I watched you storm out of yesterday, covered in flour and mumbling to yourself."

"Oh… you saw that?" Of course he did. "The owners are old family friends. Their daughter is the one I need to bring with me. Her mother lets me help out sometimes. That's why I was covered in flour."

I find myself feeling the need to explain why I was there in the first place.

"You say *need*, is it not your *want* to bring her?"

"I wouldn't say that I don't want to. It's just that we haven't been friends for some time. Now she feels there's nothing left for her here and needs to start over. I can understand that."

He looks contemplative for a moment, then nods.

"Would bringing her be an issue? Do we need to get approval from someone?" I ask, though I only feel more committed after saying everything out loud.

"Thyrvi," he says, looking down at me like he needs to explain something but doesn't know how. "You're marrying the son of a king. While he doesn't like to use his title, it does give you privileges, you could require she come. No one is expecting you to travel alone."

How had I not thought about the implications of marrying a prince? I have read about places that take titles more seriously than we do here, but that always felt like something that happened in books, and not in real life. Definitely not my life. If Gaelen's family is like that, I'm going to have to learn a lot in a short amount of time. I realize I'm spinning the bracelet and force myself to stop, as if the action could give away my secret.

"Do you think you could teach me about what will be expected of me? Or of what I should expect in Kenaz?"

"I can try, but I must admit, I'm not going to be a good teacher."

"Well, it would seem you're all I have right now," I say.

I show him the docks, brimming with merchants and people coming and going. I point out the other tavern, too, but we don't enter. On our walk back, we pass the library, and I pull him inside.

The smell of old books competes with the salty air from the water. The library is small, one room lined with bookshelves and a desk where Hulda, the librarian, sits. She's an older woman who has worked here my entire life. My father told me she'd been the librarian even when he was a child. She looks up at me but only nods. She's never been one for small talk, and I appreciate that about her.

"This is my favorite section," I say, pointing to a shelf that could hardly be called a "section".

I've never been to another library, but sometimes ships bring carts so full of books, I can only imagine their size. I'm sure the library in Kenaz could hold more than double what's in this room.

"Why is it your favorite?" Eldrin asks, eyeing it as though he were looking for something he may be missing.

"These books are filled with the old sagas. From before the Gods created our world, and early after." I pull one out and flip through it. "My father used to bring me here when I was small. We would sit on the floor and he would read them to me."

"Are you not allowed to take the books home?"

"You are. It's just more magical if you read them here. Or so he would say."

He looks around for a moment and then sits down on the wooden floor.

"What are you doing?" I ask.

"I want to experience this magic. Read one of the stories to me."

"Uh, okay," I say, a little confused by his eagerness.

Walking over to Hulda's desk, I grab two of the floor pillows she stores there. Everything is still the same as it was during my first visit. I toss one at him before sitting on my own. Flipping through the pages, I land on the story of the goddess Idun and her golden apples, one of my favorites. I tell him how Idun's apples kept the gods young, but that she was kidnapped because of a deal Loki made. She was taken to Jotunheimr, and in her absence, the gods began to age. Over time, many worked with Loki to resolve his deal and free her, granting them access to the apples once again.

"Let me read one," he says, taking the book from me after I finish.

He turns to the next page, landing on the story of Bragi, Idun's husband. It's said that Bragi was actually a famous bard, and upon his death, Odin ascended him into godhood. Odin appointed him as the poet of Valhalla, as he couldn't bear the thought of no longer experiencing Bragi's poems.

"These aren't what I was expecting."

"You don't know the stories of the gods?" I ask, shocked.

"I know the basics. I don't know all their stories. We didn't all have parents that read us bedtime stories, Love."

I guess that makes sense. Hagen didn't spend as much time reading these with Father as I did. But I'm sure he knows all the sagas by now. Adulthood led him to become well-read.

He stands, reaching out his hand to help me up. I place the book back on the shelf as he takes the pillows back to Hulda's desk.

We almost reach the tavern where he is staying when a flash of red catches my eye.

"I should go tell my friend her plan of escape is approved," I say, gesturing to where Saoirse is sweeping the bakery's front steps.

"Will you join me for dinner? I can introduce you to the rest of us."

"Sure. Here?"

"Well, the only other option you showed me didn't look sanitary."

I laugh, "Fine, see you at dinner."

## Chapter Five

Saoirse eyes me as I make my way toward her, likely having watched the whole time. She never missed anything when we were younger, and if there was gossip to be known, she always knew it.

If you don't know her, it would only be fair to assume she has an army of spies running around, but the truth is she's always been a great listener. She's also a great secret keeper, even of the secrets you have yet to realize you have. She hears the things people say, and what they don't. The bakery opening so early in the morning, and in the dead center of the village square, means she always has fresh news.

"What are you doing with that one?" she asks.

Her eyes narrow, and she tilts her head toward the tavern.

"Giving him a tour. He's teaching me about Kenaz."

Though he hadn't actually told me anything, she didn't need to know that.

"Anyways, you coming won't be an issue."

"Why did you think it would be?"

I throw my hands up and sigh. "I don't know. I'm clearly naive about how all this works."

"Which is exactly why you need me."

My eyes roll uncontrollably in response.

"Your mother wants to make my dress. Would you want to help me pick out fabric in the morning?" I try to change the subject as a smile lights up her face.

I feel guilty for not inviting Saoirse to dinner. She should meet the group from Kenaz as well, but I know she will pick up on things I'm not ready to acknowledge.

Content to live in denial a little longer, I push open the tavern door. I find Eldrin sitting at a table with three other men. He spots me right away, waving me over. I move toward the only empty seat, which happens to be next to him. Before I can sit, he stands, pulling out the chair and using the opportunity to introduce me to everyone.

"Thyrvi, you already met Bjark, but this is Soren and Rorik," he says, gesturing to each of the men.

I'm starting to wonder if all men from Kenaz are gorgeous, and what my chances are that Gaelen will be the same. Soren has the same sandy brown hair as Bjark, but where Bjark is built like a bear, Soren is slim, with a physique built of long, lean muscle. Handsome, but in a calculated sort of way. Keeping his hair short and his face clean-shaven, he has the sort of eyes that don't miss anything.

Rorik has a darker complexion than even Eldrin, though he has a full beard and the sides of his head are shaved, the top pulled into long braids. He has a rugged look about him, but the most inviting smile I've ever seen. Rorik stands, enveloping me in a hug.

"Nice to meet you, I've heard great things," Rorik says as he releases me.

"Is that so?" I can't help but mirror his smile.

"Yes, our friend here is normally a man of few words, but

lately he hasn't shut up," he says.

"I knew I shouldn't have invited you three," Eldrin grumbles.

"Right, because you want to keep her all to yourself. I'm on to you!" Rorik points in his direction.

"There's enough of me to share." I joke in an exaggerated flirty voice before I realize it's probably inappropriate for me to say.

Soren chokes on his ale before he and Rorik burst into laughter.

By the look on Eldrin's face, I'm assuming he didn't think it was funny, and I remember Bjark mentioning he was closer to Gaelen than the rest. But they can't be that good of friends if he's been flirting with me unless I'm reading it all wrong. Maybe I should've invited Saoirse after all.

"You're all children," Bjark says, making the three of us laugh.

More ale comes, and eventually stew with bread. The tavern fills with locals and travelers alike, many sitting at the bar. A rowdy group playing a game occupies a table in the far corner, and a small crowd of people watches them, taking bets. Their jeers and shouts ring out over the rest of the tavern. At this point, the lute player should probably give up—no one can hear him. Ula's is often lively, but this is rowdier than I have seen in a while.

"Tell me, Thyrvi, are you excited for your coming nuptials?" Soren asks.

"You didn't have to bring that up," Rorik snaps.

"What? I don't understand why we're all dancing around it like it's not the reason we're all here," Soren says.

Eldrin looks like he might reach over the table and strangle him.

"No need to dance around it," I cut in. "To answer your question, yes and no. Obviously, I don't know Gaelen, so that makes me a little apprehensive, but I'm excited for a change of scenery, as much as Thurisa will always have my heart."

"What a diplomatic answer," Soren says, nodding in my direction.

"It's not diplomatic, just the truth."

"Leave it alone," Eldrin says.

His tone carries a notion of finality, and I get the feeling this isn't the first conversation they've had on the subject.

We spend the next hour chatting about Kenaz, its size, the various types of shops, bookstores, and libraries it has, and the sheer number of bakeries. Apparently, some bakeries only sell cakes, some only bread, and so on.

I recommend they check out the Branton's bakery tomorrow, Rorik promising to do so. I start to understand that I won't be able to comprehend the actual size of Kenaz until I see it myself, but if they have multiple versions of the same things, it must be huge. Bjark explained it'd be impossible to walk the full length of the city in even two days. The thought of exploring it only renewing my interest in leaving.

As our conversation trails off, I notice that most of the locals have left, leaving only us and the loud group in the corner.

"I should probably be heading home. Thank you all for spending your evening with me. I had a great time," I say, beginning to stand.

Eldrin joins me. "I'll walk you home."

"Thurisa is nothing like your city, and I've lived here my entire life. I can walk myself home, but thank you for the offer," I say in protest, making my way toward the door.

I have to push through the group that has taken occupancy of the corner table, as they are partially blocking the door. One man, a few years older than me, grabs my waist and pulls me against him, breath reeking of ale.

"Leaving so soon, *Mara?* Realized none of your friends over there can meet your needs?" he asks, voice filled with disdain as his hand gropes its way lower.

*Mara.* The word causing me to pause. It hits me that I know this man, as well as a couple of the others. He ships cargo for Thurisa, traveling often, so I haven't seen him in years. I almost didn't recognize him, and if he didn't use that word, I wouldn't have. It's been a long time since someone has called me that to my face, and the fear that shoots through me reminds me that I need to move.

"My needs are none of your concern." I shove at him, but I fail to gain any space.

His face moves closer and closer to mine, when suddenly, he disappears, and someone else grabs me. Looking back, I see Rorik, his hands on each of my shoulders as he begins to usher me out of the tavern. Eldrin has the man slammed against the wall, his arm twisted behind his body. The man's friends catch up to the situation, standing to defend him. Ula, noticing the fight that's about to start, starts to yell, grabbing a club from behind the bar.

"If you ever fucking touch her again..."

That's all I hear Eldrin say before I'm out the door.

"Shouldn't we help him?" I ask Rorik.

"No. Soren and Bjark won't let anything happen to him, don't worry. Let's get you home. Your presence is only going to make matters worse."

I don't see how three men could defend themselves against that crowd, but he pulls me along before I can make another protest. Ula is good at handling these situations. I just hope she doesn't hit any of them in the process.

The events of last night jolt me awake. Comments made, looks shared, Eldrin's anger on my behalf. I think I might be letting this get out of hand.

Then, there was that word. Rorik was mostly silent as he walked me home, and if he heard what the man called me, he made no mention of it.

Shit.

Still slightly shaken, I realize too late that I'm supposed to be with Saoirse, shopping for fabric. Jumping out of bed, I throw on a pair of pants and a light sweater, pulling my hair into a braid and shoving my feet into boots.

Running through the door, I practically crash into her.

She takes a step back, eyes narrowing as they take in my appearance. "Out late?"

"A little later than I intended to be. I overslept."

"Here?"

"Yes, here!" I'm not sure my eyes could roll any harder.

"I heard Ula had some trouble in the tavern last night," she says unceremoniously, as if she's not fishing for information.

"You hear too much."

"Probably, but I also heard it started because Ketill grabbed you, and the man who's been *just teaching you about Kenaz* lost it."

Oh yes, Ketill. I was having trouble remembering his name.

I give Saoirse what she wants, recounting what took place last night, but leaving out specific details along the way.

"I was wondering when you'd be stopping in!" Brynja says, poking her head out from the back of the shop. "Need me to clear my schedule, or will Earie be making your dress?"

"Earie offered to do it, but I appreciate your offer," I say.

"I assumed as much. I took the liberty of pulling some fabrics I think would be good options for the day, though." She gestures to a table where bolts of cloth are laid out.

The bright colors range from light yellow to pink to even a soft green. I look between Saoirse and the fabric as I try to hold back a laugh, bracing myself for when she springs to action.

"Thank you so much for your efforts. I have a specific vision in mind, though. We're going to need to see all of your darker options," Saoirse says.

Brynja hesitates for only a moment before nodding and going to pull more fabric.

"I could just do something blue or green. That's probably what he's expecting anyway," I whisper to Saoirse, not wanting to overcomplicate things.

"And that's exactly why you can't. Besides, he should be used to people dressing differently than we do."

Once Brynja returns, it doesn't take long for Saoirse to land on the most unconventional option available, then becoming mesmerized by the idea of beads.

"I don't think we have enough time to incorporate beading," I say, trying to move her along.

"You'll just have to trust me. How much do you think we can spend before we piss off your brother?" she asks, smiling.

"Oh, Hagen isn't paying for this. Someone came by and paid for everything in advance on behalf of a 'G. Langavin'. I dare say you have a ways to go before you run out of funds," Brynja cut in.

"Do you remember what they looked like?" I ask.

"They only came by this morning. A skinny blond one; I

didn't catch his name, but he mentioned he was staying at Ula's. I explained Earie would most likely be the one making your dress, that I wouldn't need this much money, but he insisted and asked where he could find her."

Maybe she's referring to Soren. Which is interesting because I got the feeling he wasn't overly fond of me last night. I wonder if Eldrin isn't the only one close to Gaelen, then. Maybe I had the wrong impression from the start. Bjark only said that Eldrin knew him more than he did. I just assumed that meant more than Soren and Rorik, too. Regardless, this is an unexpected gesture. But what does it mean?

After shopping, we head back to Saoirse's family home to take my measurements. It turns out Soren showed up here as well, and Earie refused any payment.

"So, what exactly are you planning with this color?" I ask Saoirse.

She smiles widely. "It's a surprise! Just know that mother

approved after some convincing, and Gaelen is going to be speechless when he sees you. Also, it's going to piss Hagen off."

"Thanks for doing this. You really didn't have to."

"It's my fault you weren't here to help with mine, but we're going to do it right this time!"

Once my measurements are taken, she and Earie politely kick me out. I almost make it home before I hear my name being called.

## Chapter Six

"I was starting to worry I wouldn't get to see you today," Eldrin says, walking up to me.

"So, you went looking for me?" I don't see any other reason he'd be standing here.

"I was taking a walk, but yes, the notion that I would have a better chance running into you if I was outside, wasn't lost on me." He pauses for a moment. "I wanted to apologize for last night. I should've insisted on walking you home. I was trying not to be overbearing since this is your home, but the whole thing could've been avoided had I done so."

"I've walked home late at night probably a hundred times. There just happened to be a few drunk idiots."

I want to ask if he knows about the fabric and the payments, but I don't want to bring up the hand-fasting. It seems to be a topic we've mutually agreed to try avoiding—a problem for me to acknowledge later.

"Well, how long of a walk were you hoping to take?"

"I have nothing but time," he says with a half-smile.


"Are you going to tell me where we're heading?"

"My favorite place," I say, glancing back at him with a wink.

Once we are out of the village walls, I lead him onto a path that enters the woods. It's a bit overgrown from the summer, but I also haven't come through here in some time.

"Are you going to let me show you my favorite places when we leave?"

"Would you want to?" I ask as if I don't already know the answer.

"I will give you a tour of the whole city, even the places I don't like."

Okay, maybe I'm attracted to him, at least a little. That doesn't make me a terrible person. I've never even met Gaelen, and sometimes these things just happen. Am I seriously trying to justify this to myself right now?

"And Gaelen won't mind you doing so?" I wish I hadn't said

it, but we can't avoid it forever.

"No, I don't think he will," he says quietly.

"Is he only interested in men or something?"

If he is, then we could both have lovers, and maybe I could have this one—the sound of choking interrupts that thought.

"Um, no, it's not that. However, his older brother is pretty open when it comes to gender. I've walked in on him in a few situations I'll never be able to unsee," he says, clearing his throat.

"Some people get to have all the fun."

We walk a little farther until the tree line begins to thin, giving way to rocks. I reach the edge of the cliff, close my eyes, and take a deep breath. From this height, the air is crisp, filled with the scent of the ocean. It's a different smell than at the docks with all the people and ships.

I can see Thurisa, down and to the left, but I'm too far away to hear most of the sounds. There's a clear view of the bay and then the ocean. It's beautiful. The kind of place that makes you feel like the world is full of wonders, that your problems are small in comparison. If only you could get out there and see it, you might be meant for something more.

"This is amazing. How long have you been coming up here?"

"My mother used to bring me here when I was small, but after she died, I would come alone. My parents started to come here before they were married. I don't think he ever came back without her, though."

"I never knew my mother. She died shortly after my birth," he says, looking out at the sea.

"I'm sorry. It must be hard never having gotten to know her."

"Probably not as hard as knowing her before losing her," he says before changing the subject. "So Thurisa has always been run by someone in your family?"

"As far as I know."

"It's ancient, you know. They say this area was one of the first inhabited. It even predates Kenaz."

"Well, it's a strong location for trade via the sea, and offers access to the other towns and villages."

"Yes, many of us wonder why your father kept it closed off for so long."

"Raids were bad when my father was growing up; he lost people, and I think he became paranoid after my mother's death. There were rumors of poison. He was never the same after she was gone. I'm sure you can understand."

"I think my father has always been the same hateful bastard. I've never heard it said that he loved my mother. Theirs was an arranged marriage."

"Having an arranged marriage doesn't mean you can't fall in love. I've seen it happen with couples here," I say.

"And are you hoping to fall in love, Thyrvi?" He turns to look at me.

I watch as his eyes momentarily travel to my mouth before returning to meet my gaze. I'm not sure when it happened, but he's so close I can feel his breath on my skin. His hand caresses the nape of my neck, making its way into my hair, the other on my waist, pulling me closer. His eyes beg me for approval. He's going to kiss me, and in this moment, there's nothing I want more.

So, it pains me as the words leave my mouth. "We shouldn't do this."

I hesitate, making sure I'm committed to that statement before I start to pull away.

"I'm so sorry. For a moment, I—" He takes his hands off me and runs them through his hair and over his face, seeming to realize what almost happened.

"We got carried away. It's the view." I try to make the situation lighter. "It might be best for us to head back."

I immediately turn to make my way through the trees.

"Of course."

Our walk back to the village is silent, and I decide this will have to be the last time we're alone together. I'm barreling toward the Great Hall and the sanctity of my room behind it, where I can unpack everything that just happened, when

Eldrin calls out to me again.

"Can you slow down for a moment?" he says from behind me.

"I have things I still need to get done today."

"Listen, we need to talk." He grabs my hand.

We both look down at the connection, but I'm the first to pull away.

"Not today."

Of course, I avoided it as much as possible; now I'm in over my head. I need to figure out how I'm going to handle this before I can see him again. Eldrin only nods in response, not moving to follow me this time when I walk away.

## Chapter Seven

I close the door to my bedroom and sink to the ground, mind racing. He almost kissed me, and I nearly let him. Worse than that, I wanted him to do it. What the hell am I doing? As if I don't already have a mess with Erik, I'm going to start another one?

There were men before Erik, mostly men coming and going through the port, never anything serious—a night or two, at best. So, I've never allowed myself to develop feelings for anyone, and definitely not whatever this is with Eldrin. If I didn't genuinely enjoy spending time with him, this would be so much easier.

But I'm having... fun. Our conversations are easy; I find myself not wanting them to end. The fact that he looks like that also isn't helping.

Fuck.

He's here because I agreed to marry someone he works for. The contract is signed. There's nothing I can do. Maybe I'm making a big deal out of nothing. Besides, Gaelen will be here soon. I need to clean this up. Tomorrow I'll talk to Erik, and then I'll tell Eldrin we can't spend any more time together.

I spend the rest of the evening hiding in my room, preparing for my departure, when a note arrives from Len. He asks to meet in the morning; the request couldn't come at a better time. Training has always been a great way to clear my mind. And the last few days, I have skipped training more than I have in years. Though if Len is expecting my skills to have improved, he will be disappointed.

"I thought you had been working on this?" Len asks, disarming me for the third time this morning.

"I have, it's hopeless."

"Do me a favor. Make sure you always keep a dagger on you in Kenaz, and wear practical shoes."

"I seriously doubt people are going to be attacking me in Kenaz."

"For the sake of this conversation, we'll pretend Langavin turns out to be all we hope he will be. You realize, in a city as big as Kenaz, that there are people who survive, and survive well, by stealing from others? That bodies are found in alleyways, and no one ever finds out what happened to them?"

I assumed there would be some level of crime.

"And Thyrvi, I know you, and I know my daughter. You two will be out there exploring the first chance you get. So, what are you promising me?"

"A dagger and practical shoes."

"Perfect. Now, ready your stance again."

After my session with Len ends, my eyes land on Erik talking with a group of men at the edge of the field. I stick around once Len leaves, pretending to look at training swords until he gets the hint and breaks from the group.

"Thyrvi."

"I was hoping we could talk?" I ask awkwardly.

"Of course, but let's go somewhere more private. With everything going on, they'll ask questions."

He gestures toward the Great Hall. Why couldn't it be him? My life would be so much simpler if it could have just been him.

We are halfway there before I realize he's leading me to my room, quickly, I duck into the kitchen instead. It's empty at this hour, especially on days with no events or festivals. I turn around once I reach the huge wooden cutting table in the center of the room and find that he's followed too closely, not leaving enough space between our bodies.

"You changed your mind about going through with it then? Even if Hagen disapproves, I'm ready to leave whenever you are."

Erik sighs, and some of the tension seems to leave his shoulders. His hand reaches for my face, as if he plans to kiss me.

"What? No. You know Hagen announced it to the village. I can't change my mind now, even if I wanted to."

My only apprehension lies in who I'm leaving with, but I've already accepted I want to go. He grabs my arm, pushing me against the table and pinning me there with his body.

"I've spent half of my life in love with you. You knew that when you started fucking me. We didn't spend the last year together for you to go off and marry some other man. That isn't how this ends." He squeezes my arm.

"Let go of me!" I shout, trying to wiggle free.

I don't want to hurt him, but I also don't know if I physically can. He's trained with me from day one. He knows any move I might try to make, and I know I'm partially to blame for his reaction.

"This ends because I say it ends, regardless of any other man. You knew all along I didn't share your feelings. You knew it would never be more; I was clear about that. You're acting like an asshole right now, Erik."

"No, Thyrvi. I thought you'd see reason. I thought you'd grow up and stop looking for whatever it is you think you need. And I don't even think you know! I thought you'd realize you could have a place with me. That we would be happy!" he yells, and the stench of alcohol on his breath is too pungent to still be from the night before.

"You have one chance to remove your hands from her," a voice says from the doorway to my right.

I recognize the voice instantly. Erik releases me and turns to face Eldrin.

"Aren't you one of the prince's errand boys? Here to fetch him a wife? Is Kenaz not big enough to find someone willing to do the job? Either way, it's too late. Ask Thyrvi about how I've spent the last year with my hands all over her. Let's see if the prince still wants her then."

"Honestly, I've never been fond of using that title. It has always felt like something that belonged to my brother," Eldrin says, the words not coming together correctly in my mind. "You'll be sad to know the only thing your little declaration has changed is the amount of time I dedicate to erasing your touch from her body."

Eldrin's eyes remain glued to Erik as he takes a step closer.

"And if you ever touch her against her will again, I'll rip the lungs from your body while you still breathe."

The truth of what he just admitted burns through me as Erik takes a step away from me. He must have figured it out as well.

"Well, this is just rich. Don't waste your time expecting her to return your feelings," Erik says, walking out of the kitchen.

I'm not sure if he thought better of picking this fight, or if he feared my brother would kill him if he did. With Erik gone, Eldri—Gaelen turns his attention to me.

"Did he hurt you? I assume you want him alive, but all you have to do is say the word."

I can't wrap my head around his words, as if he believes I'll ignore the fact that he's been lying to me this entire time. All I can do is glare at him, so many thoughts running through my mind, I don't know how to pick just one. I should've realized the truth, each of our interactions replaying in my head. It was always right there in front of me.

Sighing, he runs his hands through his hair, meeting my glare with soft eyes.

"Thyrvi, I can explain."

"Do not follow me," I say, pushing past him.

## Chapter Eight

Gods, I must look so stupid. How did I not see it?

With all the questions he avoided, never giving me any real information, that should've been my first clue. A concern, at the very least, but I chose to ignore it like everything else with him.

My body hums in anger and frustration, but something else is trapped there as well. Something that isn't big enough to look at just yet.

I am at the Branton house before I even realize I made it to the other side of the village. Despite the history between

Saoirse and me, there isn't anywhere else I can go. I obviously ruined my only other friendship.

Saoirse answers the door, and her assessing gaze running over my body.

"What's wrong?"

"I need to hide here for a little bit."

Her eyes narrowed on me.

"Tea or wine?"

I give her a glare that clearly means wine as we walk into the dining area. Their home has always been filled with just enough stuff, somewhere I've always felt comfortable, the decades of love that form their family clearly present.

Saoirse grabs a bottle and two glasses, guiding me to sit at their table.

"So, what happened?

"Eldrin has been lying the entire time. He's Gaelen," I say.

"And you're mad about that?" She says slowly, as if she isn't surprised, and is trying to decide how I feel. The look on her face giving me pause.

"Did you already know?"

It's precisely the type of thing she would find out before everyone else. But the idea that she wouldn't tell me leaves a sinking feeling in my stomach.

"No, of course not! But you didn't think the amount of time he was spending with you was odd? He claimed to be here so you could marry another man, someone he knows, might I add. And you've been seen both dancing and going into the woods with him. The village has been gossiping about you two since the betrothal announcement."

I close my eyes with a sigh. I really am an idiot.

"And have you not noticed the way he looks at you?"

"No, Saoirse, apparently I haven't."

Or I did, and just liked it. That feels more like the truth than anything else I've been telling myself.

"Why didn't you say anything?"

"We haven't been friends again for very long, and honestly, it didn't seem like you wanted to hear it. How did you figure it out anyway?"

"I was training with your father and saw Erik. I wanted to clear the air before we left, so we went inside the hall to speak privately. He thought I was ready to end everything and run away with him. Eldrin must have seen us walk in and followed—or he was already there, I have no idea. But Erik got mad when I said that I wasn't calling anything off and grabbed me. Eldrin walked in to put a stop to it and revealed who he was, quite dramatically. He even offered to kill him."

Recounting the story for Saoirse frustrates me more than I expected, and I find myself rolling my eyes again.

"I'm going to be honest… with the exception of Erik getting rough with you, this story is everything I hoped it would be."

"You're a menace."

"I know, but while we're here, can we entertain the idea that you might like him, that this might actually work out for you?"

She must be insane.

"No, we can't. He lied about who he was, forcing me to rethink every interaction we've ever had. Everyone in the village is going to think I'm an idiot. So no, we can't talk about me liking him."

"No one even knows. I'll make sure they think you were aware the whole time. I need to casually drop the information in front of one or two town gossips; it will be fine. But you know he's going to look for you tonight, don't you?

"I'm not ready to talk to him. I need time to figure out how I feel about everything."

"Are you going to cancel the hand-fasting?" she asks.

"No, Hagen would never let me."

"Well, I heard pretty recently, actually, that a certain someone would run away with you," she jokes. "But really, you can hide here. You'll be getting ready here tomorrow anyway, and you know my father will send anyone away that comes looking for you, Hagen included. We can finish your dress together. It's already beautiful."

I smile at the idea of Len shooing a prince away.

Earie and Saoirse spend the morning being lazy with me, and Len works the bakery alone. Earie recounts her wedding day, and I'm surprised when Saoirse starts to share hers as well. I didn't attend, but my father, as jarl, officiated their ceremony.

"Were you happy?" I ask when she seems to get lost in her thoughts.

"Yes. As much as I knew how to be at the time."

I raise an eyebrow.

"We were young, and it was everything I thought I wanted. I loved him to be sure, but looking back, I wonder if I wouldn't have wanted more at some point. I want to see things; I want an adventure."

I nod, at least able to understand those wants. We don't mention what happened yesterday in front of Earie. I'm having a lovely time with them. I don't want to ruin it by making her worry.

When evening arrives, we start getting ready for the hand-fasting. It's easily the most nerve-wracking thing I've ever done. My dress is beautiful, of course; I have no idea how Earie and Saoirse found the time to complete it so quickly. It's like nothing I've ever seen.

The fabric is the darkest shade of black; the skirt is long and flowing, with a slit cut to my hip. Apparently, Saoirse had to convince Earie on that feature. The bodice is tight with light beading scattered across it. The same small sparkling beads Saoirse and I attached to pins last night and are now strategically placed throughout my hair, which we left unbound. It all reminds me of stars against the night sky.

The ceremony will be held just outside of Thurisa, in a clearing in the forest. We often hold important ceremonies there, or close to the water, should the gods choose to attend. The village and the path to the clearing are near empty, most of those attending likely already there. Saoirse leads the way, her red hair cascading down her back. Her parents walk with me in place of my own.

"Know they're watching," Earie whispers. "Just because your path is different than what they chose doesn't mean it won't be filled with as much love and happiness as they shared."

"What matters is what you put into it," Len adds, looking at his wife.

The size of the crowd is the first thing I notice through the trees, followed by the numerous lanterns. Before we turn the last corner, Len and Earie both kiss me and walk ahead. The whole crowd turns upon their arrival. If I want to run, this would be my last chance.

I feel as though I could throw up, and I might have, if I'd eaten anything today. Despite that, my feet carry me forward. There's an audible gasp from those present, and I feel a bit self-conscious. I knew the dress was too much.

Hagen is standing at the end of the path, ready to officiate the ceremony. He looks annoyed. Saoirse one, Hagen zero. On Hagen's left stands Gaelen, also dressed in black, who doesn't look to be breathing at all. I walk toward them, and before I know it, our hands are clasped together and wrapped in rope. Gaelen's eyes never leave mine, and he misses his cue.

"Gaelen?" Hagen says before clearing his throat.

"Oh—right, I do," he blurts out.

Hagen continues with the ceremony.

"I do," I say, and then Gaelen is moving closer, our hands still wrapped in the rope.

His free hand comes to caress my cheek before lifting my chin, and then his mouth is on mine. Our lips meet for the briefest moment before he pulls away, looking down at me. A pang of disappointment runs through me at his withdrawal, but someone clears their throat—my brother—and I remember where we are.

And then it's done.

## Chapter Nine

With the ceremony over, the formality gives way, and everyone gathered becomes more alive. People dancing, drinking, and eating. It feels like someone is making a toast in our honor every few minutes. If the night continues this way, I'm considering switching to water.

The men of the village keep talking to Gaelen as if they've known him for years, coming up and clapping him on the back. He hasn't left my side yet, but with all the excitement, we haven't had a chance to speak to each other. Eventually, Gaelen looks down at me, tilting his head in the direction of our table. I nod my agreement, and he leads me to our designated table, his hand at the small of my back.

"You're always beautiful, but tonight exceptionally so. Was your dress designed to torture me?" he asks, eyes following the path the slit makes up my exposed leg.

I'm confident that was one of the many goals, but I decide it's better to ignore his question. He pulls out my chair, and I sit before taking another sip of wine.

"I just want you to know I looked for you last night to explain. I should've followed you the moment you walked away, but I thought if I gave you space, you would come yell at me when you were ready." His voice carries something I can't place.

"Perhaps I'm still not ready to yell at you."

At that, he lets out a sigh and a breathy laugh.

"As long as you're planning on it, Love."

"You want me to yell at you?"

"I would choose your anger over indifference if I had the choice. We can solve anger," he says with a wink.

I look at him for a long moment before turning back to those dancing. It would be so much easier to stay mad at him if he didn't say things like that.

"Here, take this before I'm having too much fun and forget to give it to you!" Saoirse says, catching me off guard when she hands me a bag.

"What is it?"

"Your clothes for tomorrow."

I must look confused because she rolls her eyes before continuing.

"Were you planning on wearing your wedding dress tomorrow, too?"

With how focused I was on Gaelen's true identity and making it through the ceremony, where I'd be sleeping tonight hadn't occurred to me. But of course, it wouldn't be at home.

"Thank you, that was very thoughtful of you," Gaelen says, taking the bag from me and placing it under our table.

She shoots him a glare in response before walking away.

"I assume she's mad at me, too?"

"I don't think so. She's just putting on a show in solidarity."

"I'll never understand the friendships women have."

Hagen approaches me for a dance. I sigh, knowing it'll be awkward, but also knowing that it's not something I can get out of.

"Did you know he was here the whole time?" he asks once we start dancing.

"It's complicated."

I don't elaborate. What I knew or I didn't know is really none of his business. I'm trusting Saoirse to handle this.

"Well, I wanted to thank you for going through with this,"

he says just before Len interrupts.

Len doesn't speak, just takes my hand and leads our dance. I know he must be thinking of my father and how he should be here. He was my father, but sometimes I think losing him impacted Len more than Hagen and I. It was inevitable that one day we would have to live without our parents, but no one considers what happens to their friends when they go.

Len and Earie knew my parents longer than I did; it's a strange thing to think about. It wasn't long before there was a tap on Len's shoulder. To my surprise, Rorik stands there. Len nods, returning to his wife.

"Welcome to our little family," Rorik says, taking my hand.

"Do you initiate all new family members with lies?"

"We never have new members. You'd be the first. But if you want, we can make it a tradition," he says, and a laugh I greatly needed leaves my chest, taking some tension with it.

"No, it's best we don't make a habit of it."

I can already tell I won't be able to continue this all night, especially in these shoes, but the next person who asks me to dance is Erik. Rorik seems to hesitate, unsure if he should retreat. I smile to let him know it's fine, and Erik takes his place. I don't have to look to know that Gaelen is watching us, along with multiple other people.

Annoyed, I whisper, "What do you want?"

"I want to apologize. I was an ass; I should've never spoken to you like that. You're my friend before everything, and I'm struggling with this, but I also can't let you leave without saying sorry," he says before nodding his head in Gaelen's direction. "If this is what you want, then I'll find a way to be happy for you."

Yes, Erik's an ass, but I did play a role in this. He's also one of my oldest friends—and I only have two.

"Did Hagen force you to say that?"

He smiles but shakes his head no, his eyes momentarily moving to something behind me.

"Congratulations, Thyrvi, you look amazing in that dress." He lets me go with a bow and walks away.

I turn to go back to Gaelen, but I find him standing behind me instead.

"Will you dance with me?"

The way he says it reminds me of the first time I met him. I give him the same response I did that night.

"I don't even know you."

"I don't think that's completely true, but either way, will you?"

I slip my hand into his, and heat rises through me at the contact. He keeps one hand clasped with mine, and the other on my back, holding me against him, but we don't speak as if words would ruin the moment. Thankfully, the band seems to take pity on me, and when the song ends, they transition to a faster song.

People make their way back to the dance floor, but we break apart, not making eye contact while we walk back to our table. I grab a new glass of wine on the way.

"If you would be more comfortable, we could stay in your room tonight."

"What?"

"I don't think we can get away with being separated for the evening if that's what you were originally hoping."

"Oh. Um. No, I just hadn't actually thought about it, to be honest."

Obviously, we would be expected to be together tonight. A lot more would be expected, which is fine. It's not like I hadn't thought about sleeping with him before, when he was Eldrin. I'm sure I would enjoy it, it's just that this isn't how things were supposed to go.

"The tavern is good," I say, realizing he's watching me go through my entire thought process.

He smiles. "You can use the evening to yell at me."

We stay a while longer, enjoying the festivities. Once I start to yawn, he insists we leave. Walking through the crowd, people notice that we're leaving, and they begin to cheer, clapping as we make our way through the crowd and back towards the village. I feel the flush of embarrassment as it heats my face.

Gaelen's room is dark, but his familiar scent greets me at the door once again.

I take back the bag he carried on our walk over, and he starts lighting each of the candles. As the room begins to fill with light, I open the bag to see what Saoirse packed. The emptiness surprises me for a moment, but she did say it was clothes for tomorrow, and knowing her, she probably "forgot" tonight on purpose.

"So how do you want to do this?" I ask.

Maybe if I keep it transactional, it'll be easier for both of us.

"Do what?" He lights the last lantern before turning to me.

"We were just hand-fast. I assume we have to consummate it for the contract to be complete."

He looks around the room for an uncomfortable amount of time before running his hand through his hair. Unless he's totally revolted by the idea, which, the longer he takes to speak, is the impression I'm getting.

"Thyrvi, you don't even like me right now. I don't give a fuck about formalities."

His tone is defensive. It's not that I thought he was that kind of person—I didn't. But I also don't know him at all, and the person I thought I knew was a lie.

He walks over and lifts my chin. "The first time we're together isn't going to be because you felt obligated."

His voice rests at an almost whisper before he turns to shuffle things around on his desk.

"Besides, I was hoping we could talk about yesterday. Then maybe we could just be ourselves and start fresh tomorrow. I know you have questions."

"Some of us were ourselves the entire time. But you know what, I would like to hear how you thought this was going to work out."

"I didn't expect anything. I didn't have a plan. I never intended to meet you before the ceremony."

"So what? You were just going to hang around for a few days, never introduce yourself, get married, and leave?"

"Not exactly... I wasn't supposed to get here this early. I had something to attend to nearby, and it was resolved faster than we had planned. Bjark was here handling the contract, so the rest of us decided to come straight here. I thought I would lie low until the ceremony."

So, he was content to be in the same place but didn't want

to get to know the person he was going to be legally bound to?

"Why did you even agree to this?"

"I didn't. I probably had less input in this marriage than you did."

He says it casually, but the admission catches me off guard.

"Wait, you were forced into this?"

My mind reels. I assumed he was in a similar situation. Marriage to a stranger—not exactly my top desire, but more of a reluctant acceptance than it being completely against my will.

"I get the impression your life has been somewhat unconventional for a woman in your position. Typically, when your family members hold positions of power, you don't have many choices. You do what you need to, or what you're told, to serve your people or as a means for your family to claw their way into more power."

I don't miss the hint of disdain slipping into his voice, no matter how reasonable he tries to sound. It would all make sense. An alliance with Hagen would give Kenaz access to an established port, and at that point, Hagen would be unable to refuse access.

"And how did you think this was going to go between us?"

"Honestly? I expected to come here, have the ceremony, find you incredibly boring, but still take you to Kenaz. We'd only have to see each other for the short periods I'm there, and I would find a way to dissolve it at Yule."

I don't know what I was hoping for, but the pit forming in my stomach tells me this wasn't it. I don't want to be left alone somewhere. I'm alone here.

Would trading one scenery for another be enough? I hoped Gaelen and I would at least be friends. I don't even have time to process my disappointment and what this means for us before he's closing the distance again.

"But then Bjark pointed you out as you rushed out of that bakery. You were covered in flour and muttering to yourself, looking as though the gods could've stood before you in that moment, and you would have damned them all for the interruption. I was intrigued. So, I attended a party I shouldn't have, and ever since you sat down next to me, all I do is try to find ways to be in your presence. I have no intentions of leaving you anywhere."

Damn it if my breath doesn't hitch at his words.

"And if I don't want to follow you around as you travel?"

I ask, knowing very well how much I would love to see anything new. The corner of his mouth lifts, his hand moving to play with one of the beads pinned to my hair.

"I think you misunderstood. Not intending to leave you doesn't mean you're forced to come with me. It means we can build whatever kind of life you want to live."

"You just explained that you don't get to pick your life, that you have to do what is required. Is the king going to let you walk away from whatever it is you do for him?"

"No, that will be a fight." His hands move down my neck to caress my collarbone.

"And if I don't want a life with you at all? Maybe I want you to leave me and keep traveling," I say, and a low laugh rumbles through his chest.

"You don't. You liked me before you learned who I was, or you wouldn't have been so mad at me. And you certainly wouldn't have worn this dress."

He takes me in again. His arrogance isn't a surprise. He strikes me as someone who knows the impact his jawline has on women.

"Speaking of this dress." I gesture down at it with a smile. "Can you help me get out of it?"

I see his body tense and his eyes dart to mine before he recovers.

"Although, looking through my bag, it doesn't seem that Saoirse hoped we'd be sleeping tonight," I say with a shrug.

"You're an evil woman," he responds before moving over to his bags and pulling out a tunic. "I'd prefer the thought of you sleeping naked, but I guess in my shirt would be second best."

He hands me his shirt.

"Turn around and I'll unlace your dress for you."

I hesitate; whatever courage I did have fleeing.

"Just trust me."

I do as he says, feeling bumps rise on my skin every time his fingers lightly touch me as he loosens the laces.

"I'll hold the dress up, put the shirt on."

Once I'm decent, he lets the dress fall. Turning around, I step out of the dress, and he picks it up for me, laying it over the desk.

"Thank you."

I stand awkwardly. The shirt reaching my thighs. His eyes travel over my body before returning to my face.

"I should go. I'll be in Soren's room tonight. It's just across the hall." He starts gathering his clothes.

"You could stay here," I say, wincing at how quickly that came out. "I just mean I wouldn't want to inconvenience Soren. I don't think he likes me as it is."

"Thyrvi, I intend for this to work between us. I don't want to risk that by pushing you into things you're not ready for. You've had a lot of wine, and I'll have plenty of nights to spend with you. It doesn't have to be now."

"Well, I'd like an explanation for your lie."

I try to sound annoyed, hoping he isn't going to make me protest his departure any longer. It would be embarrassing, and this is the best reasoning I have. His eyes squint, but a smile crosses his face.

"If you don't want me to leave, you could just say so."

He puts his clothes in his bag and walks over to the bed. Pulling back the blanket, he pats the mattress.

"Come on then."

## Chapter Ten

I climb into his bed, quickly sliding under the blanket to hide my lack of pants. We both remain on opposite sides. What feels like a few feet of forbidden space lies between us, neither of us daring to touch.

He turns to face me, head propped up on his elbow. "So, what do you want to know?"

"Why the lies?"

"I only lied about my name; the rest of it was real."

That doesn't feel like much of an explanation.

"You're going to have to give me more than that. Why

bother lying at all then?"

"Bjark was being polite when he said we wanted to wish you a happy Name-Day. I didn't plan to speak to you, so when you sat down at our table, I panicked. But I also couldn't remember the last time I had so much fun. You were so open, it felt natural and refreshing. I knew as soon as you found out who I was, it would all be over. I planned to tell you at the end of the night, but the second time you asked my name, I still wasn't ready to give it all up."

I guess I can understand being treated differently, even if it's for different reasons. That's why I preferred men who only dock here, or are passing through. They don't know me.

"So, you quickly made up a name?"

"No, Eldrin was my mother's last name. I use it when we travel, when I can. It just makes things easier." He exhales, hand running over his face. "I intended to tell you many times, but there was always a dumb reason to put it off, so I did. I knew you were going to be mad. Then we went on that walk to the cliffside. When I almost kissed you, I knew I had lost control of the situation. I wanted to tell you then, but you were upset, and I didn't know what to do."

"And you thought the best time for me to learn the truth was in front of Erik?"

I don't know if I would've handled it any differently, but finding out privately would've certainly been preferred.

"I was coming to explain everything when I saw you two walking into the hall together. I thought about turning around and leaving it alone, but I was jealous and it got the better of me."

At that, a snort leaves my body, followed by uncontrollable laughter.

"Of Erik?" I manage to get out.

"You said you two grew up together! He obviously knows you well. You train together and have some romantic relationship going on."

I can't control the laughter that continues, and by the look on his face, he clearly thinks I'm the one being unreasonable here. It wouldn't be so funny if it were not for the timing.

"We don't have anything going on." I wipe the tears from my eyes and roll onto my side to face him.

"I'm glad you're finding this so humorous."

"If you understood the situation, you wouldn't be jealous. And we might have grown up together, but that doesn't mean he knows me." Recent events have made that clear.

Gaelen is pressed against my back, one arm under my neck and the other wrapped around my stomach. We remained on our separate sides last night, facing each other, sharing stories of our childhoods.

He spoke at length about his older brother and the trouble they'd get in together. Their relationship seems vastly different than what Hagen and I share. I get the feeling he doesn't have the best relationship with his father, but we stuck to happy topics.

When we got to the topic of his friends, he explained that he and Rorik grew up together, like Saoirse and me. They both met Bjark during training, though Bjark was a few years older and always ahead of them. He and Soren met about nine years ago, traveling together ever since, for whatever task the king sends them on.

I don't remember when I fell asleep. I must have nodded off while we were talking, but I can guarantee we were not this close. I need to find a way to sneak out of bed without waking him. As if he can hear my thoughts, Gaelen pulls me closer, angling his hips. His length presses against me as he takes a deep inhale of my hair. A second later, the rest of his body stiffens.

Great, he's awake now too, probably trying to figure out what to do. That makes two of us. I suppose I'll just have to embrace the awkwardness.

"Good morning."

I roll over and tilt my head up to look at him. His face is softer, having just woken up; he looks younger.

"Good morning."

His voice comes out as a whisper. He doesn't seem to know what to do, but hasn't made any moves to let me go. His eyes travel across my face, as though he is studying it. He is only inches away, and I'm surprised by the urge to lean up and kiss him.

"What would you like to do today?"

I respond by reaching up and running my fingers through his hair, pulling his face down to meet mine. It's as if his body has been preparing for this exact moment, all of him seeming to spring into motion. One hand grips the hair at the nape of my neck, and the other goes to the space behind my knee, pulling my leg over him as he pushes me onto my back.

Heat flushes through me at the motion. Deepening the kiss, he grinds against me. A moan escapes my mouth at the sensation, seeming to encourage him. My hand roams under his shirt, feeling his skin and the muscles that lie beneath. I thought about this moment so many times last night while watching him talk, and a few times before that, if I'm being honest. But it's more than I expected it to be. It's more than it has been before.

His hand slides down my leg and up my side, stopping just below my breast. He releases a frustrated growl just before he breaks our kiss. He looks down at me for too long before speaking.

"I thought you were beautiful last night, but I don't think anything could top the way you look right now."

Before I can respond, he is moving off of me and out of the bed. The loss of his body weight is more disappointing than I expected.

"Why?" I don't even try to hide my disappointment.

"I have to make sure you're not using me for my body, Love." He winks at me. "Let's get dressed and find food."

His arrogance is going to become insufferable at some point, but my stomach grumbles on cue.

I sit up quickly, pulling his shirt down to cover my hips. "Pastries!"

"I mean, I was thinking something with more substance, but if that's what you want."

My breath catches at his smile.

We freshen up, and I put on the leggings and sweater Saoirse packed me. He slides on his pants and a black sweater; the lines of it are softer than anything I've seen him wear yet.

Lying in his bed was intimate, but it kept the awkwardness that comes with not knowing each other well at bay. Having left its solace, the novelty of our relationship becomes apparent.

On the way to the bakery, it's clear that both of us want to be close to each other, but neither of us is sure if hand-holding is appropriate. He was just on top of me, but out in the real world, holding hands is an uncertainty.

The sweet scent of sugar and bread assaults my senses as we make our way onto the bakery steps. We push open the front door and see the center case of pastries. Always a work of art, fresh loaves of bread lining the back wall.

Saoirse is working with her mother today. Upon seeing us enter, a questioning eyebrow goes up. I respond with an almost imperceptible shake of my head, but she knows. Her gaze narrows as it moves to Gaelen. Her mother comes around the counter with her arms raised to hug me.

"Thyrvi, congratulations again! Len and I are so happy for you." Earie says, pulling me into a motherly embrace. "Your parents would be so proud."

They might have been watching, but I don't know that I would go that far.

"Do you know when you're set to leave?"

I turn to ask Gaelen, but find Saoirse and him speaking quietly, so I shake my head no.

"Make sure you let me know as soon as you figure it out!" She releases me and moves back behind the counter. "We know what you want, Thyrvi. What about the gentleman?"

"I'll have whatever she's having," he responds.

"Handsome and smart," Earie says to me with a wink.

They refuse to let us pay before leaving, and we walk to my preferred bench. Everyone seems to be back to their everyday lives; the square is busy with people determined to fulfill the day's responsibilities, and merchants are heading toward the docks. It's a stark contrast to how empty it was last night.

"Okay... I'll admit this is delicious," he says, devouring his pastry.

"I told you!" I take a bite of mine, savoring the bread and sugared cheese.

"Is there anything you need to do today?"

"I should probably start packing. Otherwise, no." I haven't made much progress there.

"You have time for that, I think we'll be staying a few extra days if that's okay with you?"

"Why?" I assumed he'd want to leave right away, or rather, that the king would expect it.

"I think it's better if we have more time to get to know

each other before the reality of Kenaz sets in."

He clears his throat, but something in his tone suggests he is uneasy about leaving.

"What will it be like when we arrive?"

He exhales, hand running through his hair.

"Honestly, I'm not sure what to expect at this point. I'm hoping we can get through the formalities and then avoid my father as much as possible."

"Why would we need to avoid your father?" Their relationship might be worse than I thought.

"It's complicated. Anyway, let's get away for the night. I'll walk you home to get ready. Dress for hiking and pack a bag of clothes for tomorrow. I need some time to make arrangements, but I'll come get you around noon."

"Are we going alone?" I asking, hoping the answer is yes.

"Worried about being alone with me?" The corner of his mouth lifts.

"No, I think this morning proved you've either mastered self-control or you're celibate."

A small laugh escapes him as we stand, and his arm wraps around my waist, pulling me in as he leans down to whisper in my ear.

"I'm not celibate, Love."

I wasn't prepared for the surge of excitement that courses through me.

## Chapter Eleven

"You do know, I grew up here, right? You could just tell me where we're going instead of using your secret map," I say.

We've been walking through the woods for about two hours. Sometimes on a trail, sometimes on what might have once been a trail. And despite what I said, even if he told me where we were going, I likely wouldn't know where it is. I was never allowed to leave Thurisa growing up, and even when I did, it was never this far.

Still, I know there are no other villages this direction, unless we're planning to walk for a very long time. If that's the case, I want to protest while we still have the opportunity to turn around.

"No, it's a surprise, and my map is fine. I got it from a friend."

"You don't have any friends here."

"Fine, I got it from your friend. So, unless you think she's willing to lose you in the woods, I think we can trust it."

He can only mean Saoirse. Which also means she likely told him I wouldn't know how to find anything.

"How do I know you can read a map?"

He side-eyes me before letting out a sigh and looking forward. It's enough to tell me that he found that question insulting.

After what feels like another hour of walking, we come upon a small clearing in the woods. Clearly, a common spot for camping from the thick logs surrounding a burnt spot in the middle. Gaelen sits, starting to unpack his bag, a tent being one of the things he unravels.

"We're sleeping here?"

I'd never technically slept outside of Thurisa. I've never been out of the village after dark, except for that night. This could potentially be the farthest I've ever been from home.

"Do you not like this spot? I don't think we'll find anything else this flat or open. Plus, there's a hidden spring nearby. Which was the whole point of the trip."

"The spring is here?"

I knew it existed, but I'd only heard people talk of it. It's said to belong to Freya. I knew it was only a few hours from Thurisa, but only lovers and couples come here. Usually after they are hand-fast, or hoping to be. The rumor is that those visiting the spring will have their union blessed by the goddess. Erik brought it up once, but I refused. I'm surprised Saoirse would tell Gaelen to bring me here.

"Yes, just a few minutes' walk."

"Do you know it belongs to Freya?"

"It was mentioned. Does that bother you?"

He stops building the tent, eyes on me, watching closely. I can't tell if he's looking for something unspoken, or if he's waiting to see what I might say.

"Why would it bother me?"

The flex of his jaw is the only hint that my answer isn't what he was looking for.

"I thought we could set up the tent, cook, and visit the spring this evening? The view of the night sky from the spring is supposed to be worth the hike."

I wonder how much Saoirse actually told him about the purpose of this spring.

He pulls out smoked fish and small vegetables, which I start cutting while he gathers wood for a fire. His bag is significantly larger than mine, and I'm glad he thought to pack so much since I only brought clothes.

We eat in an almost uncomfortable silence before cleaning up the camp. He seems nervous, avoiding my gaze and constantly finding something to do. Once the sun moves behind the trees and the sky begins to dim, Gaelen recovers two light blankets from his bag in the tent.

"Do you want to check out the spring? The fire will be fine; we can revive it when we get back."

"Sure, do you know the way?" I smirk, trying to hide the seemingly contagious nerves starting to take root in my stomach.

"Yes, it should be just up this path, somewhere between a rock formation, apparently."

He takes my hand and pulls me with him. After a few steps of me not pulling my hand away, he interlaces our fingers. The simple action turns my nerves into something softer.

The rock formation comes into view at the same time the scent of water fills the air. The trees open up to a cliffside, where a large rock is leaning, creating a natural doorway. Gaelen has to duck to make it through, but after a few feet, the rock gives way to a circular room, almost cave-like if it weren't for the open sky above us. The room is dark now that the sun has set, and the moon has yet to rise fully. Were it not for the soft pink, orange glow from spots on the rock and from within the spring, it'd be completely dark.

"What is this?" I ask, moving to touch the glow on the rock wall.

"It looks to be some type of quartz. It probably absorbs the sun throughout the day to give off this glow. Rose quartz is said to belong to Freya; if you believe this place does as well."

I hear him moving to stand behind me, and I turn to find little space between us.

"After this morning, all I can think about is kissing you again."

"Is that why you brought me here?" I know I'm staring at his lips.

"No, I just wanted to spend time with you. Without everyone you've ever known watching us. I thought maybe you could relax. I don't have to touch you, if that would make you more comfortable."

"It wouldn't."

A piece of hair falls over his left eye, and without thinking, I reach up and run my fingers through his hair, putting it back in place. When my hand starts to fall, he grabs it, pressing a kiss into my palm. And then his mouth is on mine.

His kiss is more exploring than it was this morning, his hands finding their way to the backs of my legs, lifting me so they wrap around him as he presses me into the stone. Running my hands back through his hair, I pull him closer.

He thrusts his hips against me, causing me to moan into his

mouth. Breaking our kiss, he pulls back to look at me, moving his hips to hit that perfect spot against me as he watches the pleasure run across my face. A low sound escapes him before he's kissing me again, but softly this time.

He sets me down, taking a step back before he pulls his shirt over his head, exposing his tan skin. His eyes lock on mine as he starts to unfasten his pants, exposing a dusting of dark hair.

"Do you want some help?" he asks, kicking off his boots.

"I want you to finish," I respond, looking down at his pants and back up at him.

A laugh echoes around us before he bends down to untie my boots, slipping them and my socks off my feet. He leans forward and pushes my shirt up to just below my breasts, kissing up my side, seeming to savor each taste of my skin. I run my hands over his shoulders and back into his hair. When his mouth reaches my shirt, he starts to stand, pulling it over my head as he goes.

"Are we going to get in the water?" My voice coming out rougher than I expected.

He nods, moving closer to the pool of water in the center of the room. He turns back to me, and I don't maintain eye contact as he pushes his pants off his hips and steps out of them.

Judging by the smile on his face when I look back up, he's happy with whatever he finds on mine. He nods to the water before walking in and swimming under. When he breaks the surface, pushing his wet hair out of his face, I still haven't moved.

"It's your turn, Love."

I walk forward, my eagerness to feel his hands on my body again overpowering any nerves I might have. I take the braid out, shaking my hair free, before pushing my leggings and underwear down, stepping out of them. My bra drops into the pile of my clothes last. Being fully exposed under the night sky, with him watching me, feels like magic.

"I was wrong. This is the most beautiful thing I've ever seen."

The water is warm, and after the first few steps, the bottom gives way, allowing the water to rise just up to my stomach. Gaelen makes his way over to me, grabbing my hand and pulling me toward him. When my feet can no longer touch the ground, I instinctively wrap my legs around him. His eyes widen momentarily; I hear his sharp intake of breath before his arms are around my waist, pulling me against him.

He takes us deeper into the spring until we reach a flat rock protruding from the cliff side, the top of it breaking the water's surface. His mouth finds my throat, and he works his way down, trailing kisses across my collarbone before he sets me on the rock.

His hand cups my breast as his mouth closes over my

nipple. I let out a soft moan before he moves to the other side. Standing between my legs, his other hand caressing my thigh, his face level with mine when his hand trails higher. Finally reaching my center when his fingers start to circle my bundle of nerves. My eyes close sharply, my head dropping back.

I brace my arms behind me so I can lean back, giving him better access, and he lifts my leg at the knee so that my foot can rest on the rock as well. Then, he slides one finger inside of me, followed by another immediately after. Working those two fingers in and out of me, his thumb rubbing my clit is almost too much. Just as I'm reaching the precipice, his hand is gone, replaced by his mouth as he lifts my other leg onto the rock.

"You taste so fucking good," he says, nearly growling.

His mouth is still on me as his fingers return, sliding in and out. This time, there's no stopping the orgasm as it crashes through my body.

"Gaelen, please." The words leave my mouth before I realize I'm begging.

"What is it you want, Love? You're going to have to use your words."

"You. Your dick. Please."

I hadn't even finished talking before he was pulling me forward, placing himself at my entrance. His hands are on each of my hips as he slowly slides inside me. The stretching takes a minute to adjust to, then he pushes all the way in, and we both look down, watching him move in and out of me.

"You're so fucking beautiful."

I feel the pressure starting to build again as he moves one arm under me, lifting me while he's still inside of me and bringing us into the water. His other hand fists my hair; my back pressed against the side of the spring.

His mouth never leaves mine as he starts to thrust again. I can't help but move my hips to meet him, the action causing him to moan. The sound coming from him is the last thing I need to push me over the edge. As my climax is coursing through me, his movements speed up, becoming rougher.

"Oh fuck, Gaelen," I whine, and then he finishes with me.

A few minutes are spent regaining our composure until I feel him harden against me again before flipping me over and finding his way inside me once more.

After, Gaelen carries me to the entry of the spring and sets me down in the water as he climbs out. He grabs one blanket, drying off his hair before laying it on the ground, then he holds up the other.

"Come here, we can watch the sky until we are dry enough to put our clothes back on."

I walk out of the spring, and he wraps me in the blanket. I sit between his legs, leaning back on his chest as we look up at the stars.

"When you were pretending not to be you, you said you weren't in love with anyone, but you didn't mention if you were involved with anyone," I say.

"Is this really what you want to talk about right now?"

"You know about Erik."

"Yeah, and I really don't want to talk about him."

"I just want to make sure you didn't have to give something up because of this."

"What we just did is motivation enough to give anything up," he jokes, squeezing me a little. "But to answer your question, no. I didn't give anyone up. However, there might be someone who'll be mad. And I only mention it since you will likely see her in Kenaz."

I face him. "What does that mean?"

"There's a woman I grew up with. Her father is close with mine. She and I were once… involved. It's been over for a long time, but she has a hard time accepting that."

"To be fair, after tonight, I can see why."

We both laugh, and he leans forward to kiss the top of my head.

"As much as I never want to leave this spring, we should probably get dressed and head back."

Once we return to our camp, Gaelen rebuilds the fire so we'll at least have the embers in the morning, before we both crawl into the tent. We haven't said much since leaving the spring, but the awkwardness seems to have gone with our reservations over touching each other. We lay down, just as we woke this morning, him against my back, arms wrapped around me, face buried in my hair.

Waking in the morning, we quickly dress, smiling at each other every time our gazes meet. After repacking as much as we can, we step out of the tent to find three men sitting around the camp.

"You two look like a couple that knows how to have a bit of fun!" the man farthest away says.

Gaelen grabs my hand, pulling me behind him. The men look as though they haven't bathed in weeks, if not longer, likely living out here in the woods.

"What do you want?" Gaelen asks.

"Let us join in, give us your gold, you know... the usual," the first man says, spinning a dirty knife on his finger.

"That's not happening," Gaelen says.

"The last people who visited the spring were nicer than you.

We let them leave with their lives."

"So, you what? Wait for people to visit the spring, take what you want from them, and kill them if they fight back?" Gaelen sneers.

"That's the gist of it," the man on the right says.

Gaelen nods before pulling his sword from its scabbard. Moving quickly, he lunges, the blade going through the gut of the man closest to him. The second man swings at him with a short blade, but Gaelen manages to twist away, his movements sharp and lethal. I see his sword come up in an arc before I'm being pulled backward and around the tent, rough hands over my mouth and around my body.

Another man steps into view to try to help my attacker pull me away. Thankfully, I have the small knife I used to cut the vegetables last night. I stab it through the new man's throat as he comes closer. I pull the knife free in a spray of blood right before my vision flashes white. Pain lancing through my scalp as the man behind me uses my hair to pull me with him, covering my mouth with dirty callused fingers so my screams can't be heard over the clang of swords.

I thrash my body, kicking my legs to no avail. How far can he really get me? What if more men are hiding and waiting? I can't even see what's happening to Gaelen. A swarm of panic fills my chest, and I can't get enough air with his hand over my mouth. My chest stutters with each attempt. It's then, when my body is filled with more terror than it's ever felt before, that something deep in my bones starts to unfurl, darkness writhing at the edges of my vision.

## Chapter Twelve

I feel the man's body go rigid behind me, his grip on my hair and mouth falling away. I turn quickly, taking a few steps back and out of his reach. His eyes are wide with horror, only they aren't focused on me, or anything, for that matter. A slow drain seems to pull from all of me.

No. No. No.

"What—What is—?"

His voice breaks into shrieks before he hits the ground, hands raking at the skin on his face, tearing deep gouges down his cheeks as though he's trying to rid himself of something only he can see. The man starts convulsing on the ground. Dread fills me as my stomach starts to churn.

Run, I need to run.

My body shaking, it takes a moment before my feet catch up with the command my mind is screaming. Running through the trees, I don't pay attention to the underbrush or small branches. My only goal is to put as much distance between the man on the ground and myself. Thorns catch my sleeve, embedding in my arm. Tearing free, I keep going. If it hurts, I don't notice the pain, only the resistance. I make it a few more yards before a hand wraps around my arm, quickly spinning me around.

"Thyrvi, stop!" Gaelen grips my other arm. His hands and shirt are wet with blood. "I was yelling for you."

I didn't hear. I can hardly hear him now over my pulse pounding in my ears. I look him over, not seeing anywhere the blood could be coming from. He surveys my body as well, stopping at the cuts on my arm from the thorns. In the distance, the screaming halts.

"What was that?" he asks, gesturing back in the direction of the man.

He's likely dead now. That's how it happened before. The screaming stops, just before the convulsions end.

I only shake my head in response, unable to speak. The memories of when I met the Goddess of the Night come flooding back. The blood. The sounds. Her gift. Each time, the power responded to my fear as a child. He pulls me into him, wrapping his arms around me for a few moments before kissing me on the head.

"It's over. You're safe now."

But he doesn't know.

He takes my hand, leading us back to the camp. I don't want to follow, don't want the sight seared into my memory, but I don't have it in me to protest. As we get closer to the man, I can tell he isn't breathing, his mouth covered in foam. I look up at Gaelen, confusion written on his face, along with something else. Fear.

"How did this happen?" His tone is firm, but not angry.

Still, I can't make myself answer him. I thought this was buried. Dead. Not my problem anymore. I've spent too long hiding this. To admit it now would be to admit that it was never over.

"Thyrvi, I can't protect you if I don't know what's going on," he says, grabbing my arms.

"Protect me?" I manage to croak out.

Is he insane? The laugh that escapes my lips is more feral than anything.

"I did this!" I point to the body lying before us. "Why would you think you need to protect me? Who will you protect me from? Myself?"

His eyes lock with mine for a matter of two heartbeats. Then he's pacing, his hands running through his hair and down over his face.

"Listen, there's more going on here than you realize." Looking up to the sky, he takes a deep breath. "I know how this is going to sound, but please let me explain before you jump to being upset with me."

His brow furrows. I nod in agreement, happy to let him be the one speaking instead of me.

"I'm not sure if it was always there, hiding, but in recent years, my father has turned mad. He has this witch, Thokkra, who's always been in and out of Kenaz. He started taking her counsel. At first, I thought they were just fucking, but now she's always by his side. My father doesn't care about your port. If he wanted it, I would've been sent here to deal with your brother, and he would own Thurisa."

He takes a breath.

"He wants something he thinks you have."

I can feel my heart as it drops; it might not even be beating at this point. The silence is strange after my deafening pulse only a few seconds prior. Cold snakes its way through my body.

"I don't have anything a king would want!" I say quickly, trying to convince myself as much as him.

"He ordered me to marry you, figure out whatever it is he

thinks you hide, and bring you back to Kenaz."

I know our relationship just started, but his words sting more than I'd like. I turn around, not able to face him, but in front of me, the man whose mind I just shattered lies on the ground. I try to walk away, not making it very far when his hand closes around my wrist again, pulling me to a stop.

"I asked you to let me finish."

This time, when he speaks, anger slips into his voice.

"Fuck you, Gaelen. You should've told me this before last night!" I yell at him, snatching my wrist away.

"I didn't tell you because I thought he was insane. I thought this was another pointless mission he sent me on, or a test of my loyalty. Another way to see just how far he can push me before he has to lock one of my friends or my brother in a dungeon to get me back in line!" He sighs, taking a step back and giving me space.

This can't be happening. I've made it so many years. No one has sought me, or it. Why now? Why him?

"I didn't believe him. I thought this was nothing, that you were just a normal woman, that he'd see that and move on to some other insane rambling, and I'd be off to the north in search of some random artifact or killing some unruly noble. I didn't tell you because I didn't believe it. I just thought he was mad, Thyrvi. I promise."

He stares at me, but I have nothing to say.

"I didn't want secrets between us, I just thought it wasn't real. I don't make a habit of telling people I think the king of Kenaz has lost his mind. I minimize the damage as best I can."

We've been awake maybe an hour, and I'm already exhausted. Head starting to pound, I sit gracelessly amidst the dirt and leaves. I don't have the heart to dance around this, nor do I want to. I'm not sure if I should, but my gut believes him. I can't blame him for not believing in any of this. I wouldn't.

Gods, I've spent how many years pretending it wasn't real, that nothing happened. All while people have been looking and plotting to take this stone. A king, even. How can I stand against a king?

Ignoring the voice in my head, I speak.

"It's all real, and this has happened before," I say as he bends down to sit next to me. "When my mother was dying, she gave me something. I'd never seen her with it before, but I didn't question it. Sometime after her death, I was taken in the middle of the night by an elderly woman. She brought me into the woods. I'm not even sure where or how far. We met someone else there, someone she knew. There was a ceremony in a language I didn't understand, and the woman was killed."

"The other person told me the gods were aware that I had this item, and that I needed to keep it hidden, before they slit their own throat. I was left there, not knowing what to do or where to go. Then another woman appeared, who I now know to be the goddess Nott. She seemed mad at the gods, maybe, said the night would give me a gift. That's all I remember. They found me covered in blood in my bed the next morning. No one knew what had happened or where the blood had come from. I didn't speak for some time after that."

Gaelen sits next to me, completely still. I'm not sure if he thinks I'm crazy, too, or if he is just worried I'd stop talking. Regardless, I know how all of this sounds.

"Nott is the Goddess of the Night, right?" he asks as if trying to piece everything together in his mind.

"She's the Goddess of Night and Dreams."

I wait to see if he will ask anything else, and when he doesn't, I continue.

"Word obviously travels fast in a small village, and people started to avoid me. They couldn't say anything outright, given my father's position and the fact that everyone grew up with, or watched my parents grow up. The village respected and loved him, and they certainly loved my mother. But that feeling no longer extended to me."

I stop to pull myself back together, or I won't make it through the rest. An autumn wind blows, stirring the leaves around us. I grab one to fidget with as I continue.

"After that, my father hired a woman from outside the village to help take care of me. No one in the village other than Earie was willing, and my father didn't want to burden her. The woman he hired was young. I can't even remember her name."

What does it say about me that I can't remember? I don't know the name of the man behind me either.

"Anyways, things were fine for a while. She treated me well, and I liked her enough. At some point, she started acting strangely. One night, she tried to get me into a small paddleboat; we were supposed to see a larger ship. I was afraid, and she wouldn't let me go, even when I begged to return home. The same thing that happened with this man happened to her."

I take a calming breath, trying to hold back the tears pricking at my eyes.

"I felt the power awaken, could feel it seek her out. She saw something I couldn't, but I can still hear the screaming. She fell to the ground, shaking, and then she was dead."

"Is this why that man in the tavern called you a mara?" He keeps his voice soft, but I know he has to have a thousand questions. "A spirit of nightmares?"

"Well, it would seem my victims don't need to be asleep. And no, that started the second time."

I look down at what's left of my leaf before throwing it away and grabbing another, determined to finish this story now that I've started.

"The first time, we were at the beach by the docks. A few sailors were still awake and saw her trying to get me into the boat. They didn't understand what had happened, but they told the story nonetheless. It was accepted that she was trying to take me. It was then that my father really started to close Thurisa, and even though people were wary of me, a potential kidnapping was reason enough."

"So, what happened the second time?"

"A village boy around the same age as my brother at the time called me names, making fun of what happened. He pushed me down, and I cut my arm on a rock. I didn't even have time to think before it was happening again. Saoirse was there, though, and between the boy's scream and hers, I just wanted it all to stop. He didn't die, but what he described seeing was awful. He left Thurisa shortly after turning eighteen. That man from the tavern, Ketill, was his friend."

"Has it happened any other times?"

"No. My father started making me train with my brother and Erik. I think he knew something was happening and wanted me to have another means of protection to rely on. Regardless, I pushed it down, refused to think about it, and at some point, it was gone. Or so I thought."

He might be the last person I should be telling this to, but finally sharing everything with another person feels as if a weight has been lifted.

"Your father must have known. If not everything, I'm sure he knew something. You said your parents were in love. Would your mother not have told him?"

"I don't know. Maybe. It was made very clear that I shouldn't tell anyone during the ceremony."

"And your brother doesn't know?"

I shake my head.

"You're the only person I've told, and as far as I know, the only other living person that knows." The look on his face tells me the weight of that truth isn't lost on him. He pauses before nodding.

"This thing your mother gave you. Did they tell you what it is?"

"No, but it was referred to as a key."

"Don't tell me what it is, or where. I don't know what my father or Thokkra will do."

At his words, I realize I never mentioned it being a stone or my bracelet. I fight the urge to twist it around my wrist. He moves to stand, reaching to pull me up with him.

"Thyrvi, I don't think you were supposed to grow up with no knowledge of this. I think if your mother had lived longer, she would've passed down information. Something."

"Maybe, but I have no way of knowing now."

"Maybe not. I think we need to find a witch of our own. And I know of rumors that could lead us to one."

We walk back to camp, avoiding the second man I killed, the other still lying behind our tent. The first three men lay dead around the fire; the area littered with blood and gore. Gaelen moves the bodies away from the campsite and spring, leaving them in the woods for the crows. We change back into our clothes from yesterday, burning the ones now covered in blood.

# Chapter Thirteen

The journey back to Thurisa is quiet. Even the birds are silent as we walk through the forest, as if they know what I did.

For someone who just received a large amount of information and realized the mess he is stuck in the middle of is bigger than he thought, he isn't asking questions. I wouldn't blame him if he were trying to find a way out of this. I wouldn't be thrilled if I were forced into a marriage with me either.

I should be thinking this over as well. It would help if I knew what this stone could do that would make a king interested in it. I need a plan. Or maybe just a ship out of here. If I tell Hagen everything, will he help me? Or would that be putting him at risk, as well as Thurisa? There's always the chance he'll find a way to use this to his advantage, as a bargaining chip for whatever else it is he wants. If I turn to Erik, he will help, but insist on coming with me.

Up ahead, the village gates come into view, along with the sounds of Thurisa's people going on with their lives. I wonder what they'll think of me.

Gaelen comes to a stop.

"If you're okay with it, I'd like my friends to travel with us. We don't have to tell them everything, and they won't ask questions."

"I don't know, Gaelen. If this is happening again, people being around me is a risk. Honestly, you should consider staying away, too."

"We're less likely to be attacked on the road if we're in a larger party. Less chance of attack means you can worry less about it happening again."

"That's unlikely."

As if I'm going to worry about anything else.

"And Thyrvi," he says, lifting my chin. "I'm not afraid of you."

His lips press against mine softly.

"We'll figure the rest out; I just need you to give me time."

We briefly stop at the tavern to drop off our bags, and Gaelen asks Soren to find the others. I decide I need to tell Saoirse something at least, or it'll look like we're leaving without her. Gaelen insists on coming with me.

At the Branton's, Len directs us to the back of the house where we find Saoirse working in their small garden. Gaelen lingers at the entrance, giving us space to speak.

"How was the spring?" A knowing smile lights up her face.

"The spring was amazing," I say with a laugh.

Even in a time like this, it's impossible not to laugh when she looks at me like that.

"Thank you for helping him arrange it. I wanted to stop by and tell you we're going on another trip. The other guys are coming with us, but I didn't want you to think we left without you. We should only be gone a couple of days."

"Where are you going?" Suspicion at the edge of her tone.

"I actually don't know. To see someone Gaelen knows."

"I'm coming with you," she says, glaring at Gaelen, brows knitting together.

I should've known this wouldn't be easy. She's one of the most stubborn people I know.

"It might not be safe."

"All the more reason for me to come! Look, I like the guy, but he can't just take you with no one knowing where you are."

My heart warms at her concern, even if it's misplaced.

"It's not him that's the problem."

Just getting those words out is a strain, but I can't let her think Gaelen is the issue here.

"What's the problem then, Thyrvi?"

I close my eyes, taking a deep breath before speaking.

"It happened again," I say, looking into her eyes.

She's a year older than I am. She likely remembers the time frame better than I do, though we've never spoken of it. I can already see the color draining from her face.

"Tell me."

"You remember what happened when I was younger?" I ask quietly, as if she and Gaelen weren't the only people in earshot.

Her expression turns grim, but she nods.

"This morning, we woke to men outside our tent. A fight broke out between them and Gaelen, but two were hiding in the woods. They snuck up on me. One, I managed to stab; the other, I couldn't get away from."

Even though this just happened today, it feels as if days have passed.

"I thought it was gone all this time. It wasn't. It was just hidden, buried, or asleep, I don't know."

Tears start to form, though I try to hold them back. To her credit, she doesn't back away. I watch as she works through it in her mind, then seems to resolve herself.

"So, where's Gaelen taking you?" she asks defensively.

"He thinks there's a witch that can help, tell me how to get rid of it, control it, or at least give us information."

Despite her knowing about this, I have never told her about the stone. I don't need to put her in any more danger than I already am.

"I'm coming with you. It's not up for discussion. I'll follow you if you say no."

She says it with so much finality in her voice. I wish I had a fraction of that conviction at this point.

"Thank you." That's all I can say in the face of the dedication I don't deserve from anyone.

I walk through the door of Gaelen's room, caught off guard by the multiple trunks lining the far wall.

"I hope you don't mind. I asked Bjark to buy the trunks and have some of your things moved here while we were gone. I thought it would be easier if you didn't have to go back and forth, and one less thing for you to worry about."

"Did Bjark pack them?" I ask, wrinkling my nose, thinking of what he might have seen.

"No, don't worry. I think one of the women who works in the hall did it," he says with a laugh.

It was thoughtful of him to make sure this was taken care of, but a little strange to think of someone packing my clothes. Searching through the trunks, I feel bad messing up all the neatly folded clothes; they did a much better job than I would have. Finally, I pull out a nightgown. Gaelen kisses me on the head before making his way toward the door.

"I need to check on things for tomorrow. I'll be back soon."

I draw a bath, sinking into the warm water and bubbles. I scrub my hair and body, removing this day from it as best I can. If I wanted to say to hell with everything and jump on a ship, would Gaelen let me leave? Would he want to go with me? I have no idea how far his father is willing to go to get the stone. Would leaving even be enough?

I know Saoirse would go with me. Even if she didn't want to go specifically to help me, she would go for the adventure. When we were little, we'd imagine the trips we'd go on, seeing the lands on the other side of the sea. I know if I told her everything, she would want to help. But I don't understand why Gaelen does.

I soak in the water longer than I originally intended, lost in thought. The water starting to cool gives me the motivation I needed to finally leave the water. I comb quickly through my hair, throwing the nightgown over my head.

I find Gaelen lying on the bed asleep. He must have been waiting for me. His face is peaceful. My hand reaches forward to move the lock of hair that always falls into his face as he stirs. His arm reaches out to grab me, pulling me into bed with him, his body instantly molding around mine.

"Horses do not like me," I say, looking ahead at the six horses saddled and ready for our journey. "I can't ride a horse."

"Thyrvi, how did you think we were going to get there?" Gaelen says with a smirk on his face.

"I don't know. Walk? I didn't think about it."

He stands behind me, hands on my shoulders, pushing me toward the line of horses.

"You will be fine. Today is as good a day as any to learn."

"No, you don't understand ... I know how to ride them, or I did before everything happened. Since then, horses are afraid of me," I whisper. "You know, being a *Mara* and all that."

"You're ridiculous," he says, face softening. "You can ride my horse. He's grumpy, but he isn't afraid of anything. All our horses are battle-trained. I don't believe any in Thurisa are, but we'll get you your own in Kenaz."

He points to a dark brown horse in the middle. As we move closer, they all seem to be paying attention to me, but to their credit, the only ones that seem spooked are the two on the end, both from Thurisa. Gaelen holds out his hands, fingers interlaced for me to step into. As I do, he helps lift my body onto his horse, making sure my feet are in the stirrups and giving me a refresher as to how everything works. He rides the horse meant for me but is careful to stay next to me during the journey, talking and pointing out scenic things.

Rorik rides next to Saoirse, ahead of us. Now and then, he leans closer to her and says something, always followed by her laughter. It doesn't go unnoticed by Gaelen, who side-eyes me but shrugs his shoulders. I make a mental note to ask her about it when we stop.

"What makes you think this witch will help us?" I ask him.

"I don't know that she will. But I remember Thokkra complaining about her once. Rumors are that she lives not far from Thurisa. If Thokkra hates her, I think that makes her our best option."

That much makes sense, but something is still bothering me.

"Why are you even helping me? Wouldn't it be easier to give your father what he wants? You don't even know me. You could probably get out of this by Yule. You already know everything; he doesn't need you married to me."

I prepare my emotional shields for whatever his response will be. What I didn't prepare for was the look on his face as though he doesn't like my question.

"Thyrvi, I don't need you to open up and tell me everything to realize that you've had to deal with a lot, alone. You're not alone anymore. My father may have forced me into this, but I chose to make it real. You're going to have to accept that I'm on your side. And I think she is, too." He nods to Saoirse. "Besides, this all being real makes it even more imperative that Thokkra doesn't get your key. Nothing she is involved in can be good."

After hours of riding, we head off the road to make camp. There is a small clearing near a stream where the horses can be watered, and there's space for them to graze. The men are so used to traveling together that they have everything set up in no time without us. Bjark starting the fire and food, Soren tending the horses, and Gaelen and Rorik setting up the tents.

I help Saoirse get settled in her tent, recognizing an opportunity when I see one.

"So, Rorik?" I ask, eyebrow raised.

"Oh… yeah, he's nice." Her voice carries a hint of forced nonchalance.

"Yeah, pretty nice to look at," I say flatly.

A contagious laugh escapes her, filling the small space.

"Excuse me, didn't you just marry a man that's pretty nice to look at?"

"Oh, him? Yeah, I suppose I did get lucky there." I roll out her sleeping mat, crawling across it. "But we're talking about you!"

"Rorik has been at the bakery a lot lately, but just looking at him tells me he doesn't eat pastries. He's nice, though, and he makes me laugh," she says.

Bjark yells that dinner is ready. I haven't spent much time with Gaelen's friends, but this trip has been refreshing at least, whenever I'm able to pull my mind away from why we're here.

Now that the power is "awakened" or "unlocked", I can feel it inside of me. It's not confined to one spot; it's as though the power is coiled around all of me. I know it would be easy to call on now. I wouldn't need to be afraid to use it, which is concerning since I have no idea how to control it.

Bjark hands us each a bowl of food, pulling me from my

thoughts. Gaelen and I sit on a log, and Saoirse on another. Rorik takes the seat next to her, and she and I share a look. The group starts reminiscing about one of their prior trips, laughing and making fun of each other. Bjark is definitely the more serious of the four, and something tells me keeping them in line can be a full-time job.

"How far are we from the witch?" I quietly ask Gaelen during a lull in the conversation.

"It shouldn't take long once we set out in the morning."

I'm not sure what he told everyone the reason for this trip was, but he promised to tell them it could be a risk, even though he swore they wouldn't mind.

"Saoirse, do you want me to sleep in your tent tonight so you aren't alone?" I ask after realizing she also doesn't camp often.

A look of betrayal instantly covers Gaelen's face, and we all start to laugh.

"I would hate to make the prince live without you for an evening," she says, continuing to giggle.

"Don't worry about her, my tent is close by," Rorik says with a wink in her direction.

I don't think anyone else notices the flush creeping up her neck. It's hidden mostly by her hair, but it's always been her tell.

"Besides, we'll be keeping watch in shifts. No risking what

happened last time," Bjark says with a pointed look at Gaelen.

"We've been over this. I wasn't bringing all of you with us," Galen says.

"Would have been way more fun if you did!" Soren says, winking in my direction.

The joke catches me off guard since he seems to make an effort to avoid me, but then I realize he's goading Gaelen.

"I will kill you," Gaelen says.

"Maybe next time, Soren," I say, letting a hint of playfulness into my tone.

"Absolutely not," Gaelen growls, and the camp fills with laughter.

He pulls me closer until our legs are touching and then leans down, whispering "Mine" into my ear.

"I think you two need to go to bed before we all get in trouble!" Saoirse says.

We sit around the fire a little longer, telling jokes and stories from the past. Saoirse even joins in, telling the story about the first time we saw a whale as children. I was convinced it was the sea serpent, so we packed a bag and both set out to find it. We got lost, of course, and our parents, with the entire village, spent a long while looking for us. It was a few months before my mother's death.

When we finally head to bed, it's decided that Saoirse and I will be exempt from watch duty, something I wasn't going to complain about. With Gaelen on the last shift, we settle into our blankets, and I fall asleep to the sound of his breathing.

## Chapter Fourteen

I wake the next morning to the wind rustling through tree branches and birds singing to each other. I don't need to turn around to know that Gaelen is already gone; his absence is the first thing I sense.

It's strange to realize I enjoy waking up with him and that I like his company. I have never had one of those thought-consuming relationships. Is this what they feel like?

Outside the tent, Gaelen and Bjark sit by the fire. Bjark is cooking again, which seems to be his designated job among the group. They notice me, but I only wave and walk over to

Saoirse's tent. Pushing it open, I find it empty, her things already packed. Confused, I turn and find Gaelen walking over.

"She went with Rorik to water the horses by the stream. Also, Rorik took first shift, and Soren mentioned she was going to bed when he was taking over," he says, eyebrows raised.

"Who knew you bunch would be such gossips!" I slap his chest in jest.

"We spend a lot of time together; we have to pass it somehow." I shake my head and walk over to the fire. It might not be winter yet, but the mornings certainly have a chill to them.

Once everything is packed and the horses fed, we set out again. This time, the joking and camaraderie are absent, a grim silence in their place. The act of seeking a witch is serious business, apparently, even for those who don't have a murderous power clinging to their bones.

I don't want to get my hopes up, but I can't help the twinge of excitement that forms in my stomach. Today could be the day that I finally learn what secrets my mother held. There's a significant possibility I don't want to know them, but I ignore that thought for now.

As if sensing my spiraling emotions, Gaelen reaches over and grabs my hand, running his thumb over my knuckles.

"Are you okay?"

"What if she can't help?" I ask.

"Then we're in the same place we were before, but you left Thurisa at least."

I smile and nod at his easy attitude, not wanting to bring up the fact that she could give us answers we don't like.

We pass a few houses built close together. Not enough to be considered a village, just a few families and farmland. At the last house, a woman is outside, and a few small children are running about. Soren asks her if we're close to someone named Run's house, and though she doesn't seem eager to speak with us, she points to a small path farther down the road that veers into the trees. We travel down the path single file for about half an hour before it finally gives way to an opening.

A small yellow house sits with a garden on each side, wildflowers growing in patches everywhere else. Gaelen dismounts his horse, walking over to help me down, his hands around my waist. I don't need help with this part, but I think he's nervous and needs to do something. Once on the ground, I look back toward the house, this time to find an older woman waiting on the porch.

"I have been waiting for you, Child. You took your time," the woman says. "Leave your friends and come inside."

"How do I know she'll be safe?" Gaelen yells to her.

"Would her nightmares not ensure it?" she asks, giving us both pause.

I glance back at him before standing on my toes to reach up and kiss his cheek. I'm not sure why I do it, but it seems like he needs it. Then, I walk toward the woman, and hopefully, answers.

Once inside, the house is everything I had imagined it would be. A long table off to the side, a chair by the fire, every surface covered in herbs, jars, books, and bones. Herbs hang over everything, drying. The table is covered in those already dried, being ground and added to open jars. The smell is amazing, unequivocally of the earth. I take a closer look at the jars lining a shelf on the far wall, and they're all filled with various colors of dark liquid. I don't want to know what they contain.

The woman is shorter than I am, a little hunched over from age. Her gray hair is long and left loose, though small braids with items woven into them are scattered throughout. She pulls out a small stool and sets it in front of her chair by the fire before she sits, gesturing for me to take the stool. Her eyes lock with mine, and they're the brightest blue I've ever seen.

"Sit," she says.

I keep my eyes on hers as I do.

"How did you know I would come here? And if you waited so long, why not just come find me?"

"You might have lost your mother, but it would seem you found another in an unlikely place, Child of the Night."

"I don't think that's how it works."

"It works however the gods want it to, dear."

She takes an appraising look at me, her face not giving away any opinions she might be forming.

"My name is Runa, and I have lived here for a very long time. Most of that time has been spent as a practicing witch, but never have the gods visited me. No, not until you. Nott appeared here shortly after she met with you, Child. I expected you to come sooner after your father's death."

"How would I have known to find you? Or even that there was anyone to find?" I take a deep breath, trying to keep my composure. "Parts of me thought I imagined meeting her."

The scowl on her face makes it pretty clear what she thinks of that answer.

"I assumed you would go looking for answers as soon as the

doors were open. I did not realize you were content to live in your ignorance."

"Well, I was. And why should I trust that you can provide me with the correct answers? I was under the impression this whole thing was a secret."

"It is. Even in her ancient mind, the goddess knew you would need help. Her solution was me. There are things I know, and I am sure more I don't. But for my part, I will help you as best I can. The stone, when was the last time you felt its frost?"

I remember when my mother first handed me the stone; it was cold. I remember it being cold after, when I would sit in my room looking at it. When was the last time?

"The night of the ceremony," I say.

She nods, taking a moment to think.

"You cannot trust every witch or seer you meet; it would be wiser to trust none."

"None except you?" I ask, giving her a leveling gaze.

"Some are dedicated to the wrong side. Thokkra, for example. I imagine your prince has told you of her. She believes she has found the vessel destined to house Loki's power when it enters this world."

"I'm sorry, what does Loki have to do with this?" I ask.

Runa closes her eyes and sighs.

"I forget how little you know. What do you think the key

opens?"

"Something tells me it isn't some long-lost treasure? I don't know. I didn't think about it. I didn't even believe in it! I don't even know if I believe any of this now!"

"Well, you must believe. The stone housed the key to releasing the lock in Yggdrasil that blocks the trickster's power from entering our world. Loki is dead. He died for the same reasons our gods would have if they stayed there. His power was fractured, though. Some in the lock, and some in the key. So, the rest remains waiting."

"You're saying my mother knew she guarded the key to Loki's power?"

"Yes, had she lived, she would have started to teach you in the coming years. Since she did not, and there were no other females born in her line, the knowledge died with her."

It's hard to imagine my mother hiding something this big. She wasn't a secretive person. I suppose I technically wouldn't know, but no one has ever given the impression that she was hiding some dark secret. Not even Earie, who knew her better than anyone.

"Wait. You said '*housed*', as if it no longer does. Where is the key now?"

"You are the key, or your blood is. You are the last that will be assigned to the key, and the key itself. You will not be able to pass this down the way your mother did. She likely would not have known it would be different for you. If you die before Loki's power is destroyed, it will be freed."

She says this calmly, as if it's common knowledge, and not information that will shatter my entire existence. A pit forms inside me, my stomach falling into it. This is more than I can process. I find myself standing, walking back and forth, before I even realize I left the stool.

"Why am I the last?"

"Something has triggered this deviation from the usual path, but I do not know what."

"You're saying I have to go to Yggdrasil and destroy this power? With what?"

I feel my breath quickening as though I'm not getting enough oxygen, the sides of my body squeezing in.

"Something capable of killing a god, I would imagine. There is mention of a dagger created for this purpose, long ago. After the goddess visited, I tried to research as much as I could in preparation for you seeking me. The best I could do was find a riddle that mentions it. It is said to be hidden in halls of stone, where sun dares not and shadows cling. Bound, a wolf keeps watch, and a dagger sleeps."

"Why were you so certain I'd ever find you?"

"I did not keep my location a secret. Everyone from here to Thurisa knows how to find me. Did you not think to ask your prince how he knew I was here? Your father kept you close after they tried to take you, but he has been gone for years now. I made sure it was widely known so that you would come. Though I underestimated just how much you kept your head beneath sand."

She doesn't even try to conceal her aggravation.

"And what about the power the goddess gave me? Can you tell me how to get rid of it?"

"I need a drop of your blood."

I hesitate, despite knowing I'll agree regardless, as something tells me I shouldn't. Slowly, I nod. She gestures to the table where a knife lay next to the herbs she must have been working on. I walk over and pick it up before returning to my abandoned stool. I prick the pad of my thumb, blood welling to the surface. I squeeze the sides, pulling it forward before looking at her, unsure what she wants me to do with it. She gestures for my hand to come closer before quickly snatching hold of it, bringing my thumb to her mouth. I feel as her tongue brushes over the surface, revulsion making me pull away. She seems to get lost inside her mind for a long moment. A humming sound comes from her before she snaps back to the conversation.

"The echoes of your fate are vast; you will be faced with many possibilities, and the paths you will force are uncertain. As for the power, that I can taste. You cannot be rid of it. It belongs to you now. You have always been able to control it.

You have just feared it too heavily. It is not rational to fear it; there is nothing it can do to you."

"It can hurt people I care about."

"Sure, if you fail to control it."

"And what is it, specifically?"

"Nott is the Goddess of the Night. She is also the Goddess of Dreams. She gave you the ability to pull forth a person's nightmares. It is all they will see. As their mind fights to regain control and make sense of what is happening, it will start to fracture if left for too long. Which is what you have seen happen, I assume."

When I said I wanted to leave Thurisa, none of this was what I had in mind. Sightseeing, sure. This is too much, far bigger than anything I should be responsible for.

"And what if I just go home and do nothing with any of this?" I ask.

"Then, upon your death, the trickster's power will be released on this world. I don't know what will happen, but I cannot imagine it will forgive what the gods did. "

"That sounds like a problem for the gods."

"It is also unlikely you will ever live peacefully, even if you run across the sea. Thokkra already knows who you are. The only reason you are still alive is that she thinks you hide the key. Meaning killing you could see it lost forever."

"And why isn't that what the gods did? Just hide it

somewhere, or take it with them?"

"I do not speak for the Aesir who made these choices, Child. I only share with you what I know, and that is little. I think you have choices to make. Now return to your prince, if he paces anymore, I'll have a hole in my path," she says with a dismissive wave.

# Chapter Fifteen

I can feel Gaelen's eyes on me as soon as I walk through the door. I keep my head lowered, not willing to meet his gaze. I don't know what he'll find on my face, and I need to think things through before I tell him.

He must sense I need a moment as he doesn't try to touch me, just helps me onto his horse before he mounts the other.

"Let's find a place to speak," he says to no one in particular.

How am I going to explain to Gaelen that I'm the key to freeing the very power Odin was so afraid of that he locked it in another world? My mother hid this from me and gave me the stone. At seven years old. Seven! Regardless of whether she knew I'd become the key, leaving the stone useless or not, this all felt wrong. I was a child! She should've given it to my father, bloodline or not. I don't have many memories left from that time, but I try replaying what I can in my mind.

I've always been told how much my parents loved each other. There's no way she could've kept something this big from him unless he knew. Perhaps the training was about more than the unusual events that occurred. Maybe he knew I'd need to protect the stone, or at least myself, and did everything he could to help me.

Sure, people know of the gods, but he made sure I knew every saga, even the lesser-known deities. I know every piece of lore, every creature, every myth. I thought it was just something we shared, his means of bonding with me. My brother never had to learn it all, though. General history, politics, noble houses, other villages, the lands across the sea —these are all things he's very well-versed in. Because Hagen would be responsible for Thurisa, and I, the key. But why not just tell me?

We travel a few miles past the huddle of houses and down the wood-lined road before Gaelen decides to stop, swinging down from his horse before walking over and holding out his hand for me.

"Thyrvi and I need to speak for a moment," he says to the

group, pulling me back down the path. "Are you okay?"

"I'm still digesting everything. She told me more than I expected to hear." Just enough to leave a thousand questions, though. "It's a lot even to accept, let alone decide what to do with."

My exhale shudders out of me. I'm going to have to say it all out loud now, and the sinking feeling returns, my new reality, the weight preventing me from taking a full breath.

"You don't have to tell me anything if you're not ready. But I do want to help."

I don't know if he intends it, but his arms wrap around my waist as he speaks. I decide to start at the beginning.

"You know the story of how the gods created our world? And why they locked Loki in the old one?"

"His scheme went too far right, costing the gods their power?"

I nod in confirmation before continuing.

"Right, well, it would seem they also took some of his power to forge the lock and the key." I hold up my wrist, showing him the bracelet I've worn there longer than I haven't. "The key lived in this stone for hundreds of years."

He glances at the bracelet, his eyes roaming over the stone before returning to mine.

"And it doesn't now?"

"No. Runa doesn't know why, but she said my blood is now

the key to freeing Loki's power."

His face pales, one hand leaving me to run across his jaw.

"There's more, though. Since the key has left the stone, I can't give it away. Upon my death, the lock will fail in Yggdrasil. If someone wanted to free the power, all they'd need to do is kill me."

The muscles in his jaw tense at my words.

"No one is going to kill you."

His words sound more like a declaration than a response.

"Maybe, but I won't live forever. Not that I'd want to condemn a child to this, but I can't pass it down. If I die tomorrow, or of old age, the power will be free."

"Did she say what we should do?"

His use of *we* is a spark that pulls me back from the darkness trying to swallow me. It's a simple word, but it makes me feel a little less alone.

"Destroying it was suggested."

He seems to think about this before speaking again.

"Is this why you have magic?"

"No, Nott was pissed that the gods would leave this to a child, so it seems her answer was giving me the ability to kill people with their own nightmares."

He pulls me even closer, and his lips brush mine briefly.

"I have to go back to Kenaz."

I lean back to look at him, confused as to what I just heard.

I step out of his grasp.

"What?"

"The longer I'm gone, the more suspicious my father and Thokkra will become. I need to try to convince him that she was wrong. Maybe I can push them in another direction, just until we can figure out how to destroy the power."

"And if you can't?"

"I'll find another way. I'll kill her if I need to. He might be more reasonable with her gone."

"Gaelen, I can't ask you to kill anyone."

Regardless of his relationship with his father, I don't want to be an addition to their problems.

"You're not. I need you to give me time. I know you have to be thinking about running, and if this goes poorly, and that's what you want, I'll go with you. We'll figure the rest out together, just let me try."

"And what would we tell everyone else?"

"That's your call. I trust them with my life, but that doesn't mean you have to. If I say I can't elaborate, they'll leave it alone."

In the end, I decided to go forward with them, knowing as much as possible about what they are getting into. We tell our friends about the key, leaving out only that it's no longer a separate object and the power Nott gave me.

Gaelen feels as though it's an extra layer of protection if no one else knows. To their credit, none of them so much as bat an eye. Saoirse's eyebrows do run the risk of reaching her hairline, though, and I'm sure she'll have questions later, but in this moment, they're all just eager to hear our plan.

"I'm going back to Kenaz, and because of everything you just learned, I'm asking you to stay with Thyrvi," Gaelen says to Bjark, Rorik, and Soren.

"You can't go alone," I argue.

"She's right, at least take one of us," Rorik says.

"I've spent years thinking my father was going mad; the fact that he isn't makes this even more dangerous. I need to learn the lengths he's willing to go, and I need to appear as casual as possible."

"Let me come with you, I'll stay in the city. We both know I have connections in the castle. I would just be nearby if you need me," Soren says.

"By connections, you mean lovers?" Rorik asks.

"They're still connections," Soren says, shooting him a glare.

"Just take him with you. If you're making them stay for my safety, you can give me the same peace of mind."

Gaelen turns to me, eyes softening as he nods.

"Fine, Soren, you're with me. The rest of you go straight back to Thurisa, no stopping," Galen orders.

"Wait, you're leaving now?" I thought we'd at least have another day or two.

"Worried you'll miss me?"

I look at him without responding because I know the answer is yes. He must realize it too, the corner of his mouth lifting just slightly.

"The sooner I go, the sooner I can come back. I've been gone too long anyway, and we need to establish how much they know."

Just like that, the group of men are back to moving with an efficiency that could only come from spending many years together, moving around items from saddle bags, prioritizing who needs what supplies based on each journey. Gaelen and Soren obviously have to travel longer, but they also don't want to weigh down their horses. Our group will keep traveling after dark. We'll arrive in Thurisa after midnight.

"Take care of my horse," Gaelen says, smiling at me before his arms are around me again. "And stay in my room at the tavern. Your clothes are already there, and it'll be easier for Bjark and Rorik to keep you safe. One of them needs to be with you at all times."

The key to his room presses into my hand.

"Great, so now I have a babysitter?"

"Just give me this, please. It's only temporary."

The look on his face stopping my argument.

"Fine."

"And stay away from Erik. If he touches you again, I'm going to have to kill him."

"Some might accuse you of becoming possessive," I joke.

"Possessive would be an understatement." His hand wraps around the back of my neck and pulls me toward him, his kiss claiming.

"Stay safe, and don't go anywhere!"

"I'll be right where you found me last time," I promise.

## Chapter Sixteen

"Rorik, you're in the front. Saoirse and Thyrvi ride side by side in the middle. I'll bring up the rear. If we're attacked, you stay on your horses. You keep moving, you do not stop, you get to Thurisa," Bjark says.

He's always been no-nonsense, but his tone catches me off guard.

"And what if you're outnumbered? We leave you to die?" Saoirse asks.

Of course, his gruff attitude doesn't stop her.

"Yes," Bjark and Rorik say in unison.

Saoirse and I glance at each other.

"Don't even think about it. I've known Gaelen most of his life. And that life has never belonged to him. There's very little he cares about. If he's taking a stand now, you're not getting hurt on my watch!" Bjark says.

He doesn't know about the nightmares, though. Regardless of what he says, I know Gaelen loves his friends, and I'm not letting anyone die trying to save me.

The next few hours pass with very little excitement. Rorik is far more reserved on our return trip, constantly scanning the wilderness ahead of us. Every once in a while, he'll find something to say to Saoirse, and the two will go back and forth a little. It makes me glad he wasn't the one to leave with Gaelen. She deserves to see if this can be something. Even if it goes nowhere, she can at least have fun.

I was mad at Gaelen for lying, but I don't think we would've gotten to this point so quickly if he hadn't. I don't think I've even accepted the fact that I won't see him for weeks, but to be fair, my mind hasn't accepted anything that's happened today. It's strange how quickly I've adapted to not being alone. I've even been enjoying the guys' constant joking.

"Hold," Rorik says.

His firm voice pulling me from my thoughts. We're almost free of the tree line, the path opening to a large field before it makes its way back into the woods. He's staring at something around the corner that the rest of us can't yet see.

Once our horses have halted, the sounds of people up ahead come into earshot. The sun starts to move just below the trees.

"Multiple men, horses, and a wagon," he relays.

"It's probably just merchants on their way to Thurisa," I say.

"Cart looks empty."

"They could be picking up goods from the docks," Saoirse says.

Bjark moves his horse to pass us, stopping once he's next to Rorik.

"They appear to be getting ready to eat. Let's continue on our way, no stopping. If something goes wrong, you two get out of the area. We'll find you after," Bjark says, giving me a hard stare.

Rorik and Bjark stay to the left of us, as if blocking us from the group. I keep my head down, trying not to draw any attention.

"Bjark? Is that you?" one of the men yells.

"Fuck," Bjark says, exhaling.

"Rorik? It's Sten," the man yells and starts walking toward

us.

"Stay on your fucking horses and be ready to run," Rorik orders.

He and Bjark dismount, meeting the man a few feet away. I watch as they clasp hands and hug, appearing excited to see each other.

"I didn't expect to see you two until tomorrow," Sten says.

"What are you doing here?" Bjark asks.

"The king sent us," Sten says, causing a chill to run down my spine. "Says Prince Gaelen's taking too long. Ordered us to bring him and the woman back to Kenaz."

"You think the seven of you are going to be enough to force Gaelen into something he doesn't want to do?" Bjark asks, running his gaze over the group.

"King's orders," a man behind him chimes in.

"And if he isn't ready to go back to Kenaz?" Rorik asks.

"The king said we have to bring the woman. If Gaelen's in a mood, we're to leave him and let him come in on his own."

"Come on, Sten, you're not an idiot. Gaelen's never going to allow you to take her," Bjark says.

"Where is Gaelen, by the way? Isn't that his horse?" another man in the group asks.

"Back in the village, enjoying his wife, I'm sure," Rorik says.

"You're saying he actually likes the girl?" the man in the

back asks.

"I'm saying they've hardly left their room since the wedding night. So, if you want to go interrupt, it's your head," Rorik says.

I clench my teeth in an effort not to say anything about the way they're speaking of me.

"Maybe you can talk to him for us? You've always been able to keep him under control, Bjark. If we don't bring her to the king, well, you know how he can be."

"Who are the women with you? Why don't you introduce us?" another man from the group yells, walking over from the other side of their fire. "Why don't the four of you come join us? We'll share the ale, and you can share the women."

I glance at Saoirse. She has a dagger ready, holding it by her leg out of sight. I'm better with a bow and could fall at least two before the others could reach us, but grabbing it from where it's attached to the saddle would be too obvious.

"I don't think they'd like you," Bjark says, his tone commanding enough to give the man pause.

"We're on the king's business. Women love to fuck men who work for the king," the man says.

He moves to walk over to where Saoirse and I remain, but the second he's in line with Rorik's shoulder, his sword is drawn to the man's neck, preventing him from moving any closer.

"Sten, I know you, and I know what kind of man you are. I don't know these other men, and they obviously don't know me. Get them under control if they want to leave with their lives," Bjark says, his words almost a growl at the end.

The rest of the men standing draw various weapons. Someone, obviously emboldened by ale, yells that they only answer to the king. Bjark looks back at us, head nodding once as he pulls his sword. Before I realize what's happening, Saoirse has grabbed my reins and both our horses start to sprint through the forest.

"What the fuck are you doing?" I yell over the sound of hooves, gripping onto the saddle so as not to fly off the back of Gaelen's horse.

She doesn't respond, but after a few minutes of running, she tosses my reins back to me.

"They're outnumbered."

"Exactly why they don't need to worry about keeping us safe," she says, pulling her horse to a stop and jumping from the saddle.

She guides the horse behind a large rock and then ties it to a nearby tree.

"Are you coming?"

She looks back at me as though I am stupid for not picking up on this sooner.

"They all think we're gone. They won't be looking for us

during the fight. We can sneak back and help if needed."

Relief floods through me at her words. At least I won't have to fight her on this. I dismount and tie my horse up with hers, grabbing the bow and quiver. The closer we get, the sounds of metal on metal grow increasingly louder. I thank the gods for the underbrush that hides us from view.

One of their men is holding his side, blood seeping through his hands, and another is on the ground, not moving. It's still five against two, though.

Rorik is parrying his sword against one man while the other four are focused on Bjark. My breath catches as I watch one man manage to trip Bjark, and he falls to his knees, still meeting each swing of the man's sword with his own.

My hearing muffles with the sound of blood pumping too quickly through my body. I have to do something. Grabbing an arrow, I line myself up, but we're too far. There are too many trees. I don't have a clear shot from here.

I see the gleam of a sword raised, poised to come down on Bjark's throat as he's defending against another. Before I realize it, I'm running, the nightmares unfurling from their resting place within me, accompanied by an eagerness to be used that I've never felt before.

The sword is inches away from a killing blow, but the man falls in front of Bjark, dropping his sword as he goes down. And then the screaming starts. I watch as the other three fall at the same time as their comrade.

Rorik slashes through his opponent's stomach, entrails hitting the ground before his body. With the man dying, Rorik spins around, seeming to look for Bjark and taking in the men lying on the ground.

Rorik and Bjark notice me just as Saoirse reaches me. A dull ache sets in my head. Two of the men start convulsing, seconds away from their minds breaking.

"Try to pull it back," she says.

I look at her, not understanding.

"When will you be able to practice otherwise? I know you can do it; I've seen it! Pull it back!"

Focusing inward, I notice the tether connecting me to the four men. I can feel that two are near death, but Sten is not quite at that point. I call the power back from him and can feel it easing from his mind.

The other three are too far gone, but Sten opens his eyes, just in time for Rorik to run his sword across his neck. Rorik reaches out his hand to help Bjark stand, and together, both men turn to me. The dull ache has now transformed into a throbbing behind my eyes.

"I told you to stay on your gods-damned horse and ride to Thurisa," Bjark says, his tone low and laced with anger.

"You were going to die," I say.

"I wasn't. I've been doing this for twenty years. I had it

under control."

"It didn't look like you had it under control from where I was standing."

"You shouldn't have been standing at all!" he bellowed. "And what the fuck was that?"

"You need to stop yelling at her," Saoirse says, stepping in front of me.

"Okay, everyone, calm down," Rorik says, stepping between Bjark and us. "Thyrvi and Saoirse, get your horses. Bjark, help me put these bodies in the cart. We'll burn them in the field. We can all talk after, once we've taken a minute."

As we walk to get our horses, I say a silent prayer to the gods, hoping that Gaelen's is still there. I don't want to tell him I lost it after less than a day. Luckily, the horses are exactly where we left them.

Walking back toward the others, it hits me that I successfully controlled the power. Yes, I still killed multiple men, but they would've killed Bjark and Rorik. I'm not going to lose sleep over those deaths.

Saoirse and I gather dried sticks and leaves to help the fire catch. Once the bodies are loaded onto the cart, it's moved away from any lower-hanging branches, and their horses are then tied behind ours. Rorik takes a log from their fire to set the cart alight. We watch from a distance as it burns, but not wanting to waste any more time, we set out to finish our journey to Thurisa. We ride in silence for over an hour until Bjark finally breaks the silence.

"Thank you for saving my life."

Surprised, I turn to face him. The sun has fully retreated, but there's enough moonlight to make each other out and the few feet of road ahead of us.

"Does Gaelen know you're a witch?" he asks.

A laugh bursts past my lips before I can stop it. Being a witch would be simple in comparison to the reality of what I am, whatever that is exactly.

"I'm not a witch, but yes, he knows."

Even Saoirse has never heard the whole story. She's heard the rumors from when we were children, yes, but I never told her everything. With a sigh, I retell them the story I told less than a day ago, but this time I don't leave anything out.

## Chapter Seventeen

We arrive in Thurisa with the sun, the chilled air smelling of morning dew. A dew that's set into us as well as the grass.

The men at the gates let us through without incident, but I have no doubt they'll be reporting our arrival to my brother and Erik the moment they wake. I need to think of something to excuse Gaelen's absence before Hagen summons me to question it.

The village hasn't woken yet, but some stirring down at the docks has started. Reaching the horse stable, we startle the slumbering stable hand as we enter, leaving our horses and the extras from the king's men in his care before heading to the tavern.

I turn the key in the lock to Gaelen's room, feeling the click before I push the door open. I stand in the entryway for a moment, welcomed by that familiar smell. The room is fuller now than it was the first time I entered, but it feels empty somehow.

I close the door behind me and drop my bag and bow to the floor. I remove the dagger from my waist, letting that clatter to the ground with everything else. I don't bother lighting any of the lanterns, just fumbling through the trunk until I find something to quickly change into, not bothering to bathe. I drop into his bed, letting the scent of him surround me until I can't hold my eyes open any longer.

A persistent knocking rips me from sleep.

"Thyrvi, are you in there?" a voice from beyond the door yells.

Ugh. I feel like I could sleep for another five hours at least.

"Hold on," I yell back, hearing a continued low chatter from the hallway.

I throw on the same pants and tunic from yesterday before opening the door. I find the younger teen who delivers messages for my brother standing there. Rorik, standing on the opposite side of the hall, also dressed in a sloppy shirt and pants.

"Can I help you?"

"I've been trying to find you! Hagen would like to speak with you this morning," the kid says.

My brother wastes no time.

"Fine. I'll be there as soon as I clean up."

He seems to deem that acceptable, nodding and heading back down the stairs.

"Let me know when you're ready, and I'll go with you," Rorik says.

Right. I forgot about the babysitting. Rolling my eyes, I retreat into Gaelen's room and close the door behind me. Drawing a bath, I scrub the road and death from my body. I should've done this last night, but I wouldn't have made it through the whole thing without falling asleep. I quickly dress and comb out my hair, pinning it in a bun on top of my head.

Stepping out of the room, I make sure to lock the door. For a moment, I consider not knocking for Rorik, but I think twice about making him upset with me this soon in our hopeful friendship.

Rorik in tow, I push open the door to my brother's office, not bothering to be polite, considering he wasn't willing to let me sleep. I don't know why I was expecting there to be something different about the room, but it's the same as it was the last time I was here, smelling of old books and cluttered with papers. Hagen looks up from his desk at the intrusion.

"Sister," he says before glancing over at Rorik. "Did you think you needed a chaperone for this visit?"

I didn't think of an explanation as to why he is with me, just to explain why Gaelen is gone, but Rorik answers for me.

"She's married to the second in line to a crown that you now answer to. She doesn't go anywhere without protection. Furthermore, given her station, she will no longer be summoned. If you wish to speak with her, make an appointment."

I don't need a mirror to know that my eyes have widened. In any case, I'm sure my face looks similar to Hagen's, who clearly hadn't thought through all the implications of my marrying Gaelen.

"Well, now that we all know where we stand. Where's your husband?"

His eyes glare into mine.

"I don't see how it's any of your business."

His arrogance grates on my nerves.

"I'm simply inquiring. I wouldn't want the second in line to the crown to go missing while visiting our village. Wouldn't look good for our newly formed kinship."

"He went to check in with the king and extend his absence. We plan to travel before settling in Kenaz."

It's almost the truth, and I figure that'd be the safest explanation in the event he writes to Kenaz, or someone else shows up here.

"How nice. And to where will you be traveling?"

Gods, he's so annoying.

"Multiple places, Hagen," I say, surprised by the tone in my voice. "I will be removing the rest of my things from my room. Feel free to fill it with books or whatever else it is that you do."

Without giving him the chance to respond, I walk out of the room, Rorik behind me. That didn't go as I intended, but possibly better than I could've imagined. Once out of the Great Hall, I turn to Rorik.

"What the heck was all that?"

"Eh, you seemed nervous. I thought it'd be nice to bring him down a peg or two."

Thinking back to my brother's face at Rorik's words, I laugh.

"Well, I appreciate it. Do you have any plans today?"

He gives me a look implying that I know he doesn't.

"That's fair. Would you want to spar?"

**Chapter Eighteen**

A week has passed since we arrived in Thurisa, and though I know logically it's too soon to receive word from Gaelen, I'm still disappointed that we haven't.

I spent the first few nights alone until Saoirse started staying with me. She says she doesn't want me to be alone, but if there's anything I know, it's how to be by myself. Truthfully, I think she's worried about the king, though she'd never admit it. I'm sure the proximity to Rorik doesn't hurt either.

Spending so much time with Rorik and Bjark is what I imagine having brothers should feel like if one were older and extremely bossy, and one were troublesome with a crush on my best friend. Bjark found Rorik and I sparring that first day, and ever since witnessing my swordsmanship, he has insisted I go back to training daily.

Now I spar with either him or Rorik daily before lunch. Today happens to be Rorik's turn, who, if you asked, would say I was only terrible before because I was taught to fight honorably. He says there's no honor in being dead, so we've moved on to fighting in any manner that will keep me alive. Which means I deal a lot of cheap blows and make contact between my wooden sword and their flesh in any way that I can.

"Why don't you just ask Saoirse to dinner or something?" I ask.

"She eats with us every night."

The reminder of how clueless men can be is always surprising.

"No, I mean just the two of you. Maybe outside of the tavern we basically live in."

"Would she say yes?" His eyes narrowing in suspicion. I can't help but laugh while blocking his swing.

"I think you know she would."

"I don't want to push her into anything if she isn't ready

yet. You know, after her husband," he says.

My heart warmed, knowing it was something he was even taking into consideration.

"Did she tell you about him?" I ask, a little surprised if she had.

"No, not really. I mean, she mentioned being married before. Gaelen brought it up when he noticed me talking to her. I think he wanted me to tread lightly, with some threats of what would happen if I upset your friend."

I make a mental note to thank him for that when he gets back. Not that I think Rorik is a bad guy or anything. Actually, I think she'd be hard-pressed to find anyone better.

"Saoirse wouldn't even be speaking to you if she wasn't ready."

I went on the offensive, making him block my attacks, but gaining ground.

"Honestly, I think you should just go for it. She knows her limits, let her decide."

"I have to admit, I was worried about this whole arranged marriage thing, I mean—don't get me wrong, you're a lot with the whole 'key to a dark power' drama, but you fit with us. And Gaelen is different now. He wasn't like this with Eira."

"Who?" I ask, taking a step back and lowering my sword.

It takes less than a second for Rorik's realized error to

register on his face. Gaelen mentioned someone, but he never named her.

"It's not my story to tell."

But before he can fully get the words out, I attack, parrying with my sword in my right hand in quick movements. Keeping his attention on my sword, my left hand sneaks the wooden dagger out of my back left belt loop. I block a blow with my sword high and use the opportunity to spin inward, closing the distance between us and leveling my dagger between his ribs. I use a little more force than I intended, feeling slightly guilty for it.

"Dead," I say, stepping back.

"That's fair."

While I might have won our match, I don't forget his slip-up, so of course, he spends the rest of the day dodging my questions, telling me to wait and ask Gaelen. Which, if I had any idea as to when I would see him next, wouldn't be as frustrating.

As evening arrives, everyone meets in the tavern for dinner as usual. It's a slower night, only a few other locals occupying tables and enjoying the food and ale.

"So… There's going to be a feast tomorrow in the hall," Saoirse says, just as we planned.

"Not a chance," Bjark grumbles.

"Oh, come on. It's not like someone's going to come take

me in my brother's hall under the nose of the entire village."

"Stranger things have happened," he says, glaring at me.

He means me, and isn't doing a very good job at hiding it.

"There will be too many people. It'll be hard to keep track of you."

"I promise to stay seated wherever you tell me the entire time!"

"No."

The evening goes on like this for another hour before he finally gives in. Even Rorik argues that the risk is small. I'm not sure we'll ever know if we convinced him, or if he just wanted to shut us all up.

The next evening arrives quickly, and I find myself firmly planted at a table in the Great Hall surrounded by the village, Bjark sitting to my right. Rorik just asked Saoirse to dance, and I know the grin still plastered to my face is obnoxious as I watch them.

"Would you like to dance?" Bjark asks.

My shock must be evident since he rolls his eyes before standing and taking my hand. The song has a quicker beat, and everyone around us is twirling and laughing as dancers swing this way and that, exchanging partners before trading back. We make it through two songs before Bjark must be meeting his limit of fun, and he ushers us back to our table. I spot Saoirse and Rorik again, focused on each other as if the rest of us aren't here.

"He never really liked her," Bjark says.

"What?" I ask, confused.

Rorik undoubtedly likes Saoirse.

"Eira," he says, giving me a side eye. "Make no mistake, she's beautiful. However, they were often forced together when they were younger. I think he went along with it because it was expected."

"You could've left out the beautiful part," I say, rolling my eyes.

"I'm not going to lie to you. She's beautiful, but she's cold. He would've been more miserable than he already was," he says, taking a sip of his ale. "He never looked at her the way he looks at you."

"Thanks, Bjark." His words make me feel better, if for no other reason than he thought we were close enough to share that, or he at least doesn't want me fretting over it.

"Now, if you feel better about this, and you promise me you won't get into any trouble, you'll have to excuse me. There's a woman over there who's been staring me down all evening." He stands, and I can't help but laugh.

"I promise! No trouble from me!" I say as I cross my heart.

Only a few moments pass before all of the joy this evening has brought is immediately ripped from me when Erik sits down on the opposite side of the table.

"You wasted no time," I say.

"I just thought I'd check in on you. I heard your husband is missing."

"He isn't missing," I sneer.

"Must be something important. I can't say I'd be willing to leave you this soon after getting married."

"Thank the gods we'll never have to find out." I smile cooly and stand to leave, but his hand wraps around my wrist, stopping me in place.

"If you get lonely, you know where to find me."

How did I ever find this man attractive? The idea of it is sickening. Obviously, his apology after the handfasting was just for show. I pull my wrist away and walk from the hall.

It's strange to be walking from the hall to the tavern. Making this walk at night would generally be the other way around. So much in my life has changed in such a short time that it feels as though Thurisa should have changed with it. I guess it always felt like a part of me. Now it feels stagnant.

I open the door to the empty tavern—other than the man sitting at the bar.  My eyes race back to him, heart skipping a beat.

"Gaelen?"

No, that wouldn't make sense. He would've found me as soon as he got here. The man turns, and he looks so similar, but this man is taller, his shoulders not as broad. His features are also more refined, whereas Gaelen's are rugged. He looks out of place in his worn clothing, as if he has traveled hard but isn't accustomed to doing so.

"How do you know my brother?" Theorin asks.

"I'm Thyrvi. Is he with you?"

His face softens with my words.

"No."

## Chapter Nineteen

"I'm Theorin, Gaelen's brother. I'm looking for Bjark and Rorik. I was given the name of this tavern, but it would seem no one's in tonight."

"There's a feast in the Great Hall this evening. Most people in the village are there tonight... I don't mean to be rude, but where exactly is Gaelen?"

He looks around hesitantly at my question.

"Listen, time is of the essence, and no one can know I'm here. I need to speak with Bjark and Rorik, now."

I don't like that he's avoiding my question, but I don't miss the genuine fear in his voice, so I motion for him to follow me. He doesn't know me, but maybe he'll be more forthcoming with the other two here. There is little point in wasting time arguing with him, regardless.

"Stay in here while I go and grab them. I'll only be a few minutes."

I leave him in Gaelen's room and quickly head back to the Great Hall.

Rorik and Saoirse sit closely at a table, seeming to be lost in conversation. Guilt immediately fills me as I interrupt them.

"It's important, meet me outside," is all I say, cutting into their conversation and scanning the room looking for Bjark.

When I finally spot him, he's on the dance floor with multiple women. My jaw would be on the floor at the sight if I weren't so concerned with whatever Theorin wouldn't tell me. Grabbing his arm, I pull him from the group of women, their protests following us out.

"You promised not to get in any trouble! What did you manage this quickly?" Bjark asks, but I ignore the question.

Once we are clear of the hall and I'm confident we're out of earshot of those loitering outside, I stop.

"Theorin is here." I keep my voice at a whisper.

Everyone's demeanor instantly shifts, and gone is the relaxed ease they had prior; something sharp takes its place. My chest tightens in response to their rapid change.

"What did he say?" Rorik asks.

"He wasn't willing to say much. I asked where Gaelen was, but he avoided the question. Basically, he's in a hurry and looking for you two."

At that, he nods. We walk briskly back to the tavern, careful not to draw too much attention, but the looks shared between the men make it clear they've put things together faster than I have. Bjark is the first up the stairs and through the door.

"What happened?" Bjark demands.

Theorin pauses, glancing over to Saoirse and me.

"You can trust them."

Theorin hesitates a moment longer, but seems to take Bjark's word.

"I met with Gaelen briefly when he arrived in Kenaz. He told me of the hand-fasting and that he planned to speak with our father. He didn't say what about, just that there was a chance it wouldn't go well, and it'd be for the best if I weren't home. So, I stayed out that night. Early the next morning, I was woken by Soren. I'm not sure how he found me, but he informed me that Gaelen had been taken prisoner and that I needed to get out of the city."

He rode straight here, which explains his clothes.

"Why would they take him prisoner?" I ask.

"If Soren knew, he didn't tell me. Just that I had to get here to you two, and no one could see me in the process."

"Where is Soren?" Rorik asks.

"He stayed, he's hiding in the city, collecting what information he can for a rescue," Theorin says.

"Your father isn't going to let him go?" I ask, confused as to why there needs to be a rescue.

He can't plan to keep his son as a prisoner long-term.

"Thokkra would be behind this, Thyrvi," Bjark says.

He glances over to Rorik, and the two hold eye contact longer than would be normal.

"What are you not telling me?" I ask as Bjark lets out a sigh.

"If the king has allowed Thokkra this much power, it's not going to be good."

"But what does that mean? Is she going to question him? Come here? What?"

If my chest was tight before, it's as though there's something wrapped around me, and now it's squeezing. My breath comes in rapidly, and I can't get enough air. I feel the nightmares come to the surface, reacting to my panic, ready to come to my defense. I'm busy shoving them down internally when Saoirse puts her arm around my shoulders. Her touch grounding me. I had almost forgotten she was here, but I give her a small smile, grateful.

"Why did you need to leave the city? Surely Soren could have sent someone less notable to bring these two back," she asks Theorin, but Rorik answers in his place.

"If Thokkra has Gaelen, she likely knows he figured something out. She'll want whatever information she thinks he has, and if she can't break him, she'd resort to using people he cares about."

"The king would allow her to do this?" I ask.

"If he wants something bad enough, there's little he won't resort to. I don't think he'll allow her to kill him, though."

"Great, so just torture then?" Sarcasm spills into my voice. Rorik nods his response.

What kind of father does this? My own father would've murdered anyone who tried to touch me. It's been well over a week. How long has this been going on?

"What's Soren's plan?" I ask in a voice that's not my own.

"Getting Rorik and Bjark is Soren's plan. He'll try to get Gaelen out if the opportunity's there, but he doesn't have Bjark's connections with the guards."

"We can't leave Thyrvi here alone. Rorik, you'll have to stay," Bjark says, looking to Rorik, who's about to protest, but I beat him to it.

"There's not a chance in hell that any of you leave without me," I say, cutting them both off. "This is happening because of me, and if you try to leave me, I'll just go on my own. It's not like I can't get a map."

Before they can debate it, Saoirse speaks up.

"If you two wish to leave, go ahead… We can travel to Kenaz with one of the merchants, or I know a general willing to take Thyrvi anywhere she wants to go. It's not as though we don't have options."

Saoirse dares them to argue with a glare, which I think she'd actually enjoy, but I give her hand a squeeze, thankful her cunning mind is on my side.

Rorik sighs, and I know, regardless of what Bjark says now, he'll argue in favor of wherever she stands. From the shake of his head, Bjark knows it, too.

"Pack light. Whatever you need, we'll buy once we arrive in Kenaz. We leave at first light," Bjark says, conceding the argument.

I pack a few pairs of leggings, sweaters, and my cloak, alongside multiple daggers, and, of course, my bow. Rorik tells Ula that we'll be leaving for a time and pays to keep the rooms longer. When Saoirse leaves to inform her parents that she'll be gone, I briefly consider telling Hagen, but I know it'd just lead to more questions since I already told him Gaelen would be coming back. He can hear of my departure from the guards, and I'll deal with it whenever I return. It's not as if we're going to share a heartfelt goodbye anyway.

Once morning arrives, we meet just before dawn, horses already saddled. Theorin seems more comfortable in his skin, having bathed and wearing borrowed clothes from Rorik.

I imagine sleeping in a bed also helped, regardless of how short the night was. I'm not sure at what point I fell asleep last night, my mind filled with possibilities of what could be happening, or what'll happen once we arrive. We leave the horse he rode here on, giving it a break, and he takes one of the horses we brought back from the king's men. I wonder if the king has realized they won't be returning, and what he thinks of that, especially now. If he has one son in a dungeon, would he even care that the other is missing?

"How did your parents take the news of you leaving?" I ask Saoirse after we have made our way out of Thurisa.

"My father was suspicious, of course. Especially after the story of Gaelen leaving to extend his time in Thurisa."

"I'm sorry you have to lie to them."

"It's fine. I would never let you do this alone, and they will be safer if they don't know the truth."

Our trip to Kenaz has been miserable. Yesterday it rained all day, soaking our clothes and most of our things. We stopped to make camp at night, though we didn't put up actual tents, just built a fire the best we could with the weather and slept under trees. Thankfully, the forest is full enough to provide at least some shelter, but I still felt the chill in my bones. The fire couldn't reach the size needed to dry anything.

Each of us takes a shift of guard duty to allow for as much sleep as possible. By morning, the temperature has dropped enough to turn the rain into flurries, our breath fully visible as we quickly eat, readying ourselves to set out for the day. Theorin doesn't seem accustomed to the type of traveling the way Bjark and Rorik are, or the same way of life that they're used to. To his credit, he never complains. Saoirse and I are far from accustomed to any of this, but somehow, we are managing. It will be better once we are all dry.

I want to ask what our plan is going to be, where they might be keeping him, and if we're going to speak with the king. Or if this is more of a break-in and out situation? The tension constantly filling the air stops me from asking any of it, our trip continuing in its somber tone. The only thing keeping me from losing my mind with impatience is knowing that Bjark and Rorik don't actually know anything either, and our first step is to reach Soren.

A few hours into the day, Theorin's horse canters up next to mine on the road. His face remaining forward, watching Bjark in the lead, Rorik and Saoirse behind us.

"Something you said the other night keeps replaying in my mind," he says. These are the first few words he's even bothered to speak to me since we left Thurisa.

"What's that?"

"You said this is happening because of you. Why would Thokkra taking Gaelen prisoner have anything to do with you?"

This time, he turns, searching my face for an answer or what I might be hiding. My relationship with Rorik and Bjark might be new, but it was earned, on both our parts. He might be Gaelen's brother, but I'm not sure how much I can trust him.

"Your father forced Gaelen to marry me because he thought I had something he wanted. He was mistaken, and Gaelen went to clear up any confusion there might have been. He was trying to protect me."

"Will you be annulling the hand-fasting at Yule then?"

His question catches me off guard. I hadn't thought about that since the night of the ceremony. I originally didn't go into this planning to annul anything, though that was Gaelen's plan. He seemed to have changed his mind about things before he knew all my secrets and had been taken prisoner because of me. There could be a chance he doesn't want to continue the relationship now, after everything.

The thought doesn't sit well. We haven't even really started yet, but I guess I was interested in seeing where this went. That was before I was faced with the decision to either jump on a ship and move to the other side of the world or find a way to destroy a dark power locked in Yggdrasil by the gods— possibly both.

Looking over, I find him still watching me, eerily similar to the way his brother would watch me think through something.

"I don't know," I say sharply, turning my eyes back to the road before us.

What business is it of his anyway?

"Yeah, I can see that."

## Chapter Twenty

Another two days of travel pass before we arrive at the gates of Kenaz. Bjark's been even more on edge since we should've arrived yesterday, the weather slowing us down. I'm sure Saoirse and I add to the delay, though he'd never go as far as to say it.

We stand on a wooded cliffside, watching the walls of Kenaz, Bjark, and Rorik, monitoring the guards and their movements to form a plan. The walls are mammoth-like. Any force capable of breaching them could take Thurisa in seconds. In fact, Thurisa could fit inside of Kenaz multiple times, even in just the parts visible to me.

I feel ready to explode being this close, but not able to do anything. I can't see a way we would find one person hiding in a city this big, and we need whatever information Soren hopefully has. Bjark stands, clearing his throat. Finally, it seems this silence is going to break.

"I don't feel comfortable using the main gate. I know some of the men on it, but some are newer. We run the risk of Theorin being recognized, and if Thokkra wants us as well, we could be detained."

"We need to travel farther down, to a poorer side of the city. The gates are smaller, fewer guards, and no nobles to put on a show for. On the bright side, the gate guards don't seem to be doubled or overly alert," Rorik adds.

We don't get back on our horses. Instead, we lead them through the woods onto a dirt path that outlines the city walls from a distance. After walking a couple of miles, we seem to be nearing the gate they were referencing, and we shuffle our horses into the line of people moving toward it.

Theorin's hood has fully covered his face since we reached the city outskirts, but Bjark and Rorik have now loosely placed their hoods over their heads as well. Saoirse and I have no risk of being recognized, so we decide not to wear ours, which might ease any suspicion the men might cause.

Bjark gives the signal a few feet ahead of us to the guard he knows on duty, and we all fall in behind him to ensure that specific guard stops us.

"State your business," the guard says.

"Discretion," Bjark responds, pulling the hood back just enough that his face is visible to only him.

The man nods.

"Hurry up, you're holding up the line." He ushers us through the gate and turns to yell at the group behind us. "You, sir, we need to search your cart," he says, stopping them.

The city is overwhelming in every way. There are endless waves of people everywhere you turn. They walk down the streets, in and out of buildings, through long alleyways. Some yell for people they recognize, others yell to draw attention to whatever they happen to be selling, but mostly, they are a constantly moving sea of bodies.

I was worried we would draw attention, not being from Kenaz, but I don't see how anyone would notice. In fact, many of these people are likely not from Kenaz. I would need a month to explore the entirety of this place properly. I look to Saoirse, and though she is diligently scanning the crowd, she doesn't seem to be as awestruck as I am.

"So now what?" I ask no one in particular.

"Now we find a shit-hole tavern to lay low in until we find Soren," Bjark says.

"Actually, I have a better idea," Theorin says, moving his horse to the front to take the lead. "Our best bet is to make sure Soren can find us. Follow me."

He proceeds to guide us through the streets and down multiple alleyways. The quality of the buildings seems to improve with each step, as the roads become slightly more organized, with most people walking to the sides to accommodate the occasional carriage that makes its way down the road.

The quality of clothing improves enough to make me worry we'll stand out in our travel-worn attire, but it's then that Theorin leads us through a gate and into what seems to be a small courtyard filled with plants.

Only the ivy-laden gate is visible from the road, nestled between buildings. The four-story building on the other side of the courtyard is constructed from high-quality stone, albeit aged, and in the center of it sits a door, the loudest shade of yellow I've ever seen. From the side of the building, a young boy comes running toward us.

"Take your things from the saddle bags and leave the horses with him," Theorin instructs as the boy starts taking hold of our reins.

"Are you sure this is wise?" Rorik asks, looking at the building.

"They've always kept my visits quiet, and this is where

Soren found me last time. I think staying here is a safe bet," Theorin promises.

As we walk toward the door, it opens, and a voluptuous, well-dressed woman walks through it.

"Oh, Theo! We weren't expecting you back for a while, given your exit. Is there something I can do for you and your friends?" she asks, eyes traveling over us.

"We need a place to hide, for a time. No one can know I'm here."

She looks us over again, fully taking in the state of our clothes and the dirt covering our bodies.

"Yes, of course." She nods, directing us to follow her.

I follow just behind Theorin and step into a luxuriously decorated building. The air is heavily perfumed with hints of lilac, jasmine, and vanilla, carried by a more sensual scent. The walls are lined with an array of colors, various artworks depicting the female body on its own, and with others, filling multiple frames. The furniture is plush and frequent, as we pass several sitting rooms, all empty except for the last, where many women lounge. Some are nicely dressed, others less dressed.

"What are we doing here?" Saoirse aggressively whispers.

We don't have one in Thurisa, but from the looks of it, Theorin brought us to a brothel—a nice brothel, but a brothel.

"I told you. This is where Soren found me last time, and it's our best option for staying hidden," Theorin responds.

I look to Bjark, and he shrugs, exhaustion visible in the lines of his face. We are led up a flight of stairs, down a series of hallways, and then finally through a hidden door. We enter a seating area with multiple rooms off to each side. Through the doorways, I can see various beds in each room, and one seems to be a bathroom. The room is decorated nicely, but not as lavishly as the rest of the building; its most notable feature is the lack of any windows.

"Please make yourselves comfortable. There are plenty of bath sheets for you to bathe with, and food will be brought up right away," the woman says, smiling at Theorin.

"Thank you, and the man that found me last I was here, have you seen him at all?" Theorin asks.

"I haven't, but I can check with the girls," she says, leaving the room.

"Why would they need this?" I ask, looking around.

"Sometimes people need to be hidden. A brothel is the best place. People are already hiding their faces when they come in and out of here, so no one thinks twice about it," Theorin says.

A few minutes later, a knock sounds at the door, and Theorin lets in two women carrying trays of food. It's just soup with bread and cheese, but the aroma is amazing after the cold journey, eating smoked meats. They could've only brought the bread and cheese, and I would still be elated.

The soup is a warm broth with chunks of vegetables and meat, and the seasoning has us soaking the bread to get every last drop of broth. As soon as we're finished eating, Saoirse takes the first bath, and a different woman comes in to collect the dishes and trays. On her way out, she stops to speak quietly with Theorin.

"Your highness, Soren left me instructions as to where I can leave a message for him, should you return. Would you like me to see that it's done?"

A weight lifts from me with her words. If she knows how to find Soren, that alleviates our first hurdle. Hopefully, he knows something useful.

"Theo, and yes, that would be greatly appreciated!"

She curtsies, then leaves the room. Rorik standing to close the door behind her.

"The man has a way with women! We should never again underestimate Soren's ability to have contacts everywhere."

Over an hour later, after we no longer smell of horses and dirt, we lounge in the sitting area, too anxious to sleep despite our exhaustion.

"Should we go scout the castle or something?" I ask, unable to keep my leg from bouncing up and down.

"I don't want to risk being spotted before we hear what

Soren has to say," Bjark grumbles.

"Well, sitting here doing nothing isn't helping," I complain.

"We don't know what we're up against, or what's going to be required. Just save your energy," Rorik says, as if they're going to let me help when it comes down to it.

I'm sure I'll need to argue and threaten my way into being included, but I know for sure there's no way I'm being left in this room while they all risk their lives.

Without any windows, it's hard to gauge what time it is, but it must be well into the evening when the door finally pushes open again. Soren stands in the doorway, looking around at all of us.

"You didn't leave them in Thurisa?" he asks, looking at Bjark.

"She has every right to be here. Regardless, the options were to bring her with us and know she's safe, or let her come on her own," Bjark says.

"She would be safer fumbling through the woods right now than being in this city."

"You don't know them very well. And what if taking Gaelen was a trap to pull us out of Thurisa so Thokkra could have someone take her? We already met with the king's men after separating from you and Gaelen. They were on their way to bring her to Kenaz," Rorik says.

"And where are those men now?" Soren asks.

"Dead." Bjark doesn't volunteer any more information, and Soren seems content to leave it at that.

"None of this matters right now. What happened?" I ask.

Soren actually looks at me this time, face softening.

"One of my contacts in the castle had a friend working the night we arrived. She attended the king's dinner, but was in and out of the dining room, so she didn't catch everything. Once the yelling started, the servants were listening at the door to what they couldn't make out; a guard filled in later. Thokkra accused Gaelen of lying and withholding information from the king. She insisted he be kept in Kenaz while she ensures Thyrvi is brought to the castle. Gaelen obviously argued against that. The king wasn't in agreement with her right away. The more Thokkra pushed, the more agitated Gaelen became and threatened her. As he left his chair to walk over to Thokkra, she ordered the guards to detain him. They hesitated at first, unsure about moving against the prince. Then he pulled out a dagger, and they only managed to reach him as he sank it into her stomach. There were three guards in the dining room, and one of Thokkra's men. Apparently, Gaelen decked the guard, who ended up retelling the story. As he was fighting the other three, the king ordered him to stop, had him arrested, and sent him to the dungeons."

We all sit attentively, hanging onto every word that crosses

Soren's lips.

"So, what happened to Thokkra?" Saoirse asks.

"The pool of blood left in the dining room to be cleaned would've been enough for a normal person to die of blood loss, but apparently, she walks the castle as if nothing happened."

"And Gaelen?" I ask.

He looks to Bjark and Rorik.

"I don't know anyone with access to the dungeons. And it's mostly being guarded by Thokkra's men. However, she only has a small number at her disposal, so castle guards handle some shifts. One of the girls heard the guards say his condition isn't good. They disagree with his treatment, and it's causing discourse."

"And what do we know of that treatment?" Bjark asks, voice low.

"She's torturing him, but rumor has it she hasn't visited him in a couple of days. She's pissed she hasn't gotten anything from him, and the king is starting to doubt that he has anything to give her."

The backs of my eyes start to sting, but I blink them away. I don't have time to cry right now; I'll make time for it later.

"Gaelen's always been our father's favorite. I know he wishes he were born first, and it's because of his strength and ability to handle what needs to be done. He likely would've had me killed already if Gaelen hadn't threatened to walk away if anything happened to me. Our father is stubborn, but Gaelen won't break before he does, and they both know it. This could go on for some time before our father swallows his ego," Theorin says.

"Which is exactly why you, and her, shouldn't be here!" Soren says, pointing to me. "Thokkra lays one hand on either of you, and he'll fold, and everything he's gone through will be for nothing."

The truth of his words makes me uncomfortable.

"He hasn't even known me that long."

I didn't mean to say it; it was a reaction to the awkwardness I was feeling more than anything.

"Doesn't matter! He made a choice," Soren basically spits the words at me, unimpressed with my comment.

"So, what are we doing, Soren?" Bjark asks.

"She knows we'll come for him. The guards around the castle have doubled."

"But not at the gates, because she's hoping we make a move, to capture one of us," Rorik says, more as an observation.

"I know a few men in the guard. It might be a risk, but I can go to the tavern they all frequent. Learn when the men I know will be working, see if any are put off enough by what's happening to help us. Gaelen trained with many of these men, and they swore their lives to keeping the Langavin family safe, not a witch."

"We can't leave him there for another night!" I say sharply.

"Your friends that are servants, you trust them?" Saoirse asks Soren, and he nods. "Could they get Thyrvi and I in if we pretended to be servants as well?"

"Yes, but she isn't setting foot in the castle. Were you not listening to anything I just said?" Soren says, the grip on his frustration slipping. It's fair, though. He has been dealing with this alone longer than any of us.

Rorik stands, having not yet learned that Saoirse can handle her own battles.

"You don't get to decide where she steps, she does! And you're so busy telling us where Thyrvi should or shouldn't be that you're overlooking the one advantage we have in this situation," she says, remaining levelheaded.

"And what's that?" Soren sneers.

"That no one knows who the fuck we are."

"Sure, let's say you can walk into the castle and pass as servants. I don't doubt your ability to do that much. You would then have to navigate the castle without knowing its layout, past the dungeon guards, unlock his cell, and get him out. What will you do if he can't walk out? For that, you would need at least two of us. How are you getting us in?"

I hadn't allowed myself to think of how bad the damage might be. My stomach churns as all the possibilities run through my mind. I stand, unable to sit any longer, needing air to get through the nausea.

"If your friends can get us in, I can handle the dungeon guards," I say, and watch as Soren and Theorin's faces both fill with doubt.

I've only ever used the power when there's a perceived threat, but I feel it awake and ready beneath my skin. I have no doubt it'll answer if I call. Bjark nods in agreement with me.

"I believe you can get into the castle. I know you well enough now to say you'd even make it to the dungeon, and you'd kill the guards, but your method wouldn't be quiet. Now you've alerted the castle from the screaming. You would have maybe two minutes to unlock his cell and get him out. How are you managing that?" Bjark asks, staring at me, ignoring Soren and Theorin, who are looking at him as though he had grown another head.

"I'll find a way," I say, fully aware that I sound like an insolent child.

"Not good enough," Rorik says. "You're not risking your life, and Saoirse's, on a half-assed plan."

"She doesn't have to come. Regardless of whether I have a whole plan or not, some things aren't going to go the way we think they will."

"I can decide when I risk my own life," Saoirse says to

Rorik.

I feel bad for being the cause of any potential arguments between them, but I can't say I blame him for wanting to keep her safe.

"He didn't mean it like that," I say, but she cuts me off with a glare.

"I know how he meant it."

"Fine," I say, moving on from the issue. "Can someone draw a rough map of the outside and the inside of the castle? Soren, when does your friend usually arrive?"

Theorin volunteers to draw the maps, knowing the castle better than anyone else here. Soren's contact is part of the evening staff, meaning we won't be able to get in until tomorrow night. I'm not thrilled with this information, but it does allow Bjark time to meet with some of his friends in the guard.

With the extra presence around the castle, if Rorik, Bjark, and Soren can dress as guards and go unnoticed, that'll allow them access to a door on the outside close to the dungeons. Assuming all of this goes well, we'd have to kill the guards in the dungeon, get Gaelen out of the castle, through the walls, and to a carriage that Theorin will be waiting in a few streets away to bring us all back to the brothel.

With less than twenty-four hours before we have to act, the men waste no time putting things in motion. Soren arranges to meet his contact and bring us back uniforms to wear tomorrow. Bjark and Rorik head to the tavern to meet with the guards, and Theorin makes arrangements with the brothel to borrow a carriage. Saoirse and I are left with very little to do, other than going stir-crazy.

"I want you to use your power," she says after a prolonged period of silence, during which I've been pacing back and forth, feeling trapped in our windowless room.

"Excuse me?" I must have misheard her.

"I want you to test your power on me. We need to know you can use it at will. Not just when you're afraid." She looks at me as though all of this makes sense and I'm the crazy one.

"I'm going to be terrified. It'll be fine."

"But we don't know that. I'll feel better knowing you can call on it."

"And if I kill you in the process?"

"You won't. I know you won't. Besides, we already saw that you can pull it back. You did it with those men, and you did it when we were younger; we didn't realize it then."

I look at her, eyes wide.

"Fine, don't make it attack me, just see if you can reach out to me or something. What if we get stopped before we even make it to the guys tomorrow?"

I sigh.

"I know I can do it. It's hard to explain, but the power's

aware of you. It senses your mind in this room. When everyone else was here, it sensed them as well. I know I can reach out with it. When we traveled here, it didn't recognize birds and small animals. I think you have to be intelligent enough for it to sink into." I say, and she seems to think about it before nodding.

"So, it doesn't pick up on Soren then?" she asks, and we both laugh.

# Chapter Twenty-One

The day crept by at a painful pace, Bjark drilling and re-drilling the plan into our heads. Evening arrives just as the anticipation might kill me.

Saoirse and I dress in the dark blue dresses Soren returned with last night, servants' attire courtesy of his friend, Jane, who we're supposed to meet in an hour, a block away from the castle.

I hardly slept last night, waiting for everyone to come back and not able to relax until they were all accounted for. Every hour since we woke to trays of breakfast being brought in has been agony. The possibilities of every bad thing that could happen run through my mind. We get caught, we get killed, we get tortured. I have to watch them be tortured. Gaelen is already dead. I die in all of the scenarios, and Loki's power is released on our world, throwing everything into chaos—the one thing I was meant to prevent from happening.

I try braiding my hair into a bun, but my hands shake and my fingers keep slipping, missing the strands, and I have to start again. Eventually, Saoirse takes over braiding and pins my bun at the nape of my neck.

We make our way out of the brothel through a side door, bland and unassuming, and go down an alley and into the accompanying street. We were given a list of streets and turns to take, some of which are already forgotten due to my being unable to focus when they were being given to us. I know Saoirse likely had them memorized the first time Rorik listed each one. I also know there's zero chance that Rorik and Bjark aren't following us right now.

They returned late last night with enough gear for them and Soren to pass as guards today. Bjark was able to meet with a few of his friends, who, as he expected, were not in support of Gaelen being taken prisoner and were willing to help. They pulled in a few of their trustworthy friends, making it so there would be enough guards on the walls tonight willing to ignore our retreat, instead of us being shot by arrows. At least, that's what I keep telling myself.

Every new street we turn onto is an improvement from the last, wooden buildings phasing out completely until everything is made of clean stone. Even the carriages are covered in embellishments. I can't even begin to describe the things people are wearing. It's not so much that it's outlandish, but the quality is so far above anything that would be worn in Thurisa. Their daily attire must cost a fortune.

Though I practically gawk, they all seem content to ignore servants making their way to the castle, not worth a second glance at, or even a first. The large sum Gaelen left with the seamstress makes so much more sense now. He's used to daily dresses costing a small fortune. Of course, he thought my wedding dress would.

I feel small next to all these people in this city, surrounded by their extravagant luxuries. He grew up in this world, used to all these things, and women who dress far differently than I do. How could he ever have expected me to live here? He certainly didn't try to prepare me. He didn't say we need to stay here, though, and that he doesn't spend a lot of time in the city. I remind myself of this, knowing I'm trying to ease my newly found insecurities, even though doubt still takes root.

Finally, we spot the woman who must be Jane. She stands in her blue dress, with soft blonde hair pulled into a bun, and is carrying two baskets full of flowers that she must have purchased on her way in. We nod to her as she hands one basket to Saoirse and links arms with me.

Without skipping a beat, she proceeds to gossip and giggle, nudging us to join in as we pass through the outer wall of the castle, through what is clearly the servants' entrance. The guards take their time looking us over, but make no motion to prevent us from entering.

Once through, we enter a dirt courtyard just as full of life as the city outside of it. People loading and unloading carts, horses being moved to stables, and day servants saying their farewells to friends on the night staff. I know Kenaz is significantly larger than Thurisa, but the number of people it holds shocks me at every turn. This city is just layers upon layers of people.

Walking toward a small door in the side of the stone wall, we enter an incredibly large kitchen. It's also filled with people, boasting two hearths already cooking meats that smell divine. Pans and cooking stones fill the shelves that line the walls, followed by multiple large tables of breads, pies, and piles of vegetables.

We follow Jane through another door into a hallway where most servants seem to leave their cloaks and other belongings. The baskets are deposited onto a small table here as we make our way deeper into the castle.

Jane pushes her way through another thick door, leading us to a set of stairs and into the main castle. Where the servant's area is made of plain stone and wood, the central portion of the castle is a stark difference. Stone walls are adorned with rich tapestries, and the floors are covered in ornate carpets, so thick that you can't hear our footsteps. Each piece of furniture or decoration is either polished or plush, and it isn't lacking in either, though it feels cold—the kind of cold that can't be removed by lighting a hearth.

The impression the castle gives is harsh, and my mind is having a hard time imagining either of the brothers growing up in such a place. Theorin, who asks everyday people to call him Theo, and Gaelen, who was happy to sit on the floor of a library reading with me. My library is probably smaller than the size of a bathing tub in this place.

The memory of Gaelen reminds me why we're here in time to realize that Jane is leading us through yet another door into what must be an unused seating area, all the furniture covered in cloth, and—a closet?

"I'm going to leave you here for the moment. All staff members report for assignments at the start of each shift. I can't take you there; they'll realize you don't belong. Stay here, and I'll be back in less than an hour to get you to where you need to be," Jane says, closing us in.

The closet is dark, with only a faint light making its way

through the bottom of the door. It's pretty cramped as we try to turn around, but we manage to sit, although squished, on the floor with our backs to the wall.

"If anything goes wrong, promise me you'll run."

"You wouldn't," Saoirse whispers back.

"I don't think this is exactly the adventure you were looking for when you signed up."

"No, but maybe it's the one I'm supposed to be on."

We sit like this for what feels like forever, so much adrenaline coursing through my body, I can't stop fidgeting, only the fear of being caught keeping me firmly in the closet. But the urge to pace grows greater by the minute.

Suddenly, the nightmares are aware of someone outside the closet, just before a foot darkens the light coming in under the door. I can hear our collective inhale as we hold our breath, our hands clasped tightly. A ruffling can be heard before the door swings open, Jane looking down at us, arms laden with sheets.

We exhale at the sight of her, helping each other to stand in the small area. She gives us both a stack of sheets as we walk through the hallways, apparently on our way to restock linen closets after the laundry was washed today. It's hard to tell where we are based on my memory of Theorin's map. I tried to commit every detail, but I'm not sure he included all the extra doorways and alcoves. But I believe we're moving closer to the door that should give Bjark, Soren, and Rorik entry.

After stocking a few closets, our bundles are almost empty, and I'm certain we're close now. When the hall comes that should house the door we need, I turn down it to find the door exactly where it should be. I feel a second of relief knowing we've made it this far, all according to plan, but that relief is fleeting as I hand my sheets to Saoirse and slowly walk the length of the hall.

First, I remove the wood barring the door, hiding it next to a nearby table that sits under a painting depicting what could only be the Aesir-Vanir war. I only read about the battle, which included small depictions. I've never seen anything this detailed. It took place before our world was created.

I wonder how they have this here, or who painted it? A voice clears, and I turn back to the door, twisting the bolt through the mechanism, and the inner bar retracts. I'm careful not to open the door, should it draw the attention of someone passing by.

I'll just have to trust that the guys will find it. I make my way back to Saoirse, heart pounding with every step, and reclaim my bundle. Her eyes stay locked with mine for the length of my retreat.

"We've got this," she says, voice barely a whisper, but I hear the shake in it.

She's scared. I never thought she'd be afraid of anything, except that once. I shouldn't have brought her here. I should've pushed for her to stay. Everyone else is here because of me, and she only came to support me, but we could all die; she could die. How could I have let her come here? She gives me a tight smile, and we go back to following Jane.

Once we near the hallway that should lead to the dungeons, we step into another room. Jane immediately closes the door behind us, hands her sheets to Saoirse, and drops to her knees to look through the keyhole. A few minutes later, we hear a shuffle and clatter from the other side of the door.

"It's hard to tell, but I'm almost certain that was Soren," she says, turning to us.

She opens the door to check the hallway, then takes the remaining bundles from us.

"This is where I leave you. Good luck." She nods before going back to her assigned task.

By the time we arrive outside the door to the dungeons, Bjark, Soren, and Rorik are there, helmets off, and two men in different colors lie on the floor. Judging by the difference in attire, they aren't castle guards, so they must have been Thokkra's.

The men aren't bleeding, but I'm very sure they're dead. It was swift and quiet. Bjark was right, my solution for this would've drawn significant attention in no time. Soren and Rorik drag the bodies to an alcove farther down the hallway, where they can remain hidden if someone were to glance by. However, the lack of guards might still draw attention.

"Thyrvi, there was no key on these men," Bjark says to me, eyes grave.

"Maybe it's inside," I say, my voice too high.

Bjark nods and enters first, sword drawn in case any guards are waiting inside. Once through the entryway, we're met with a metallic tinge in the air. We have to descend a staircase, going down more stairs than we went up in the servants' area, delving deeper into the earth. The stone walls seem to weep, water dripping down them.

Once down the stairs, we enter a larger room, which is dark and cold, with only a single torch lit on the far wall. A series of cells line the walls, and my eyes search them one by one, finding each empty. Did she know we were coming? Did she have him moved? My entire body turns to lead as a cold sweat breaks out across my skin. Of course, this was a trap.

## Chapter Twenty-Two

My eyes land on Bjark, and I know we both come to the same conclusion. This was a mistake.

I spin, my heart not willing to accept what my mind already knows. I search each cell again, one by one.

Empty.

Empty.

Empty.

I keep looking, heart sinking further and further with each one I pass. Finally, I reach the last one and notice the shape I missed the first time, blocked by shadow.

"Gaelen," I say, but there's no movement.

I can't fully see him, but I know. Frantic, I look back to Bjark, who's already searching.

"Do you see a key?" I ask, voice cracking.

I sweep my gaze over the room, looking for anything that could hold a key. There's nothing. I already know from my prior scans of the room, but I look regardless. Everyone else has made it down the stairs, taking up the search. The king or Thokkra likely has it.

There's no way I'm leaving him here. I drop down to examine the lock.

"Maybe we can pick it? I have hairpins," I say, pulling them from my hair and turning to our friends.

The friends I'm going to get killed tonight because I pushed for this, because I couldn't wait. Soren seems like someone who can pick a lock, so I offer the pins to him first.

"I can try," he says, looking unsure.

I sigh, looking at the hinges. They're on the outside of the door but seem to be bent back, preventing easy removal from this side. With time and proper tools, we could do it. It wouldn't be quiet, though.

Soren walks over to me, holding out his hand for the pins. Handing them to him, I move out of the way, grabbing the torch and bringing it over so he has more light. I notice freshly etched runes around the lock that I couldn't see before.

Each second Soren spends on the lock feels like minutes passing by. Minutes we don't have, and didn't account for. Sweat breaks out on his forehead, and I know it's not from effort. With each click of the mechanism inside, he shakes the bars, nothing budging. Gaelen still hasn't moved in the corner, despite the clatter.

"Fuck it, look around for something we can use to ram the lock. I'll fight my way out of here before I leave him," Bjark says, moving around the room.

"We could probably find a loose chunk of stone to pull out," Rorik says, looking at the walls.

A loud click sounds in the lock, and Soren lets go of the pins to shake the door, but it doesn't open.

"Fuck!" he yells, forehead against the lock. "I'm sorry, Thyrvi," he says, looking up at me. "Maybe we can wedge something between the door and the bars to pry it open before we resort to ramming."

He stands, pulls his sword out, and examines its thickness. I know it'll eventually bend or snap before the lock gives. I bend back down, looking at the runes and running my fingers across them. There are remnants of the old language still throughout our world, though not enough information remains to learn it. Usually, when you find them, they're aged. It's curious that these are freshly scratched into the surface.

Thokkra must know the old language. I wonder if that means Runa does as well? I use part of the door as leverage to pull myself back up, but the door pushes open, and I trip inside, catching myself on the cell bars before I fall.

"Soren! It's unlocked!"

A warmth floods through me, and as I look back at Soren, I feel like I could laugh and cry at the same time. I hand the torch to him as he follows me into the cell. The elation and relief I was just feeling fade with each splinter shooting through my heart. I'm not sure how I was expecting to find him, but I wasn't prepared for the sight before me.

Gaelen sits in the corner, knees raised, head on the wall to his left, covered in dried blood. He isn't wearing a shirt, and his body is covered in cuts, bruises, and burns. His eyes are open, looking at me, but one is clearly swollen, almost shut. His lip is split, and bruising blooms across his cheekbones. I kneel next to him, feeling the tears forming in my eyes.

"Gaelen," I say again.

His eyes remain on me, but he doesn't speak. Despite the chill in the room, he looks to be sweating, beads of it mixing in the dried blood, likely from infection. I reach to feel his forehead, and the moment my skin touches his, his whole body flinches.

"You're actually here?" he asks frantically, voice hoarse. "You can't be here. She wants you; she'll kill you."

His hand tries to push me backward.

"No one's killing me, remember? And I'm not leaving without you."

I try to keep my voice soft, holding my fear back from spilling into it. It takes him a moment to focus, taking in the situation and looking around at his friends. I think he just now understands that we're here to rescue him. I turn to Soren and Bjark, who are now both standing in the cell, Rorik remaining behind with Saoirse.

"Can you help him stand up?"

Gaelen grabs a chain hanging from the wall and twists it around his hand. Grunting, he uses the chain to pull himself up, cradling the burns on his side. Bjark grabs his elbow to steady him, and together they walk out of the cell, Gaelen limping.

Rorik runs up the steps to make sure the hall is still clear, Saoirse and I following behind him. It takes a few moments for the other two to make it up the stairs with Gaelen, but they do. The movements reopen injuries, now bleeding across his stomach and chest.

I look up to find him watching me watch him, and even in his state, he tries to wink, giving me that half smile. The way he always does when catching me looking at his body. A small smile forms on my lips in response, but with my heart almost jumping out of my chest, it can't grow any wider.

We're so close. We just need to get outside. We make it through the first hallway, past where we hid with Jane as she watched through the keyhole. We just need to make it to the next hallway, a short walk away, and then out the door. Finally, we make our last turn, finding five guards standing at the door waiting for us.

Fine. We can handle five men. It won't be quiet, but we're already at the door. I hear Bjark and Soren draw their swords from behind me. Saoirse, at my side, pulls the dagger we both have strapped to our left legs. For a second, I consider pulling mine and handing it to Gaelen, but if we have to resort to Plan B, it's better that he's unarmed.

"I would like to know how you got that cell open?" a female voice from behind asks.

My heart stops beating altogether as I turn to find a woman standing in a black dress next to a man, who, based on the resemblance to his sons, is the king. Accompanying them stands another four guards, one with a blade to Jane's throat.

"You need better locks if they're all able to be picked with hairpins," I say with a confidence I don't feel.

The power that has been ready for days now stirs, eager.

"Impossible," she says, looking me over, her voice cold. She is younger than I expected, younger than Runa for sure. Her blond hair is left down, a contrast with the dark makeup around her eyes.

But I just shrug, the response seeming to annoy her.

"I'm impressed you made it this far, but this is a family matter, and I cannot allow you to leave with my son. I admit I expected the other three to come for him, and will, with their cooperation, excuse their insubordination," the king says, giving Bjark a pointed look, likely knowing he would lose Gaelen forever if he did anything to them. "However, I have no idea who you ladies are."

His eyes roam over all of us.

"If you all take another step toward the door, or move to attack my men, I will have your friend here killed."

His hand gestures to Jane.

"Just let them leave, I'll go back without a fight. When I know they're gone, I'll tell you what you want to know," Gaelen says, taking a step toward his father.

Is he serious? I didn't go through all of this, or make it this far, for him to voluntarily walk back into that cell.

I hear laughter, and I think the pressure from all of this has cracked me, because with horror, I realize my chest is vibrating with it.

"You will do no such thing," I say to Gaelen. Looking back at the king, "You have no idea who I am? But you worked so hard to get me here. Funny, don't you think?"

Taking advantage of the realization dawning on him and Thokkra, I move forward, making eye contact with Bjark as I do.

I hear his sword returning to its sheath as I pass Gaelen.

"Listen, I don't know her," I say, gesturing to Jane. "Killing her would be a waste of what I assume to be a competent servant. But I intend to do whatever is needed for the people I care about to walk out of that door."

Satisfaction crosses his face with the fact that what he wants has been delivered before him.

"Kill the girl," the king says to the guard.

Not a second later, the knife slides across her throat. The blood spray hits the king on the side of his face. He doesn't flinch. I hear Saoirse's gasp, and Soren struggles to get by when a guard grabs him; the rest draw their swords.

"I told you I didn't know her!"

"Regardless of how well you know her, she helped you gain access to my home. That deed was never going to go unpunished," he says.

Thokkra eyes me intently, reminding me of a predator watching its prey.

Fuck.

Fuck.

Fuck.

We miscalculated this greatly. I was hoping for fewer people if it were to come to this.

"I'll make you a deal," I say, my voice coming out with

none of the fake confidence I had prior.

"Thyrvi, no," Gaelen protests, but Bjark is already holding him, and between the blood loss and infection, he's weak.

"I know what you want, and I have it. Let them all leave, alive and unharmed, and I'll give it to you," I say.

A smile crosses the king's face, but Thokkra is as still as stone.

"Done. I did not enjoy knowing my son was being tortured anyway. I am glad you're more reasonable than he," the king says, gesturing for the guards to stand down.

I look back at Bjark and give him a nod that he reciprocates before firmly locking his arm through Gaelen's. Soren is confused but puts away his sword, mimicking Bjark. Gaelen tries to fight against their hold, yelling for them to let him go, and I wince at the thought of what this is doing to his injuries.

"Get her!" Bjark yells at Rorik, looking to Saoirse.

He doesn't understand what's happening either, but he disarms Saoirse in a second, swinging her over his shoulder as she also begins yelling. I watch as each of them safely crosses through the door before the guards move, using their bodies to block it.

# Chapter Twenty-Three

I fumble with the bracelet tied to my wrist. It's just leather, but it hasn't been untied in some time.

Once I get it loose, I take one brief glance at the stone before I cover it in my fist. This stone is the reason I'm in this mess to begin with, but it's also been with me for so long and is still the last thing I have from my mother. The idea of letting it go is harder than I thought it would be.

"You and my son seem fond of each other. I'm glad the arrangement worked out then! Your father should've agreed years ago," King Langavin says, driving yet another splinter into my heart.

"What does my father have to do with this?"

"You will have to take that up with the young jarl," he says. "But for now, I would like my key."

"You mean my brother?"

"Hand me the key, or this man will run you through, girl," Thokkra says, gesturing to the guard dressed in her colors, standing by her side.

He can't mean Hagen. What could Hagen and my father have to do with any of this? He's trying to upset me, and this is a distraction that I don't have time for. I release the hold I have on the nightmares, feeling them emanating from me as they seep into each mind of the guards behind me. The screaming starts as I watch Thokkra, her eyes widening in horror. I just have to buy time until they start falling.

I know the power extends its way toward the king, and the guard who killed Jane starts to scream. Everyone else remains untouched.

Gods damn it. It's as if a wall stands in front of them, the power not able to penetrate it. I hear as the men behind me start to hit the ground, and I turn to see two already convulsing. One seems to have bit his tongue, blood pouring out of his mouth. Another claws into his eyes, and I turn away at the sight of fluid, but I know it will stay with me.

"What are you?" the king asks.

"I think you should've figured that out before you forced your son to marry me, don't you?"

The remaining three guards seem to think about attacking, but are afraid to leave Thokkra's boundary. They shouldn't be. I feel the drain already.

"I'm going to give you what you want, and then I'm going to walk out of here. The power will reach you if you follow me."

Truthfully, I don't know how far away I can get and it still work on the men it's already latched into. One of the men to my left just died. The corners of my vision darken. I've never used it on so many people at once.

"And you," I say, looking to Thokkra. "The next time I see you, I will kill you. I swear it to the gods."

I don't know which, since they all seem to have damned me. In the same breath, I throw the bracelet to the king, not waiting to see if he catches it, before I run out the door into the night air.

My first gulp of crisp air helps to ease some of the panic flowing through my veins, but running in this dress is awful. My vision starts to darken further from the drain of power. I should've called some of it back.

Assuming I don't pass out, I have bigger problems. I sent them ahead of me, and I have no idea how to get back to the brothel. I didn't listen to this part of the plan. I could never focus my thoughts by the time we got this far, convinced we'd all die, or leave together. My plan B was never supposed to be a real possibility. I would've even sacrificed myself to get them all out.

By the time I reach the wall, I'm barely running; it's more of a brisk stumble. I follow the wall, trying to stay in its shadow as I make my way toward a gate. I basically fall through the outer gate, which is significantly smaller than the others, only meant for walking, not carts. It also, coincidentally, appears unguarded at the moment.

I make my way down the side street, which we all discussed prior. Unfortunately, that's the only part of the plan I can remember. I watch the walkways until I spot a group of younger people walking and talking amongst each other. I fall in behind them, trying to keep their pace and blend in, but eventually I start swaying on my feet too much to keep up. The world begins to spin as a pain strong enough to split my skull open creeps its way in.

I manage to reach the stone wall of a building, using it to brace myself. I need to make it out of this section at least. It's too nice. If I were to pass out here, it would cause alarm, but I have no idea how to make it back to the brothel. I don't even know if I'm where I should be.

I should've stayed by that first side street, but I was afraid to stay so close to the castle in case they came after me. I hold onto the walls for another block before I'm sliding down one, unable to force my body to go any farther. I spot an alleyway a few feet ahead and crawl to it on my hands and knees. I don't make it far into the alley before I have to stop, sitting with my back to the wall.

I feel something warm on my lips as the taste of iron reaches my tongue. I wipe my hand across my mouth, and it comes back coated in blood. My nose must be bleeding. I hope that didn't start while I was still on the street. There's no way it wouldn't have drawn attention. Maybe if I just stay here a few minutes, I'll regain enough of my strength.

But I'm so tired.

Slowly, I start to lose the battle to keep my eyes open. I just need to close them for a little while, and then I know I'll be able to move again.

The sensation of falling wakes me, my head dropping backward as arms lift my body into the air. A bolt of panic shoots through me.

I didn't make it far enough—a guard found me. I don't know that I have enough energy to fight back as I lift my head toward my captor, but I find Bjark carrying me.

"You're fine. I got you," he says as he ducks into a carriage.

"Where is Gaelen?" I ask as he deposits me onto one side of the carriage before taking the other.

"He fought us the entire way out of the castle grounds and through the gate. It took Soren and me both to get him outside the walls. Once we were down the side street, I got him to listen long enough to explain that we had a plan, that I couldn't go back to get you if he was acting like an ass. He calmed down enough. Once he heals, he's going to kill me for letting you do this, and for stopping him."

"He'll get over it."

"Yeah, maybe."

"Thank you for coming back for me. I would've never made it that far even if I knew the way."

"Yeah, well, I went back to the castle for you, but the guard said he watched you stumble through a few minutes prior. You went down the wrong street, I think, or I would've spotted you sooner."

"Whose carriage is this?"

"It's just a carriage for hire. They're all over in the nicer areas. I flagged it down. The driver will take us to the brothel, and no one will know it's us; they all look the same."

The surety in his words and the movement of the carriage lull me back into darkness once more.

I wake as the carriage comes to a stop outside the brothel. We go around through the side street, entering through the stable doors to prevent any patrons from seeing us enter.

I'm still exhausted and have a pounding headache, but knowing I'm this close to everyone, to confirming we all made it out safely, and finding out the extent of Gaelen's injuries has adrenaline fueling me enough to make it up each step and through the halls to our secret room. I don't even have the door fully open before Saoirse engulfs me in a hug, immediately followed by Rorik on top of her.

"I was so worried," she says, pulling back to look at me. "And I'm going to kill you! That was not okay!"

"Yeah, you both should've told us!" Rorik says, looking to Bjark and me. "Are you hurt?"

"I'm fine, just drained," I say.

Theorin comes in for a hug next, which catches me off guard at first.

"Thank you! They told me what you did," he says, stepping back.

I smile and look over to Soren. He's the only one still seated.

"Where is he?" I ask.

"He's asleep in the other room. Any wounds that had started to heal reopened in his struggle to get to you. He eventually passed out. A healer will be here soon," Soren says.

"A healer from where? Can we trust them?" I ask.

"It's one of the women from the brothel. Sometimes they need a healer, unfortunately," Theorin says, a grave look on his face. "He looks pretty bad."

I nod in response and walk toward the other room. I look down at my shaking hand as it reaches to turn the doorknob, and pause for a moment, bracing myself before walking in.

## Chapter Twenty-Four

Gaelen lies on the bed in what would look like a peaceful sleep, if you ignored all the damage done to his body. He'll likely live, thank the gods, but the senselessness of it all consumes me.

He didn't need to do this for me, and I don't want people I care about risking their lives to keep me safe. I need to figure out Runa's riddle. Finding the dagger and ending this is the only way I can keep everyone safe. We can't remain hidden here forever, and going home isn't an option right now either. It's something I'll have to dissect later; my mind can only handle so much at a time.

I step closer to him, kneeling on the ground next to the small bed. Up close, I can see the sweat breaking out across his skin. It reminds me of how I sat as my mother died, sweating from fever. The festering burn on his chest likely causes his.

I don't know enough about healing outside of the basic knowledge Earie taught Saoirse and I as girls. I was never interested enough to learn more. I look over all his visible injuries again, so many that could be infected. The dungeon was disgusting and so damp. My vision blurs as my eyes fill with the tears I've been fighting back for days, promising them they would have their time. They seem to be claiming it now.

He could have died at any point. Any one of us could've not made it out tonight; an innocent person just trying to help us actually didn't.

I can't imagine the pain and mental torment Gaelen must have gone through. I wouldn't have stayed this strong. I'm sobbing into my hands when I feel him caress the nape of my neck, and then his fingers sink into my hair, still pulled into a loose braid, though the pins are missing.

"Love," he says softly, his voice breaking.

I don't want to think of the reasons why.

"I'm fine." He gives me a slight smile when I look up at him.

"You're not! I can see you!" I say, and he starts to laugh, followed by a wince.

"How did you get out?" he asks.

I run my hands over my face, wiping away my tears.

"I used the power; I think I killed most of the guards. I would have killed Thokkra and your father, but she had some way of blocking me. The effort of using the power on so many people started to drain me, so I gave up the stone and ran."

"Did Bjark find you?" His voice may have been hoarse, but I could still hear the notes of anger in it.

"Yes, I passed out against a wall in the city. Don't be mad at him."

"You scared the fuck out of me," he whispers, closing his eyes.

His hand stays in my hair, unraveling my braid.

"I'm sorry. It wasn't really part of the original plan, but Bjark knew I'd try to buy you all time if I had to, and then I'd get out. He was always going to come back for me."

He doesn't say anything for a time. I hope he's not deciding how mad he should be at Bjark.

"Bjark trusts you." He says it more as an observation.

A knock sounds at the door before a woman walks in carrying a basket of supplies. She introduces herself as Sylvi, the healer that Theorin mentioned would be coming. She hands me a tonic and tasks me with convincing Gaelen to take it, and then sets down her basket to go and fill multiple basins with water.

"Why would I need a sleeping tonic?" he asks.

"I'm going to help her clean all the blood off your body, and then she's going to clean out and stitch your wounds."

"I lived through getting them, I think I'll be fine."

"This is going to hurt, your burns are infected, and you won't sit still once I start working," she says over my shoulder, dropping off the first basin of warm water.

He doesn't look convinced.

"Please? I need you to heal quickly. We're going on a long journey, and if you don't heal, I'll have to leave you behind."

"You're not leaving me anywhere, first of all. But where are we going?"

"You'll have to drink the tonic to find out, I'm afraid," I tease him, but he doesn't seem to buy that either.

Sighing, I use the last thing I have.

"This is going to be painful, and even though you might be able to handle that, I won't be able to handle watching it."

He exhales, and I know I've won.

"Fine. But don't leave."

"I wasn't really going to leave without you!" I say, smiling.

"No, I mean now. When I'm asleep, will you stay?"

"Of course." I nod, heart aching.

He pulls my mouth to his. I hadn't kissed him yet. I didn't

want to hurt him. I taste the blood from his split lip, but this kiss seems to carry more than those that came before it.

Afterward, when the basins of water are no longer clear, and an insurmountable number of rags drenched in blood are piled into one, all his wounds are finally clean. Sylvi was able to stitch multiple wounds closed, some not needing it. Two burns required infected skin to be cut away, but are now covered in salve and wrapped. She examined his swollen eye, and the bone didn't appear broken. Thankfully, she doesn't think anything is. The biggest concern is still infection.

Another knock sounds at the door as Rorik walks in.

"I can sit with him, if you want to get cleaned up and change."

I look down at myself for the first time, realizing I have blood-tinged water dried to my hands and halfway up my arms. My servant dress is covered in dirt from the dungeon, and sleeping in an alley. And I can only imagine what's in my hair, but still, I shake my head.

"I promised I wouldn't leave him."

He seems to have been expecting that answer since he retreats without further protest. But only a few minutes pass before he returns, followed by Bjark, Soren, and Theorin.

"Did you go for reinforcements?" I ask.

"We know you didn't do that just for him. You did it to save all of us. This is the least we can do," Rorik says.

"He's a brother to all of us; we have him," Soren says.

"Some of us more than others," Theorin interjects.

Rorik gives him a side eye.

"Saoirse has a bath ready for you. She'll help you, and you can come right back. He probably won't even wake up while you're gone."

Reluctantly, I agree. It'd be nice to get out of this dress, and I know if I keep arguing, they're just going to carry me out.

I bathe quickly. Even though the warm water feels amazing, I don't want to linger.

"Is he going to be okay?" Saoirse asks.

I sit in front of a mirror in the bathroom as she combs through my hair. The headache isn't as bad as before, but it still lingers, so she works through one small section at a time.

"As long as the infection stops, I think so. None of the wounds on their own would have been fatal. There are just so many," I say, closing my eyes.

The image of him sitting in that cell, covered in dirt and blood, is seared into my mind. I change the subject.

"I hope you're not mad at Rorik for carrying you out of there."

"No, I understand why he did it. It was really hard thinking I would never see you again, though," she says, giving me a look.

"I'm sorry. Gaelen was pretty upset over it, too." I sigh,

feeling bad for scaring everyone, but I would do it again if I had to.

"Hmm, he seems to care deeply about you," she says, searching for a reaction in the mirror.

"He might, I don't know."

"And might you… care for him?" she asks.

I stare at her for a moment before speaking.

"What are we doing right now?"

"We're assessing your feelings after a traumatic event. You just found him covered in blood, scary things happened, you could've died. I want to know how you feel about it all. You never look at your feelings enough, and it's not healthy. This is what friends do."

"Well, maybe you look at them too much."

"You mean a healthy amount?"

There's no winning with her.

"I haven't thought about it," I say.

She only sighs in response.

"Fine. I'm happy it's him. I missed him when he left. I had a feeling of dread the entire trip here. Finding him was heartbreaking. I was terrified the entire time we were in that castle that you'd all die, and were my death not likely imminent, I could've killed myself for bringing you along. Is that what you wanted?"

"Well, you should probably get back in there then before he

wakes up," she says with a knowing smile, putting the comb down. "But for what it's worth, I wouldn't have been okay if you died either."

"This feels like fucking hell. Next time, just kill me, and get out." I hear Gaelen's voice say through the door, followed by laughter.

"Not a chance! I'm way more afraid of Thyrvi than I am of you!" Rorik says, followed by murmured agreements.

I knock on the door before pushing it open and walking in. The guys stand quietly, pick up the extra beds, and carry them out. I sit in the chair next to Gaelen's bed, where he's obviously pretending to be asleep.

"I know you're awake," I say.

His good eye opens, the other trying. I raise my eyebrow.

"I woke up a few minutes ago. They told me what they did. They didn't want you to be upset."

I scoff, rolling my eyes.

"They care about you. Seems like I missed a lot," he says.

"We became friends. Well, I became friends with Bjark and Rorik at least. I don't know about Soren and your brother."

"And us? Are we friends?" he asks, the corner of his mouth raised in a smirk.

But I sense the truth in his question. I watch him for a moment before responding.

"No, we were apart for two weeks, and I forgot all about our arranged marriage and our trip to the springs. I actually met a farmer. Though not a prince, I think we'll be rather happy. I traveled all the way here, risking my life and my friends' lives to tell you it's over," I say, tossing my hair back and smiling.

"You couldn't at least wait till I was healed before breaking my heart?" he asks, but the joke doesn't do enough to lessen the reality of what happened.

"Thank you," I say, telling myself I will not cry again, trying to spin a bracelet that's no longer there. "All of this happened because you were trying to keep me safe, and you didn't have to."

"I took an oath to keep you safe, Thyrvi."

Our eyes remain locked, but I don't know what to say in response to his words or the fluttering in my stomach. He rolls onto his side in an obvious struggle.

"What are you doing? You're going to pull your stitches!"

He lifts the covers, gesturing for me to get into the bed next to him.

"I'm not getting in that bed. I'll hurt you."

"I'll be fine, just lie with me."

I only hesitate for a breath before I slide in next to him.

## Chapter
## Twenty-Five

In the morning, my body is stiff from being in the same position for so long, but Gaelen no longer feels feverish.

At some point, Sylvi stops to check in on his wounds and orders him to take a real bath, but not to soak the stitches for too long. Then leaves me with more of the salve to apply after. Once the new bandages are secured, I help him put a shirt on. We spend the rest of the day eating, talking, and napping. The drain of power took more from me than I realized.

The next few days are spent hiding in the brothel, giving Gaelen time to heal, as I try to decide on our next steps. Soren,

Bjark, and Rorik are the only ones who leave regularly, Saoirse going out a few times with Rorik. I'm starting to go a little stir crazy, but just relaxing with Gaelen has felt like a dream.

At some point, Rorik starts sleeping in the same room as Saoirse, though I must have missed when. I make a note to have another *feelings check* with her.

"Before, you mentioned we were going somewhere?" Gaelen asks, sitting on the edge of our small bed.

"Not until you can put on your own shirt," I joke.

"But I like when you do it," he says, grabbing my legs and pulling me onto his lap, my legs on either side of him.

"You're going to get hurt."

"I'm already hurt. You're making me feel better." He places light kisses on my neck.

"It's not happening." I pull back to look at him. "But if you cooperate and promise not to pull any stitches, I'll tell you where we're going."

"Promise."

"I've been thinking about Runa's riddle and playing the old sagas through my head, and well, I only know of one wolf that is bound."

"Fenrir?"

"You do know some!"

"I said I know the basics."

"He was bound in Gleipnir, made by the dwarves. There's

only one place I know of with stone halls that the sun can't reach. And why wouldn't you hide a magic weapon with the only ones capable of crafting it in the first place?"

"The dwarves?" he asks.

I nod.

"No one has seen the dwarves in ages. We don't even know if they still exist," he says.

"Their stronghold was said to be in the Stengrost mountains. They don't have to still be alive for the dagger to be hidden there."

"People have gone into the Stengrost mountains. No one has seen a fortress or ruins of one."

"Well, they wouldn't, would they? It'd be inside the mountain, Gaelen," I say.

He looks at me like I'm insane. When I don't say anything, he only nods.

"Okay, when do we leave?"

"That's it? You just believe in the dwarves now?"

"No, but I believe in you. Even if you weren't the key to some dark god's power, blessed by a goddess, and having less than a week ago snuck into a dungeon to save my life, I go where you go."

I softly press my mouth to his, trying to be careful of his healing lip.

"You need a few more days to heal, and we need to gather

supplies."

I think about the things we'll need to trek through the mountains. Then I remember Theorin's question about Yule.

"I don't know if we'll be back for the Winter Solstice."

I hope he wouldn't want to annul the hand-fasting, but it can't hurt to check. A lot has happened.

"I'm good, Love," he says, shaking his head as if to answer my unasked question.

His use of the nickname makes me feel as though I'm melting. It strikes me how much I missed hearing him call me that. He must confuse whatever he sees on my face, prompting him to continue.

"Unless you were hoping to attend? I'll agree to annul it if that's what you want. But you're not getting rid of me. I'll expect us to do it all over again. If you were serious about the farmer, I'm going to have to kill him."

I just smile, and without thinking, my fingers dive into his hair, pulling his mouth back to mine. But I'm not soft this time. His hands trail under my shirt, pulling it over my head.

"We shouldn't," I weakly protest, knowing I don't want to win this battle.

"I'll be fine," he says, biting my bottom lip, making me moan.

I stand, sliding off his shirt as he carefully moves up the bed, leaning his back against the headboard. I remove my leggings and bra while he slides his pants down, his cock freed and waiting.

His eyes roam over my body, a smile spreading across his face as I crawl over to straddle him. His arms wrap around my waist and pull me closer to him as he angles his hips. I carefully lower myself onto him, trying to be aware of his injuries. His hands grip my waist as I start moving.

"Gods, I missed you," he whispers against my neck.

We wait for our friends to finish their food before we break the news of our plans to leave.

We all sit together in the main room of our hidden space inside the brothel. Honestly, with some of the sounds that make it through these walls, it's a small miracle Gaelen and I have managed to keep our hands off each other this long.

"After everything, you seriously think we'll let you go without us?" Saoirse asks.

I knew she'd be the first to argue, and the hardest to

convince. Unless she knew there was a good reason.

"I don't want us to separate, but we need people we trust watching the king." I take a deep breath. "And I need someone to watch my brother."

I can feel Gaelen's eyes on me; I didn't tell him.

"What does Hagen have to do with this?" she asks.

"I don't know. There was something the king said about my father and the deal that was made with my brother. If I survive everything else, I'll need to deal with that next."

"You will," Gaelen growls.

I watch Saoirse as anger and determination threaten to take over her.

"I'll go to Thurisa. It wouldn't make sense for anyone else to go, and I can talk to people, see what I can find out," she says.

"Don't do anything to draw attention to yourself. I don't know how far this goes, and I don't want you getting hurt," I plead.

"I'll make sure she stays safe," Rorik says with a nod in my direction.

"Your father was family, and my father's best friend. I know he'll help us should we need it," she says.

Needing Len would mean something big, that there's something we need to sway the judgment of the village for. And it'd mean undermining Erik's control over Thurisa's militia.

"You're going into the mountains right as winter starts with the hopes of finding the dwarves' ruins, and within them, a magic dagger? This doesn't sound like a fool's journey to you?" Soren asks.

"I know how it sounds, and I've played the witch's riddles over and over in my head. This makes sense. And we don't have time to wait until spring."

"Don't we? We can move you three. You can stay in hiding until the ice thaws."

"That'll give my father and Thokkra too much time to prepare. They'll realize Thyrvi's bracelet doesn't house the key soon, and he won't respond well to being tricked. It's better we act now than risk them finding us while we wait out the weather."

I didn't expect him to defend my plan.

"We need to get Theorin out of the city until our father is dealt with," Gaelen adds, looking at Soren and Bjark.

"Soren has more connections here; it makes sense for him to keep an eye on the king. I can get Theorin out, and keep him alive until he's crowned," Bjark says.

"I can keep myself alive," Theorin retorts.

"Sure, in a city where you can buy things and duel people. You managed a three-day journey on your own with a bag Soren packed for you and one road to follow. Yet you still looked like death when you arrived," Bjark says firmly. "Either way, it'd be good for you to get out and see the people whose lives you'll be impacting once you're king."

I think those two are going to have a great time together. But truthfully, Theorin wouldn't make a bad king.

We spend our last couple days gathering supplies for our separate trips. Snow is starting to fall regularly now that we're getting closer to the Solstice, but it hasn't stuck yet. I know once we're in the mountains, it'll be everywhere, and we'll be miserable. We pack extra items for warmth, and Bjark brings back extremely thick coats. So dense, it severely limits my range of mobility. Between that and the boots, it's going to take us years to make it into the mountains.

When the time comes to leave, it's harder than I thought it would be to say goodbye. Hugging each of them, my heart aches knowing it could be the last time I see them. When I reach Bjark, he grabs me in a big bear hug.

"I'll see you soon. Be safe!" he says before clasping Gaelen's shoulder. I move on before I can hear what they say so that I don't cry. Standing in front of Saoirse, I don't have the words to give her, so we don't say anything; we hug each other. She then turns to Gaelen.

"If anything happens to her, I'll come for you."

The look on her face scares me a little. I feel better knowing she's going back to Thurisa, where she'll be safe, and where she and Rorik can have time together. I also know there's no one better for the task she's assigned, and if she does find anything, and I don't make it back, I do not doubt that Len will do whatever needs to be done.

"I would expect nothing less," Gaelen says back to her before hugging her.

## Chapter Twenty-Six

We walk the city donning cloaks with hoods covering our heads. It's early, and the streets are as empty as I imagine they ever get. Only a small number of people are awake at this hour, bundled up to keep out the chilled air, likely heading off to whatever it is they do for work.

This is the first time we've been outside of our rooms since the castle. Even though the sun hasn't yet risen, my eyes are still adjusting to its brightness. As we make our way farther out of the city, colorful doorways give way to drab wood and crumbling stone; cobbled streets turn to dirt. Finally, we reach one of the smaller gates that lead out of the city, and Gaelen takes my hand, pulling me closer. Outside of the walls, I can see people congregating, waiting for their turn to be let in. The guards look exhausted, not really paying attention to anyone leaving. My breath comes easier with each step we take away from Kenaz. A giddiness comes over me, and if it wouldn't draw attention or potentially injure Gaelen, I could skip. Instead, I settle for smiling.

Gaelen still has bruises, but the cuts look a lot better, and all signs of infection have long since cleared. The extra salve Sylvi made for us is still packed in our bags just in case.

I was surprised to hear him ask Rorik to take his horse back to Thurisa, assuming he would have brought it with us, but apparently, normal horses are not the best option in mountain terrain. Rorik and Soren had our supplies smuggled out of the city last night with a merchant, while we're meant to meet with someone a few miles northeast of the city to grab our things, and with three horses of a different breed, one extra to help carry everything we need to stave off the cold.

When we finally reach the horses, I don't know what I was expecting, but their short stature and dusting of fur is not it. I'm not sure if it's their personality or the better hold I now have on the power, but they don't seem to be bothered by me, content to nibble on the patches of grass still holding on to life. The man provides us with a few small bags of dry feed, but ensures us they are hardy foragers and will find things to eat under the snow and from trees, given the opportunity. They are trained to stay close to people and each other, and with there not being any real predators in the mountains, we shouldn't have reason to worry about letting them graze on their own.

We ride through the thick birch forest, hoping to put as much distance between us and Kenaz as quickly as possible. It takes a full day of riding to get into the foothills of the mountains, where we dismount. The horses are surefooted, but we don't want to risk any injuries.

We continue on foot for a few miles over a rocky trail, horses tied together in a single file behind us. Cliffsides block us in on both sides as the trail continues to wind. Night has fully taken over the sky before Gaelen finally feels comfortable enough to stop. The snow is starting to thicken, but it still hasn't reached its full depth. We will likely need to wear the additional gear tomorrow as we make our way deeper into the mountain range.

Gaelen makes a fire as I set up our small tent. I'm not looking forward to the nights where this is the only thing between us and the freezing winds; it looks a little pathetic. He had more success with the fire than I did with the tent, already unpacking the blankets from saddle bags and bringing them over. He leans over me to lay everything out inside, and his lips lightly brush mine.

He's been quieter than normal today, which I guess is expected after everything. Hiding out in our room was like living in our own little bubble, safe and surrounded by our friends. Now that we're back in the world, we can no longer avoid reality, and my mind continues to replay what the king said about my father and brother.

"Did you know your father tried to arrange our marriage before, but mine wouldn't agree?" I ask.

Gaelen emerges from the tent to look at me. "No. I didn't know it was happening until it was agreed to. That's why I thought your brother forced you into it. But they'd already agreed, the document was just a formality."

"Hagen acted as though he had just received the offer when he told me."

"Is there a reason you didn't want to talk to me about this sooner?" he asks.

I knew he was going to overthink it when I didn't mention it before I told Saoirse.

"No, I just had a lot to think about already. And I was worried about you. I didn't have room to think about what it all meant yet."

"Do you think it's strange that he refused without at least telling you? You would've had to be an adult at the time."

"I didn't think about that part yet. I told you I didn't have room for any of this. But no, I guess not. He would've wanted me to marry someone I chose."

Nodding, he unpacks our food for the evening—some bread, the first thing that will start to go bad, and salted meats. Honestly, if I never had to eat salted meat again, I could die happy. We need to watch for small animals we can hunt along the way.

I wake feeling his body warmth pull away; he must have been waiting for me to fall asleep. The shifting of wood sounds from outside, and firelight filtering through the fabric seems to grow. For a moment, I consider getting up to make sure everything is okay, but sleep reclaims me before I can muster the energy.

The next few days pass similarly. We ride where we can, lead the horses when we can't, and try to cross as much distance as possible. Gaelen doesn't sleep most nights. I know he's worried someone will find us, so I don't argue.

I wake early each day, making him rest while I prepare things for us to set out again. Occasionally, he takes small naps when we stop to let the horses graze or get water at a stream.

Now that we are farther away from civilization, he's started staying in the tent longer at night. Last night, he fell asleep before me, and our shared body heat had us both sleeping longer than intended. Folding our bedding, I try fitting it all back in the bags to strap to one of the horses, but it's never easy to fit back together.

I catch Gaelen looking up to the mountains where we passed the day prior, seeming to focus on something.

"What's wrong?"

"I thought I saw something move up there."

I squint in the direction he points.

"Up by those large rocks."

"I can hardly see them." It was about midday yesterday, if not earlier, when we passed that spot before making the descent down the winding path. "It's probably just an animal."

"Maybe."

By the time evening approaches, I'm exhausted, and my calves burn from walking up a steep incline all day.

I have heard it said that our mountains are small in comparison to some of the lands across the sea, and if that's true, I hope I never have to climb them. He hasn't mentioned why we haven't stopped for a single break, but he keeps glancing into the distance and at the trail behind us.

Whatever he saw this morning clearly has him more worried than he's letting on. His paranoia rubs off on me, and I catch myself looking back. When I'm not looking behind us, I'm watching a peak in the far distance.

I hadn't noticed before, but this morning, there was a small peak between several others in the distance, only this one had far less snow. My curiosity is the only reason I don't insist on stopping. I know at some point we'll need to leave the main path, and I'm hoping this might be a sign. I don't know if the dwarves still exist, but I know we have no chance of finding them or where they were, on the most frequently used trail through the mountains.

Stepping onto the ridge of our smaller mountain, my breath catches as I take in the view. The setting sun behind the mountains gives the sky a pinkish glow, only broken by clouds and snowcapped peaks.

This journey hasn't been easy. I've hardly been warm since we left the brothel, my body is tired and sore, and I would love to eat normal food, but this view makes it all worth it.

Across the birch forest below are two mountains covered in snow, and behind them sits another, this one with a dusting of snow in comparison, the earth and rock still visible.

Looking back to where Gaelen stands with the horses, I find him watching me. Smiling, I take a few steps toward him, wrapping my arms around his waist and snuggling my face into his jacket. His arms slide around me as we take in our surroundings.

"It's that one." My gloved hand points to the peak hidden behind the two closest to us. His eyes squint to focus on it, and a smirk forms on his face, the first of the day.

"Why that one?" he asks, eyebrow raised.

"It has almost no snow."

"Do dwarves keep away snow?"

"No, but heat does."

I have run the possibilities through my head countless times since I spotted it. Of course, their mountain would be warmer than the rest. Their forges are that of legend, and even if an average forge is hot enough to melt steel, I don't know how hot a forge would have to be to create magical weapons. If stories are true, their fortress would host plenty. What they might be doing with them, as isolated as they are, is another question entirely.

We need to leave the main trail after this descent. Cross through the forest and around a large lake before reaching the front two mountains. Anyway, if I'm wrong, it will at least be warmer that way.

"The horses are carrying less weight now, so I think we

should ride. We won't make it down before dark at this rate," he says before kissing my forehead and pulling my hood up more.

"Gaelen, what's going on?"

He looks at me for a moment before sighing.

"I think we are being followed."

"By what?"

"I'm not sure. I caught a few glimpses of something moving in the distance, but I can never get a good look."

My mind went to what he wasn't saying. Nothing is out here. We have foxes, rabbits, and birds, but there are no animals that would follow us all day, and certainly none big enough to be a concern. He doesn't just think we're being followed, he thinks someone is hunting us. I don't know how they could follow us and remain hidden this far out. They would need the appropriate gear, food, and a tent. Those aren't things that allow someone to be stealthy.

I stare up at him for a long moment. The green and yellow remnants of bruising are still on his face, mixing with the circles forming under his eyes. He's been through a lot recently. I don't know if I believe we are being followed, or if I think this is an aftereffect of everything else, but he never doubts me.

"What do we do if they catch up?" I ask.

"I think there's only one. We kill them quickly and go. I

don't want to fight them on the side of the mountain, and we can't sleep until this is dealt with."

With the sun setting, and the way the path twists, it's impossible to see anything but a few feet ahead of us. We make it to the bottom sometime in the middle of the night. Dismounting, we lead the horses off the trail and into the woods, the trees closing in around us.

The silence of night is a very different experience from what we'd grown accustomed to on the mountain pass. It almost feels eerie compared to the open sky. The hoot of an owl sounds just before one flies overhead in the same direction we're going.

"Aren't owls an embodiment of your goddess?"

"She isn't my goddess, but yes."

Part of me does wonder if she's sending a message, and of course, why she has bothered to help me at all.

We continue walking, exhaustion sinking in, but every time a twig snaps in the distance, my body finds a new reserve of adrenaline and fear to keep me moving. The sun starts to rise somewhere behind the mountains, and the sky lightens.

We still aren't out of this forest after an entire night of walking. I peer over my shoulder, and my eyes sweep over something before my mind can register it. I do a double take, and my heart feels as though it's falling out of my chest as my blood thunders through my veins.

Something that resembles a person stands twenty yards behind us. It's dressed in furs, an axe in hand, but its face—its face is covered in a mask of bones.

## Chapter Twenty-Seven

The nightmares reach out, triggered by my fear, whatever control I hoped to have, faltering with the ice that snakes its way up my spine. The figure doesn't move. I feel no pull on the power, but there isn't anything blocking me like with Thokkra. It's as if nothing stands before us.

"The nightmares can't find it," I whisper.

"I don't think it's alive," he says, eyes searching the woods around it for any others. "Leave your bow on the horse, make sure you have your sword. We're going to free the horses and run."

"There's only one. Why would we run?" I ask, but the thing chooses this moment to make its move.

"Go!" Gaelen yells, cutting the rope tethering the extra horse to his.

To my surprise, the horses follow, eventually passing us as we run through the trees, dodging branches and jumping over logs. My foot catches on a root, the world tilting with my fall. Gaelen is there to grab my elbow, pulling me up before I hit the ground. His pace stays with mine even though I'm certain he could outrun me.

Ahead of us, the horses break through the tree line and run straight onto the frozen lake. Once Gaelen and I exit the forest, I hesitate, but he doesn't give me an option, pulling me onto the ice with him.

Ideally, we would've taken the long way around. The mountain starts midway through, so at some point, we would need to walk on the ice due to the mountain sides, but it would have been at least shallow water, not deep like this.

The horses' hooves thunder on the ice ahead of us, causing small fractures to start running along the ice.

"Just keep moving!" Gaelen yells.

I mistakenly glance over my shoulder and find the thing gaining on us.

"Keep running. Do not stop. I'll handle this and find you," Gaelen says before coming to a stop himself.

"What are you doing?" I try to stop slowly to avoid sliding on the ice.

"Thyrvi, go! I can't fight this and worry about you!"

His words and my instincts force me to run before my mind has made sense of it. From behind, I can hear the clatter of steel as Gaelen's sword meets the thing's axe. If I can just get to my horse and grab the bow, I might have the time to line up a shot. But they're too far ahead of me.

I spare another glance backward, just in time to see Gaelen lose his sword, it sliding in my direction. He tackles the thing, both of them landing on the ice with a resounding crack.

Fuck. If we live through this, he's going to kill me.

I start running toward him. The thing notices and seems to focus on me, now busy trying to escape Gaelen's grasp as opposed to fighting him.

I'm so close to reaching his sword. I look up to where they struggle against each other, so many cracks in the ice as Gaelen fights to get the axe out of the thing's hand. I hear another crack just before the ground disappears from under me.

Plunging into the freezing water, it's as though a fist was just pound against my entire body, the breath rushing out of my lungs in an instant. Chunks of ice float past me as I sink, making their way back to the surface where I entered seconds prior. I try to follow them, but I'm not used to swimming in winter gear. However, the frigid water stabbing every inch of my skin makes me work extra hard for any space I gain.

Finally, I reach that break in the ice ceiling overhead and reach up, trying to find purchase in the surrounding ice. I can't tread water with the extra weight, my fingers grabbing the sides of broken ice and sliding off. Getting my arms over the side is another story.

Knowing I won't be strong enough to pull myself out, I try to undo the buttons of my jacket to remove some weight. I'm halfway done when a hand wraps around my arm, dragging me out of the frozen water. I want to lie on the ice coughing, but without waiting even a moment, Gaelen forces me to stand, then pushes me forward.

"We have to get you off the ice and out of these clothes. Now," Gaelen growls.

With my constant shivering, I can't even respond. We make it to the frozen river, and a strip of small rocks running along each side allows us to move off the ice. The horses, having finally stopped, can be seen up ahead.

Apparently, they'd decided there was enough distance between them and any trouble. Gaelen whistles, and three heads perk up from where they foraged under the rocks, then they begin trotting back toward us. I can hardly keep my eyes open long enough to see their arrival.

My thoughts come in slowly. Gaelen pulls a blanket from

the saddle bag and lays it on the ground, rummaging around until he finds the extra clothes I packed. He takes off my jacket, dropping it to the ground in a wet heap. My sweater and shirt are pulled from my body, and my soaked bra too, before I even realize what's happening.

"What are you doing?" I try to say through my shaking, wrapping my arms around my chest. The words are barely audible.

"You're going to freeze to death."

A dry shirt and sweater are forced over my head, not even waiting for me to put my arms through them before he moves on. He takes off my boots, socks, and pants, making me step onto the blanket before he starts replacing everything he removed with dry versions all over again. Even if I weren't so exhausted, my cold fingers wouldn't be able to move at the speed his are.

He starts to undo my braid, shaking my hair free and removing as much water as he can before using one of his shirts to remove the rest. He takes off his jacket, putting it around me and grabbing dry gloves for my hands.

I try to protest, "Gaelen, you can't give me your jacket."

"I'll be fine," he says before putting on an extra sweater.

He wrung out the arm of his jacket, but it's still wet from grabbing me, the rest still holding on to his body heat. My boots are cold, the water that was in them frozen, but the extra socks he gave me are helping. I can already see the frost starting to form on my hair.

"There's nothing on this side of the lake to start a fire with. We have to keep going, and you have to walk. I know you're tired, but we have to keep your blood moving."

He steps in front of me, so close our bodies touch, his fingers sliding up my neck and into my wet hair. The warmth from his lips is a stark contrast to my frozen ones. He shakes his head at me before he picks up the blanket and wraps it around us both, and we start walking again. We don't bother to hold onto the horses, but they follow nonetheless.

At some point, we stop, Gaelen trying to get me to eat, but I can only manage a few bites. He checks my toes and fingers, warming them in his hands, and then we continue, repeating the process every few hours. By nightfall, I can't remember the second half of the day.

"Thyrvi," he whispers into my hair.

The sun is gone, and he's carrying me.

"Why didn't you put me on a horse?"

"You needed warmth."

Looking up at him, I can see the exhaustion in his face and the blue setting into his lips. I wiggle around, forcing him to put me down.

We're at the base of the mountain. The one without snow, it was so far away last time I looked at it. Looking at it this closely, I can see that it's just a mountain. No gates, no doorway, no signs, nothing. I don't know if we can survive walking around this whole fucking mountain looking for a door. We need a fire. The horses need to graze. Why would I think it was going to be as easy as just making it here?

I look back at Gaelen. After everything he's done, I can't hold it back any longer, and my eyes fill with tears.

"I'm so sorry. I never should've made us come here. You saved my life, you kept me warm, you even carried me for gods' sake, and now we are going to die out here because I was so fucking stupid," I manage to get out between sobs.

"First of all, I'm not going to let you die. Yes, you made a mistake on the ice, and I'll be mad at you for that once I know you're safe, but you were not stupid about this." He grabs my shoulders, spinning me back around. "Look!"

There's nothing there. Just the base of a mountain I risked everything to reach.

"What am I supposed to be looking at?"

"There are runes carved into the mountain."

"Gaelen, it's the old language. It's not unheard of to find runes carved into equally old things!" I yell and hear a small laugh escape his lips.

"Humor me and go touch them."

I start to wonder if the lack of sleep is getting to him. We might not be able to make a fire, but we can set up the tent.

We might produce enough body heat between the two of us to keep us from dying before the sun rises. It does feel slightly warmer here. At least, there's less snow.

I storm over, ready to prove him wrong as I slap my hand down on the stone.

"No, take it seriously. Will it to open."

I roll my eyes but look to the mountain. The truth is, I do want it to open. I don't want to have been wrong about this, or the dwarves being real. What will our friends say when they find out we froze to death because I was an idiot?

Though I know how this key thing will likely end, a small part of me was holding out hope for more time with them. But right now, I'm so tired, and I'm so fucking cold.

From the corner of my eye, I see a shiny ripple run through the mountain. Startled, I look back, and I swear, even half frozen, he looks a little smug. Quickly, he grabs the reins of the horses and walks over to me. Grabbing my hand, we walk through the mountain.

## Chapter Twenty-Eight

The heat is like an assault to my frozen body. Going from one extreme to another feels like pins pricking my limbs as my blood starts to thaw.

"I knew you could do it," Gaelen whispers, just before his mouth meets mine.

"Did you just walk through that fucking wall?" asks a voice on my left.

A dwarven male, with dark hair and a long beard, stands there. Looking around, I can see that we have entered a large, open room connected to multiple hallways on each side. Directly in front of us, the floor ends, giving way to the rest of the mountain. I bring my attention back to him.

"Um. Yes," I say.

His eyes close with an audible sigh.

"Why did it have to be me?" he asks, seemingly to no one, and shakes his head. "How did you get through? The magic prevents human entry."

"I'm not sure. I just touched the runes." I turn to look at Gaelen. He knew this would work, that I could get us through. But how?

"And why exactly are you here?" the dwarf asks.

"I'm looking for a dagger. I heard it might be hidden here."

Being this direct is a risk, and not a well-calculated one either, but I'm exhausted, and honestly, we can't afford to waste any more time.

"Oh no, no, no. They're not going to like this."

"Who isn't going to like this?" Gaelen asks, losing his patience with the frantic dwarf. "We almost died getting here, and we're exhausted."

"Right, I'm not being very hospitable. Nora wouldn't like that," he says, looking around, seeming satisfied with whatever he finds. "My name is Skorri. I'll take you to my home until someone can decide what to do with you. You're just going to cause a spectacle out here."

"I'm Thyrvi, and this is Gaelen." I look over at Gaelen, who doesn't look amused. "Would you have somewhere we can put the horses? They also had a long journey."

"Oh, yes. We have a barn, mostly for goats. Tie them over there and grab what you need. I'll have someone fetch them." Skorri gestures to a notch in the wall.

Human visitors may not be completely unheard of then. We tie the horses to the notch and grab our bags, following Skorri as he leads us through a series of hallways. My body is starting to thaw from the heat inside the mountain, but it's also making room for my hunger.

The cave-like hallways seem to stretch on forever, and I quickly become aware that I won't be able to find my way out. Was it two lefts before the right or three? Hopefully, Gaelen is doing a better job at remembering than I am.

We approach a door, and Skorri pushes it open, gesturing once more for us to follow. The dwelling has the same cave-like feel as the hallways did, but considerably homier. The floors are covered in rugs, wooden furniture fills the room, books and paintings line the walls. The most amazing smell is coming from somewhere inside, and it makes my stomach rumble.

"Nora, I need to tell you something!" Skorri yells.

"Skorri, is that you?" a voice I assume to be Nora's yells back.

"Yes, now can you please come here?" The yelling continues.

"Do you believe in dwarves now?" I whisper, glancing up at Gaelen.

He smirks. Listening to the conversation between Skorri and Nora unfold, I realize this will never be the type of relationship Gaelen and I share. Not that it's something I would've ever wanted before, but a bit of the mundane would be nice right about now. A comfortable routine that we could fall into, not worrying if the other would die today. I wonder if we'll be disrupting Skorri and Nora's routine, the happy, safe life they've built here together.

"Oh, my gods," Nora says as she rounds the corner.

She's somehow shorter than Skorri, but her hair is a mass of red curls falling all around her.

"Now, Nora, I was minding my business. I was walking by on my way home, and these two just walked straight through the mountain wall as if it weren't there. I thought about leaving them, of course, on account of how the council is going to react, but I thought, no, Nora would think that's not polite. So now they're here, and it's your fault, so you can't be mad at me about it."

"Skorri, shut up, would you! This is the most exciting thing that's happened in the last hundred years by far!" Nora says, clapping her hands. "You did well bringing them here. Can you imagine what would happen if Gilda found them? I would've never heard the end of her bragging!"

Nora smiles at us.

"Well, you two look absolutely dreadful. Come have a seat, and I'll grab us some food."

She points to the chairs at their table before heading off in the other direction.

"Please, sit," Skorri says quickly, not bothering to look at us before following after her.

We sit down at their table, which is somewhat shorter than the average, and after only a few minutes and some muffled tones, the pair walks in carrying a pot, bowls, and loaves of bread. The smell making my mouth water. Sure, we ate a little bit on the way here, but seasoning was not a luxury we had space for.

Nora starts to fill bowls and passes them around, followed by bread. The bowls are filled with a brown liquid and chunks of meat and vegetables. When the first bite touches my tongue, I almost cry.

To someone who hasn't spent the last few weeks traveling through mountains, it might not be that good, but to me, in this moment, it was the best thing I'd ever eaten. I look over at Gaelen to see him watching me, no doubt making sure I eat.

"Well, let's hear it then! Tell me who you are, then we can get into why you're here," Nora says.

"My name is Thyrvi, and this is Gaelen." I gesture to him.

"Mm-hmm, and is he your brother? I don't see any resemblance. Friend then, maybe?" she asks.

"He's my... We are—hand-fast, we're hand-fast. I don't know if you're familiar with the term."

Gaelen shuffles uneasily at my words. It does feel like a minimization after everything that we've been through, but anything else feels overwhelming. By the raised eyebrow, I think Nora picks up on it.

"Where do you think humans got the tradition, dear?

She takes us both in, her gaze more measuring than the first time.

"Was it an arrangement then?"

"How can you tell?" Gaelen asks.

"Just the little things. You two don't seem completely comfortable with each other yet, so your relationship must be newer, but at the same time, newlyweds normally can't keep their hands off each other."

Gaelen doesn't say anything in return, and I don't know what to say either. There are times he always seems to be touching me, his hand always in mine, at the small of my back, or toying with my hair. But do I ever do the same?

"Oh, but I meant no offense. Arranged marriages are less common with the dwarves, but they do happen, and they've led to happy unions."

"Nora reads a lot of romance; you'll have to forgive her. Young couples are exciting."

"How long have you two been married?" I ask.

"Ninety-two years, this year. We're young for dwarves, though," Nora answers.

"Regardless of how you two ended up together, you made it all the way out here. How did that happen?" she asks.

"I'm looking for a weapon; I have reason to believe I'll find it here."

"We are dwarves, there are thousands of weapons here, dear," Nora says, sounding perplexed, as if I am looking for a needle in a haystack.

"A witch told me about a dagger and gave me a riddle. She said it would be found in 'halls of stone, where sun dares not and shadows cling. Bound, a wolf keeps watch, and a dagger sleeps.' Sound like anything you know of?"

The couple looks at each other for a long moment before Nora clears her throat.

"The council will never let you near that dagger, and even if they did, there's no way you'll get to it," Skorri says with an apology in his eyes. "I know you traveled a long way, and this isn't what you want to hear."

"Maybe if I explain it to them. There's more to it. I haven't told you everything," I say, a sinking feeling settling in my stomach.

"The council isn't going to agree to see you, dear. They'll demand Skorri tell them how he came upon you, and then they'll likely send you back the same way you came," Nora says.

"I'm not leaving here without the dagger."

"I think you should tell them, Thyrvi. Maybe they can persuade their council somehow," Gaelen says, to my surprise.

If he was upset by my prior comments, he must have moved on since he grabs my hand, lacing our fingers together in my lap. It took us too long to get here. I can't risk leaving empty-handed. Besides, I wouldn't know where to turn if we did. So, I take a breath and nod.

"I assume you know the story of how the Aesir blocked Loki from coming to this world?" I ask, and they nod in response.

I proceed to tell them everything how the key is now me, how Loki's power will be freed upon my death, and how I now have to find a way to destroy it. Grave expressions on their face, Skorri and Nora sit in silence after listening to me.

"That dagger was crafted and hidden at the request of Odin. Taking it won't be an option," Skorri repeats.

"The dagger lies on a stone behind the bound wolf, Fenrir. You'd have to get past him to get it, and that won't happen," Nora adds.

"And where is he?" I ask.

"He's locked in the bowels of this mountain. He was bound shortly after this world was made. Odin didn't trust him, being a creation of Loki, and what is said to happen at the world's end. The dagger was placed there before Fenrir was bound, and it hasn't been touched since," Skorri says.

"Can you tell me how to get there?"

"Yes," Nora answers.

"Nora, no!" Skorri yells, slamming his fist on the table.

"Skorri, don't you take that tone with me! You heard the girl, we don't have a choice. You know what the council will do. Maybe you were fated to be the dwarf that found them. The goddess is older than the Aesir. If she's helping, this is big. I won't be on the wrong side of history when this saga is sung," Nora says in a manner that lets me know she won't accept further disagreement from him.

"We'll have to act soon. Maybe tomorrow. Word will spread because of the horses. The council will send someone to inquire, but they're not normally quick to convene," Skorri says.

"What can you tell us about Fenrir?"

"When this world was created, and our realm linked to it instead of the old one, Odin asked many things of the dwarves. You know about the dagger, but he also asked the dwarves to create Gleipnir. When Odin took Fenrir from the land of giants, tricking him, he was brought here and bound in Gleipnir. It is stronger than any chain, created from impossibilities. We've never seen his prison, and I can't tell you what to expect should you get inside," Skorri says.

"Maybe we can use his being bound to our advantage," Gaelen says.

I already knew of the Gleipnir, having read about it years ago. There's nothing they tell us that'll help prevent us from being ripped to shreds.

"Why are the dwarves hidden? From what I've read, it wasn't always this way," I ask.

"Access to our fortress was always hidden, but yes, it's true that a long time ago we interacted with humans more freely. Now, it's not often we leave the mountain. You have too many political quarrels. Senselessly killing each other and drawing imaginary lines to deem who claims the land. It would be unfortunate should our abilities or creations fall into the wrong hands," Nora responds.

"It's likely many of those in powerful positions, or strong magic users, know we still exist, but humans cannot find their way here without a dwarf's approval. Well, except for you, apparently," Skorri adds.

"But humans do come here?" I ask.

"It's scarce, and only a select few."

Nora shows us to a room in their home where we can sleep and a small bathing area to clean up. I lost track of the days we spent out on the ice, not knowing how long it's been since I took a bath, but washing in the warm water feels amazing. My toes are red when I pull them from my boots, but I think they'll be fine, thanks to Gaelen's efforts.

Nora takes our clothes, insisting on washing them. I feel bad until I realize we probably stink, and she's doing it for her benefit as much as ours. Sitting on the small bed that I know for a fact Gaelen will be too tall for, I wait for him to return. I know we're both exhausted, but we haven't had much of a chance to speak alone.

"What was chasing us on the ice?" I ask as soon as he closes the door.

The sight of him is distracting. He emerges shirtless, only wearing loose-fitting pants.

"There are clans that live in the mountains north of Kenaz. They tell stories about dead men that can be controlled by magic, faces covered in bone. I believe that's what it was, and that it was hunting you. I assume that means Thokkra knows you tricked her," he says without hesitation.

"How did you kill it?" I ask, remembering he'd lost his sword. I didn't get to it before I fell.

"It was dead already. Killing you was its only purpose. That's probably why your nightmares didn't work. There wasn't any intelligence for them to latch onto. When you fell, it stopped, it just watched to see if you would come back up. I took the axe from its hand and removed its head."

A chill runs through me at the thought of being in that water again.

"I know you're mad at me for going back, but I was worried you were going to die," I say.

He looks down at me for a long moment.

"If saving a life, even mine, comes at a risk to yours, you have to choose yourself," Gaelen says.

The firm look on his face catches me off guard.

"Because of this stupid key? That's not fair."

"No, because I'm selfish and I don't want to live in a world that you're not part of."

It's more than either of us has said up to this point. I hate myself for it, but I break eye contact. My heart racing with the implication of his words.

When I look back, I can already see the perceived rejection written on his face. I don't know how to fix it from here, and I haven't had time to process anything to say something equally heartfelt. So, I ask my next question as he pretends to fix our bags.

"How did you know I could get us through the mountain?"

"It was a hunch," he says, not looking up at me.

"Care to elaborate?"

He sighs, continuing his fake task.

"My cell. The first time Thokkra visited me, I remember her

unlocking it. I was unconscious when she left. After her next visit, she never locked it on her way out. I checked it as soon as I knew she was gone, but it was still locked somehow. It had to be magic. And she was the only one who could open it. When I saw you walk down those stairs, I thought I was dreaming. I watched you panic when you couldn't find a key, making Soren try to pick the lock to no avail, and then I watched you push it open. But it wasn't a dream. It opened because it's what you wanted," he says, finally looking up at me.

I remember how shocked he was to find that I was real. All the blood and injuries that covered his body, now just small remnants of what they were.

"Odin only needed a lock. There was no reason to make a key as well. I believe he made a key in case he ever needed to use Loki's power, and then he hid it away. But he fucked up and made a key that can undo any magical lock, not just Loki's."

The weight of what he says tries to settle on me, but I don't have the energy. If I survive tomorrow, I'll deal with it then.

"Gaelen, we can handle whatever it is you're doing with the bags tomorrow. It's been a long day, and you carried me for part of it. You must be tired. Can we just go to sleep?"

He nods, standing and getting into bed next to me. I fall asleep the moment my head hits the pillow, and I remember nothing else until Nora lightly taps me on the shoulder. Opening my eyes, I give her a slight nod, and she silently retreats. As I very carefully extricate my body from the larger one wrapped around it, I only hope he'll forgive me.

## Chapter Twenty-Nine

On any other night, he would've felt me leave. I know he'll be pissed when he wakes and realizes what I've done. Hopefully I'll be back by then, but if not, I likely won't be back at all.

He wanted to do this together, him fighting and distracting the wolf while I grabbed the dagger and snuck out unharmed. It wasn't a bad plan, except that he cares about me, and I can't let him continue to put his life in danger because of that.

The mountain seems to be sleeping, not that we saw many people on our way in. Last night, when it was Gaelen's turn to bathe, I quickly went in search of Nora, and she agreed to help me, leaving Skorri out of the equation as well. Nora assures me there won't be any guards, explaining that all the dwarves know where Fenrir is kept, but none are stupid enough to enter. Just me, apparently. We've been descending through the halls for what feels like twenty minutes at least, when Nora grabs a torch from the wall. We leave the stone hall and enter a spiral stairwell that appears to go on forever. We must be moving away from the forges, the air growing colder the farther we go.

"So, were you looking for an arranged marriage?" Nora asks, likely trying to fill the silence.

"No. I wasn't looking for any of this. Technically, his father is a king. He arranged the marriage because he wants Loki's power, and his witch somehow knew I had the key." I decide to leave out my brother's potential involvement and any implications. "We didn't find out the reasoning until after."

"A prince, though! That's exciting!" She's clearly trying to look for a bright side. "But answer me this: why exactly are you sneaking down here without him? I didn't ask before, because it's not my business, and I believe we're meant to help you, but that doesn't stop me from wondering."

"People I care about keep ending up in danger because of this key, him more than most. He was forced into an oath, and I know he cares about me, so because of that, he's going to continue to put his life in danger to save mine. I'm not going to watch him do it again."

I don't tell her the rest. My silly thoughts about how this has felt like fate since I saw the mountain in the distance. The soft pull I've felt to come down here, knowing it's something I need to do on my own.

"Why did you come without Skorri?"

"Truthfully, he gets in enough trouble with the council. He's always tinkering with something and making things they disapprove of. If we get caught, it's better he's at home asleep."

"Dwarves were known for being innovative, though, so why would he get in trouble for that?"

"Well, he's blown a few things up over the years, but mostly, this council has grown too old."

Finally coming to a door, we enter on a floor where unlit torches line the walls.

"This is as far as I can go, dear. You'll just need to head through that door," she says, gesturing to the one in front of me. "I hope you know what you're doing, and I'll pray the gods keep you safe."

She takes a torch from the wall, lighting it and handing it to me before taking a seat on the steps. Looking at the door, it doesn't look too intimidating. Surely, they would need something stronger to keep him in if the stories were true.

My mind goes back to Gaelen, and I wish I were better at all of this. I hate that I hurt his feelings right before my potential death, and that this could be his last memory of me.

"Nora, thank you for doing this. And if I die, will you tell him... tell him I'm sorry."

She nods with a small smile.

"Do try not to die, dear."

Walking forward, I wrap my hand around the cold doorknob and turn. I didn't think to check for magical locks until I'd already opened the door. The room is dark, the only light coming from my torch. The air is cool with a persistent damp smell. I search the walls near the door and find a few other torches hanging. Carefully, I light each one while trying to get a good look around the room. None of which is easy to do while keeping my back to the wall.

It's still dark even with the additional torches. I can see huge rocks toward the center, but I can't make out any finer details. Then slowly, as if sputtering to life, two yellow orbs appear near the ground, the light from the torches reflecting in them. Unease sets in with the realization of what they are, of the only thing they could be. Eyes.

The eyes start to move, raising as the deepest growl I've ever heard echoes through the room. They're level with my chest when they finally stop moving. The torchlight reflects off the Gleipnir around his neck, and I realize he can't reach me from where I stand. Equally though, I won't be able to get the dagger until I move closer. Knowing this, I decide to light the remaining torches while I form a plan.

With everything now lit, the room is slightly more illuminated. I can make out Fenrir's body, which is much larger than any dog I've seen, and covered in thick, black fur. Unfortunately, I see no way to get to the dagger without going through him. I'm not even sure that a regular sword would do the job.

The sword strapped to my back feels inadequate in this room, against a myth. I might need to get the dagger first and then stab him to get away. Surely its magic would work on him. It occurs to me then that I don't know exactly what he is. Everything I've read names him a wolf, but it's clear he's no mere animal.

I test his reaction by moving closer, and he lets out another growl but makes no move to reach me. He likely knows the length of his chain, content to let me mess up and get too close. I'll have to be fast; I don't have another choice.

The nightmares uncoil as I move closer, having sensed him from the other side of the door. I held them back, waiting for the right moment. Running forward, I shove the nightmares toward him as I try to reach the first boulder. He lets out a whine, but manages to block them somehow, lunging forward and snapping at the air in front of me.

From the sound of his jaws coming together, I know there's no way he couldn't remove my head from my body in a single bite. His canines are longer than my fingers.

In his effort to reach me, his claws slash out, ripping down the skin of my arm and shoving me into a boulder. My head slams against rock, blood dripping into my eye. The pain is dizzying, and I try to right myself on the rock, just outside of his reach.

His lips are pulled back in a constant snarl now, loud enough to fill the cavern. I manage to stand, but everything begins to spin. When my vision finally rights itself, I push out with the nightmares again, moving closer to the dagger. This time, heat and an uncontrolled fury rage through my body, more disorienting than the hit to my head. My mind darkens, and I see Fenrir, the day he was bound. Like the dagger, he was feared by Odin, but Odin saw more in them. So, he hid them away, waiting for the day when he would need to use them. When my vision clears, I see the wolf, ready to pounce again.

The rage filling my body isn't mine. It's his. Once I make that distinction, it's easy to separate our emotions. He's pissed that I'm here, that he's here, pissed at the gods, and rightfully so. So much time wasted hidden from the light, unable to run, to hunt. An idea comes to me, reckless, and a risk I cannot afford to take. But just maybe...

I move forward, letting his massive body slam into me, the air knocked from my lungs at the impact, and I'm pushed to the ground. Just before his jaws close around my throat, I reach up and touch the Gleipnir, feeling it slip through my palm. He pauses, realizing the pull is no longer around his neck, and backs away, growling and watching me. I sit up, wiping the blood from my eye. Not sure yet if I've made matters worse, I do the only thing I can: I hold up my hands and start to speak.

"I have no intentions of hurting you. I only came for the dagger. I don't think you were guarding it by choice."

I slowly start taking steps to my left, toward the dagger. He watches me as I move, but makes no effort to attack me; instead, he shakes out his fur. There it is, lying unceremoniously on a scrap of leather, atop a rock. Hand shaking, I reach for it. Feeling the weight in my hand, I don't know what I was expecting, but it just feels old. I turn back to the wolf, who hasn't moved from his spot.

"You might be free of the Gleipnir, but you're still deep inside a dwarven mountain. You could try fighting your way out, but for one, I don't know where the real door is. And two, these are dwarves; the place is bound to be filled with weapons." I restate Nora's prior words.

He watches me, but I still feel his anger, though not a blind fury like before. No, now it's the cold, sticky kind of anger.

The kind that waits, demanding it be satisfied with vengeance.

"I get it. The gods fucked me over, too. Listen, if you cooperate, I'll get you out with me."

He growls a response, but I sense it's more of a begrudging agreement than a threat.

"You can't eat any dwarves. Unless they try to kill us first," I say with a pointed stare.

I don't even know if he was considering it; the growl I received gave off a hint of annoyance more than anything. The nightmares didn't work on him, but I don't think it's for the same reason they didn't work on the dead thing on the ice. No, I believe Fenrir is intelligent, and unlike most humans, knows his mind well enough to block out the magic.

"I'm Thyrvi, and I hope you don't mind, but I'm going to call you Fen," I say, receiving a huff in response.

Despite the impression he's trying to give, I can feel that he doesn't hate it. As I walk toward the door, a glint catches my eye. The Gleipnir lies discarded on the ground. It seems to have shrunk in size after being removed. I go back for the leather that the dagger laid on all these years. I wrap the Gleipnir in the leather, tucking it into the pocket of my pants where it isn't noticeable. I'm hit with a flood of suspicion from Fen.

"Not for you, but I'm not leaving it here either."

# Chapter Thirty

A mass of red curls rushes me the moment I push through the door, arms wrapping around my middle and squeezing. The strength of someone so small is surprising.

"I heard all that growling and I thought you were dead for sure!" Nora sobs.

Fen walks through the door behind me, letting out another deep growl.

"This is Nora, she's my friend," I say, holding my hand out to Fen as if that would be enough to block him. "And if this is how you respond to a hug, I'm going to need you to brace yourself for the next human you meet. He's going to seem rather hostile."

"Thyrvi, what did you do? The wolf can't be free. Odin commanded it," Nora says, fear cracking her voice as she backs away from us.

"Fen isn't going to hurt anyone, and he'll be leaving when I do."

"I don't think you understand how things work down here. The council isn't going to let you walk out with the wolf and the dagger. I hoped to sneak you out with it."

Tears start to form in her eyes, likely concerned for the trouble this will cause her.

"I promise you. I'll find a way to make this work and keep you and Skorri safe."

"Thyrvi, he could be a danger to us all, and even if not, Odin might bring his wrath down upon us!"

"The gods are not watching us, Nora. Not the Aesir, at least."

She shakes her head, starting to pace the hall, hands fiddling together before she speaks again.

"I don't know how we'll make it back up without someone spotting him," she says, drying her eyes and sizing him up.

His black fur makes his yellow eyes seem to glow, even with the additional light. Now I can see that his fur isn't just black, it has a dusting of gray and brown throughout. Though there are wolves across the sea, and we have dogs at home, I imagine none look like this. Even being chained under a mountain for centuries, there's no mistaking that he's a skilled killer.

As we reach the top of the stairway, the rhythmic sound of boots echoes through the halls ahead. Looks like we weren't as discreet as we thought. I take one look at Nora, and she lifts her shoulders, shaking her head. A group of ten dwarves rounds the corner carrying axes and wearing armor. Fen's body lowers to the ground, ready to lunge at any dwarf that comes too close, letting out a snarl.

"Nora Emberbrow, you, as well as your guest, are to be taken before the council by the order of Gralmir," the dwarf in the front says.

"What about the wolf?" another whispers.

"He shouldn't be freed; the gods will be angry." I hear one from the back say.

Fenrir brims with the desire to destroy those standing in our path. With his jaws and my nightmares, we could fight our way out of this, but I don't think it would be enough to get us back to Gaelen and out of the mountain, not to mention the trouble it would cause Skorri and Nora. I need to gain control of this before they do something we can't come back from.

"The wolf will come with me. Anyone who attempts to harm him will not receive a clean death," I announce to the group, feeling an inkling of pride from Fen.

The dwarves choose to lead us through the mountain instead, not bothering to keep us out of sight, which means I finally get to see the real dwarven kingdom.

The land of dwarves is carved from the mountain itself, with the center never appearing to end, whether from the north or south. The floor spirals down the mountain, with a small barrier wall following it, likely to prevent falls. Looking down, I can see hundreds of halls reaching out from the center walkway, traveling deeper into the mountain.

Dwarves can be seen moving along each floor carrying various items, weapons, books, and food. As we continue, dwarves remove themselves from our path, coveting distance when they see the wolf. They stop to take him in, then notice me, and the blood all over my skin. To Fen's credit, he manages not to growl at those just trying to go about their day.

I get the feeling there's a more discreet path we could've taken, but the council wanted us paraded through, for all to see what I'd done. They stop in front of a set of stone doors, two guards pushing them open to allow us entry, the dwarves encircling us remain. Walking into the room, it's much like everything else, carved from stone, torches lining the walls.

Toward the rear of the room sits a table, where nine dwarves are seated. They seem somewhat apart from the dwarves I've seen thus far, older, more formal. I find myself wondering if they were here when the world was made or the dagger placed. Have they met the gods? Nothing I've read references how old dwarves truly get, only speculation.

Against the wall, I notice Gaelen and Skorri on their knees, hands bound at their backs, a dwarven guard standing on each side of them. They don't seem to be injured, but Gaelen doesn't look happy. His eyes roam my body, pausing on the scrape at my forehead, following the blood coating my face, and then down to the scratches in my arm. Our eyes lock briefly before his go to the wolf. I should've told him, maybe asked him to let me do this on my own, but I know he wouldn't have.

"Nora, what have you done?" the center dwarf asks, tone commanding.

"This isn't her fault," I say.

"I am not talking to you!" the dwarf bellows.

From the corner of my eye, I see Gaelen stand, his assigned guard arguing against the disobedience.

"Well, I'm talking to you! You don't understand the stakes," I yell back, murmurs traveling through those gathered.

"I understand that you entered my mountain without permission. I understand that you conspired with my subjects, and I understand that you have stolen not once, but twice from this very council," the dwarf says, anger spilling through his tone.

"I disagree. Fenrir isn't an object. I could not have stolen him. I will admit to freeing him, though. As for the dagger, it belongs to Odin, does it not? If he has a problem with me taking it, he's welcome to come and tell me," I say.

A gasp echoes through the room. I know it's my own anger filling me this time. Anger at Odin, at the gods, at Nott. Anger at this whole gods-damned situation I'm being forced to deal with, the fact that I have to risk my life and those I care about over and over again for something I didn't ask for.

One of the council members, a woman with dark skin, golden eyes, and long braids, starts to laugh.

"She should've been a dwarf, so filled with fire," the woman says to what I assume is the council leader before turning back to look at me. "What is your name?"

"Thyrvi."

"And how did you get into our mountain, Thyrvi?"

"I hold the key to the lock that imprisons Loki's power. It would seem it opens more than originally intended," I say to the group.

"Can we see it?" another male council member asks.

"It's inside of me."

"Well, take it out," he says, face contorted in disgust.

"It's not like that, it's just me. I'm the key," I say, feeling an uncertainty coming from Fen at my confession.

I proceed to tell my tale yet again, starting with my mother's death, the stone and ceremony, the goddess. They seem shocked to learn of her assistance or that she would gift me with magic. I tell them what the witch told me, that the key somehow transferred from the stone to me, that if I don't destroy the power, it'll be free the moment I die, which is why I have come for the dagger.

I tell them how I used the key on Gaelen's cell, even though I didn't realize I had, and how I used it to enter the mountain. I explain there are those actively trying to free Loki's power and tell them of Thokkra and the dead thing on the ice. I tell them I need to travel to Yggdrasil to do what the gods were content to put off.

I realize this is the first time I've told the story, said out loud what I need to do, and felt committed. If this is my fate, then I can't pretend it doesn't exist any longer.

I know all of this was meant to be a secret, my own mother warning me not to trust anyone, but is that because the gods wanted it that way? Did those before me have people actively seeking Loki's power? Or were they able to live quiet lives, keeping the stone in a drawer somewhere? I'm not playing by the gods' rules anymore. It might be a risk, but I don't have another choice at this point.

The members of the council sit stunned for a moment before murmurs break out amongst them. Time passes by as the arguing in hushed tones carries on, the dwarves seeming to get nowhere, when their leader stands, stating they'll need to discuss this matter privately. I request that Gaelen and Skorri be freed, which they agree to do, but leave the guards at each door.

Nora runs to embrace Skorri, apologizing for sneaking off without him. He smooths down her hair, looking for any injuries before telling her it's alright. Gaelen watches them before turning to look at me, expression firm.

"Do you want to yell at me?" I ask.

His lips form a tight line before he shakes his head.

"You got what you came here for, that's all that matters." He looks forward, avoiding my gaze.

"But you're mad at me."

"And you would have me believe you give a fuck about that?" His words cut, catching me off guard.

"I do." Of course I do.

"No, Thyrvi, you don't. If you did, I wouldn't have woken up alone this morning, with no idea where you were or if you were safe. Right after I watched you fall through ice, worried what the moments it took for me to get to you might cost, and then carried you to this fucking mountain, terrified you were going to freeze to death in my arms," he yells, finally looking at me. "If you want out of this, you can just fucking say it."

"What?" I freeze.

That's not where I expected this to go.

"I know this relationship wasn't our choice, but I've been trying to prove to you it's what I want. Every time I think we're moving forward, you pull away. Tell me this is what you want— tell me you want to be with me. No dancing around it, no half answers."

I know he needs me to say something, anything, and I want to so bad it hurts. But I feel as frozen as I did on that ice. A dozen things I could say fly through my mind, not one of them making their way to my mouth. I just freed a wolf feared by Odin himself, but the thought of telling this man my feelings —that I want this —is paralyzing. Once I say it, I can't go back. It'll all just be out there, exposed.

My vision starts to blur from the tears threatening to spill over. I knew he was going to be mad, I knew that, and I thought I could live with it. I didn't realize it was going to hurt him, though, not like this.

He takes my silence as an answer and nods his head.

"Yule is in a few days. We'll end our hand-fasting. I'll make sure you get to Yggdrasil and safely end this, then we'll go our separate ways."

The council returns as my heart shatters.

# Chapter Thirty-One

I step forward, away from my friends. If anyone's going to be punished for this, I want to make it known that it should be me. This is my burden, and my responsibility.

It takes some time for all the dwarven leaders to take their seats, and the one I assume to be Gralmir is the last to enter. Once everyone is in place, he watches me for a long while before clearing his throat.

"The dwarves have served the Aesir for as long as time itself. We are renowned for our crafting abilities. We've crafted many items that the gods still rely on to this day. The

Allfather sought wisdom, and it is through wisdom that he bound the wolf and hid the dagger under our mountain. We cannot know if he entrusted them to us for a time, or to be kept until the end. What we do know is that the wolf, the dagger, and Loki were trapped in their prisons for a reason. We are not meant to question that reasoning."

Murmurs can be heard throughout the council, even from the guards. It's taking everything in me not to rush the dwarf along, my patience quickly wearing thin after everything Gaelen just said.

"Just as your bloodline was chosen for a reason, what you, Thyrvi, are tasked with is different from your ancestors, for a reason. It is possible Odin left the dagger and wolf here, for you to come for; we cannot know. But what we do know is that the Dream Weaver set you on this path, and she did that with intent. Thus, I declare it is dwarven duty to aid you in your quest."

I know this is what I came for, what I needed - the means to leave with Fen and the dagger, not as an enemy of the dwarven kind. But I don't feel the flood of relief I was expecting.

"And what about Skorri and Nora? Will you try to punish them for assisting me without your approval?"

Gralmir doesn't look thrilled with my words, or maybe my lack of enthusiasm. But I'm not ungrateful, just numb.

"Skorri and Nora will be pardoned for any misdoings that may have resulted from their aid," the female dwarf with the golden eyes says. "We will also provide you with whatever provisions you may need to complete your journey, and a dwarven warrior will accompany you as you make your way to Yggdrasil."

I want to argue that last part, but I don't have the energy.

"Who?" I ask.

"We will be taking volunteers, and from the pool of those that step forward, the council will pick the dwarf we see fit. You will leave the day after Yule."

Of course, wouldn't want to miss the Solstice.

Our dismissal isn't even entirely off the dwarven leader's lips when I turn to see Gaelen walk from the hall, Skorri following quickly behind him.

I curl up in a chair that's just slightly too small for me, next to the hearth in Skorri and Nora's home.

A quick bath cleaned the dirt and damp air from my body, leftover from Fen's prison. Nora helped me clean out my scratches and the cut on my head that left dried blood caked in my hair. Gaelen and Skorri have yet to return. At least, I assume so since I haven't seen either of them. Fen is laid out across a rug, finding it more comfortable than the stone he's lain on for who knows how many years. Nora walks in, handing me a cup of the tea she started making a few moments ago.

"You know, dear, I couldn't help but overhear your conversation. Neither of you were quiet after all." She takes a sip. "I hope you don't mind me asking, but what's wrong? He's gorgeous and is obviously crazy about you."

"I'm the problem," I say, taking a deep breath.

She nods as if she'd gathered that much already, and I can't fight the small smile that crosses my face.

"He knows I went into our marriage willingly, despite it being arranged, but looking back, there have been many times where he wanted me to say that things were real for me, and I always avoided it."

"And are they?" she asks, taking another sip of her tea, her eyes not leaving me.

Are they? Do I even know the answer to that? Have I taken the time to think about it? It wasn't long ago that I was having this same conversation with another nosey redhead.

This is what Saoirse was talking about, why she asked the questions she did. She already knew the answers to her own questions, and she knew I was never going to pull these feelings out and look at them. But what had I said? *I'm happy it's him.* But of course, there would be no way for him to know that. I avoided it like the plague, and then I let doubt set in when I saw Kenaz.

"Yes, but he would have no way of knowing that." I take another sip of my tea and wonder if she put some emotional enlightenment potion in here.

"Is that why you're the problem?" she asks.

I nod. "I guess I haven't had many people I could trust with my feelings, and those I could are dead. So, letting him in, letting him know how I feel about him, feels like opening everything that I am. Letting him see those hidden parts of me, and then trusting he'll take care of them. That's not the kind of strength that I have."

The tears I've been holding back finally escape. Nora sets down her tea and comes over to wrap her arms around me.

"You don't need to be strong, dear. You just have to have courage. I haven't known you very long, but I know you don't lack that. You're allowed to be afraid of getting hurt or letting him see who you are on the inside. But what you can't let your fear do is cost you the chance of truly being happy. Then no one is hurting you—but you." She runs her hand over my hair, reminding me of Skorri when he was trying to calm her.

"How did you become so wise?" I ask, laughing through my tears.

"Well, I'm one hundred and sixty-three, and that's very old for a human."

After we finish our tea, I help her carry everything back into their small kitchen, and together we wash the dishes.

"Listen, I know Skorri. He took one look at that boy, all flustered with emotions, and there's only one place he would have taken him… to the forge. It'll be a while before they're back. Why don't you take your wolf and go get some rest while you think about our conversation?"

I knew Fen made her weary.

I only intended to take a small nap, thinking I would wake when Gaelen returned. However, I feel as though I've slept for hours, and I'm starving.

My gaze wanders over the room, but there are no windows

to gauge what time it is. My heart sinks before my brain has time to register the difference in the room; the bag of Gaelen's clothes is gone. I look at Fen, taking up half the space.

"Was he here?" I ask, receiving a groan and a surge of annoyance in response, as if to tell me he doesn't care about my relationship problems.

"You know I'm the only reason you're getting out of this hole in the ground, right?"

He turns his head to the other side of his massive paws so he doesn't have to look at me.

"Fine."

Leaving my room, the smell of breakfast, coming from the kitchen, fills the air. It's been so long since I've eaten a warm breakfast. Nora's the first to notice me as she carries food to the table, a huge smile on her face. Skorri is already seated, but nods in my direction.

"Well, look who's finally awake! I was starting to worry you would sleep your remaining days with us away!" Nora says, cheery as ever.

"I slept the whole day then?"

"And night," Skorri adds.

"Sit, sit! I made pancakes!" Nora says.

I look around the room as I take my seat, no sign of Gaelen here either. When my gaze returns to the table, I see Skorri watching me, and he gives me a gentle smile.

"He thought it'd be better if you two had some space. I found him somewhere else to sleep for the time being."

The time being? He means until we leave.

"Thyrvi, the mountain is abuzz with news of you. I know many dwarves who would be honored to meet you. Might you be up for a bit of a tour? The council also sent word that Fen will need to go down to where the animals are kept for his ration of chicken," Nora cuts in, giving Skorri a look.

"Of course, that'd be nice."

I try to make myself look somewhat presentable before Nora and I venture into the rest of the mountain. I'm excited to see more of their daily life. There aren't many accounts from people lucky enough to experience it before the dwarves went into hiding. Most interactions occur in human lands.

We take Fen to the stable area where goats, chickens, and our horses are being kept. There's also a large cavern where mushrooms and some other root vegetables are grown. I assume they've adapted them over time to grow with no sun. That or magic is somehow involved, I'm sure. I get the feeling Fen finds this whole thing undignified, a vague restlessness coming from him.

"We don't have that much time left. Then you can hunt whatever you want," I tell him as we head to the more populated areas of the mountain.

On our way out, I note a few extra stalls next to the horses we brought.

"Nora, when approved visitors come, where do they stay?"

"It's not often, but when it happens, we have designated areas for them. Smaller spots were dug out of the mountain for those occasions."

"Would they be on this level or one similar to yours?"

"They'd be one level up. We'll pass the accommodations on our way to the market. You know, if you're considering revisiting us, Skorri and I'd be happy to have you stay with us! No need to be in one of those empty rooms, dear!"

"Of course! I'd love to come back."

Assuming I don't die and all that.

We make our way through the winding halls, dwarves nodding or waving as they see us walk by. Word must have traveled quickly, as they all seem excited to see me. Their eyes always pause on the dagger strapped to my waist. I worked too hard to leave it anywhere and have it stolen. After they get a glimpse of the dagger, they take in the giant wolf walking behind me, though they watch him with precaution. I can't say I blame them. They likely all grew up with stories of the vicious wolf trapped below their feet.

Fen seems to take joy from the extra space they ensure stays between him and them. His yellow eyes roam over them constantly.

"The visitor rooms are down that hall," Nora says, gesturing to a hallway off to the right.

We veer left into a massive open cavern filled with stalls and dwarves selling all manner of things. There are the usual items you would find in a market: breads, spices, fabrics, crystals, and art. And then there are darker items. Alcoves in the walls, covered in beads, where people sit with pipes, the smoke thick. Others have stalls where potions are sold, or women claiming to know your future through runes or cards. I'm tempted for a second, before I remember what the witch said.

My future is too uncertain. It's unlikely these people can tell the future at all. I don't think true power like Runa and Thokkra have is common. I still have a feeling the nightmares are a simple trick compared to the well of magic they could house.

"Do you know what you plan to wear to the Solstice?" Nora asks as we stand before a fabric merchant.

"Probably something similar to what I have on now. I didn't plan to be attending any celebrations when I packed."

She looks me up and down, not hiding her disapproval. After our tour through the market, I let Nora show me off to all her friends, and much like Nora, they all try to prod through my business. When I can't take it any longer, I ask to see the forges, to which she obliges. We pass many, most seeming to be for the making of weapons, massive axes, hammers, swords, and daggers, all created with such intricate detail it's clear no human could craft something so beautiful.

She also shows me where smaller items are made, machinery, and even jewelry. It's all truly an art form, each dwarf containing a level of skill and dedication that could only come from centuries of practice and pride in your work.

"There's one more place I hoped to show you today."

Nora interrupts me, watching me look on with intent as molten metal is poured into a mold.

I nod and follow her as she walks deeper into the center of the mountain, snaking up to a higher level.

"I know you don't have long left here, but you already know so much of our history, I thought you'd be glad for the opportunity to learn more!"

She pushes open a massive stone door into the biggest library I've ever seen.

"This is amazing," I say, breath catching.

"There are many books here that are older than this mountain itself. You'll never find most of these, or even a selection this large, in your lands."

"And it's okay for me to be here?" I ask, hopeful.

"I checked yesterday after you fell asleep. No fire, and no liquids are permitted in. There are special lanterns you must use."

I nod my agreement, still taking it all in. There are rows and rows of shelves filled with books. From where I stand, I can't even see the back of the library.

"If I leave you here, do you think you can find your way back?"

I look to Fen, who groans with indignation.

"I'll see you at home for supper then," she says, turning to leave.

Once I'm sure she's gone, I look back at Fen.

"It pains me to say this, but we can read tomorrow. Right now, I need you to help me find something else."

## Chapter Thirty-Two

Fen leads me back through the crowded marketplace and down the hall that Nora pointed out. It's darker than the rest of the mountain, only one torch aflame.

"Do any of these smell like a human?" I ask as we stand at the start of the hall.

I wouldn't be surprised if Fen hates me, but he walks up to the second door on the left. I take it that means this is the one. I pause, fist mid-air, before knocking. I have nothing planned to say. When I saw those empty stalls in the stables, my thoughts immediately turned to finding out where Gaelen might be staying and apologizing.

Only, I hadn't thought through the apologizing part. Maybe I should wait and come back after I have. At least I know where to find him now. My hand returns to my side, and I stare at the door for a moment longer before deciding that giving it more time is probably for the best.

Fen has been giving off a low growl, more of a vibration than an audible sound. I turn to find Gaelen standing at the end of the hall, watching us.

"Your wolf doesn't like me."

"He isn't mine, and he doesn't like anyone."

His eyes drop from mine to the dagger, then to his door.

"What are you doing here, Thyrvi?" He sounds exhausted.

"You left."

"You left first."

I guess that's fair. There's soot on his hands. He must have been working in the forges then. Nora never technically showed me the one that Skorri works in.

"I came to say that you were wrong."

His mouth forms a tight line. I let out a sigh. As soon as the words leave my lips, I know I'm not going about this correctly.

"Do we have to do this in the hallway? Can we just go inside?"

The room is small, fitting a small bed against the wall, a

table with two chairs, and a wardrobe. Of course, Fen comes in with us, immediately lying out across the small rug next to the bed.

"Not very spacious."

"I've had worse accommodations," he says.

My mind goes to the dungeon, though something tells me that isn't what he meant. I stand in the center of his room, not sure where to go. He hasn't asked me to sit, and he leans his back against the closed door, watching me.

"So, you came all the way down here to inform me I was wrong about something?"

"No, not exactly." I look around, as if I will find the words I need written on his empty walls. "I came to say sorry."

"Sorry for what?" His head turns to the side, as if he's listening intently, or like a predator sizing me up—maybe both.

"That my actions hurt you."

"So, not sorry for what you did then?"

"No."

His hand runs down his face and over the stubble at his jaw.

"I knew I had to go alone, and I knew if I talked to you about it, you would've tried to stop me."

"And why did you have to go alone?"

"The night before, you said I had to choose myself, even if you were at risk. So, I knew if it came down to it, you would

320

choose to die for me. That's not what I want."

He opens his mouth to speak, but I hold out my hand.

"Let me finish."

He doesn't look thrilled, but doesn't speak either.

"I also just had a feeling that I needed to do this by myself. I think I was meant to free Fen, and had you come, it wouldn't have gone that way."

I look down to where Fen lies, feeling his annoyance with this whole endeavor.

"I pushed the nightmares at him, and he was able to block them, not like Thokkra, and not like with the dead thing. They felt him and attacked, but he was mentally stronger. When I tried again, I pushed even harder, and he pushed back. I was filled with his anger, and I saw the day he was bound with the dagger. I saw Odin leave him there. None of that would've happened if I hadn't gone alone."

"Do you still feel his emotions?"

"Yes."

"And can he feel yours?"

I hadn't thought about that. Fen huffs in irritation at the question as if to say, "Yes, and it's a real inconvenience."

"I would take that as a yes," he says.

Gaelen watches the wolf for a time before his eyes travel back to mine.

"Well, I appreciate you explaining your motives behind

yesterday. If that's all, I have a few things I still want to do today."

Is this some kind of dismissal?

"No, that's not all," I say, letting Fen's annoyance spill into me. "You said I have to choose my life over yours. I'm saying that's bullshit, and I refuse to accept it. You don't get to tell me you want our relationship to be real, that you want me to care about you, and then decide you're the only one who gets to make sacrifices. I don't want people I care about getting hurt, especially not for me."

"Thyrvi, I don't think you know what you want."

"Can you stop? Just stop making assumptions." My voice is now just below a yell.

"You leave things so open, that's all I can do. If I'm wrong, use your fucking words and say so."

"You're wrong! I hate the thought of you leaving, of never seeing you again." I'm yelling at this point, but his eyes lock on mine. "I do want to be with you, I'm just—afraid of you knowing that."

"Why would you be afraid of me knowing that?" His voice softens.

"I don't know, Gaelen! What if you change your mind? What if you realize you were forced into this, that it's not something you ever wanted, and you want to be free? Everything is out now, and we know the motives. You don't have to do any of this." I wave my hands around aimlessly. "What if it's all too much? Not to mention Kenaz. I saw the people, the way they dress, the way they act."

His eyebrows scrunch at that.

"I saw the world you grew up in, and the world you live in. It's nothing like Thurisa; I could never fit there. What if I let you see me, all of me, and you don't like what you find?"

I'm still yelling, heart racing, tears threatening to spill over. Fen has resumed his vibrating growl. Gaelen exhales and smiles softly before pushing off the door and slowly walking over to me.

"I read this wrong, and I apologize. I'm sorry for the things I said, and how I said them. I get it now."

I look away, tears falling down my cheeks from the softness in his voice. I try wiping them away as his fingers graze my chin, lifting it to make me look at him.

"Love, I will only walk away if it is what you want. I'm not changing my mind. There's no freedom I want that doesn't include you. I need you to understand that I don't give a fuck about Kenaz, or what world you think I might live in. The only time I've been inside the walls of that city and not been miserable has been with you. If you want to live in the smallest house in Thurisa for the rest of our lives, I'll be there."

"Why?" It comes out as more of a raw whisper. His eyes

travel down to my mouth, and I know he wants to kiss me, but he refrains.

"At some point, when I was getting to know you, I don't know when exactly, I stopped seeing options for my future that didn't include you. Whatever plans I thought I had no longer mattered, or I caught myself trying to rearrange them to include you. It doesn't really matter; what matters is that all that I am is yours. And Thyrvi, I see you, and I want you."

His hand travels to the back of my neck, lacing through my hair. We stay like that for a moment, frozen in time, letting the weight of his words settle in between us. I know this is when I would usually deflect, but I can't, not now.

"Gaelen…" I take a breath. "I want this, and you."

I don't finish the "you" before his mouth is crashing against mine. His arms wrap around my body, lifting me until my legs wrap around him, turning to press me into the door.

"I want to do filthy things to you right now, but you brought a wolf," he says, breaking our kiss.

I start laughing and then acknowledge the disdain I feel from Fen.

"You're right, I don't think he likes you. But you said you had things you needed to do anyway."

"They have a rookery. I thought I would send messages to our friends. Speaking of which, there's something you need to understand. Yes, our friends are doing this because they care about you, but there's more to it than that. The dwarves don't care about you; they're doing it because it's right. After all, the safety of everyone and everything is at stake. If you want to risk your life, you have to let them make the same choices."

He's right. I have been so worried about what everyone is risking because of me. I didn't think about their motivations, and what happens if I fail.

"My motivation lies with you, though, fuck what's right," he adds, kissing me quickly before putting me down. "Do you want to go get your stuff and stay here?"

The thought is tempting; it would be more private.

"No, we only have a few days left, and I think it would hurt Nora's feelings."

Chapter
Thirty-Three

The story of what happened and why I'm here spread through the mountain like wildfire.

Skorri informs us that over a hundred dwarves volunteered to go on the journey. The council somehow narrowed down the list to thirty, and then met with each before making their decision. In the end, they choose a younger female dwarf with a renowned ability to wield an axe.

We send coded letters via raven to Soren and Rorik, letting them know of our plans. We don't know where Bjark is, but

Gaelen assures me that Soren will. I hope he and Theorin are safe.

Fen and I spend most of our time in the library, where it's often just him and I. I read as much as I can find on the gods, on Loki, and the old world. There are full accounts of the magic items the dwarves have crafted as commissions for both the gods and humans alike. There are many references to the world tree, but so far, I've only found one book with great detail on Yggdrasil. I try to memorize as much as I possibly can before we have to leave.

Today is finally Yule, and from what I see on my walk to the library, it doesn't seem to be any different than in Thurisa. Plenty of food is being prepared, ale is being brought out, and, of course, there will be music. Gifts will be exchanged, and the evening will start with the commitment ceremony. It's my belief we begin with that, so those not moving forward with their marriages can spend the rest of the celebration single.

Gaelen leans down over the back of my chair, kissing my neck. He must have just come back from the forges with Skorri.

"We should head back and get dressed for tonight," he says.

Confused, I look down at my clothes.

"We packed for a winter trip through the mountains. Everything I brought looks exactly like this." I gesture to my clothes.

Gaelen winks, taking my book and laying it down on the table I've been using the last few days, stacked with books I'm not quite finished with. Taking my hands, he pulls me to stand, wrapping his arm around my waist.

"Just come on."

Fen follows us, still unimpressed with Gaelen, although he hasn't been impressed with anyone yet. It's strange to think that we leave tomorrow, and I often find myself wondering what Fen will do with his newfound freedom. I tried to ask once, but I only felt a yearning in return. The moment when I saw his memories has never happened again. Perhaps I was only meant to see that Odin's actions ensured our fates were intertwined.

Pushing open the door to our borrowed room, I find a dress in the deepest shade of burgundy I've ever seen. The bodice is covered in delicate gold beading that flows up the low-cut neckline and continues onto the straps. The skirt of the dress is woven with a soft, gauzy material I've never seen before. Running it through my fingers, it feels like silk, but thinner, and would be see-through if not for the layers.

"How did you do this?" I ask, turning to him.

"Nora, of course. Do you like it?"

The dress I wore to our hand-fasting was beautiful, but it was a statement, and though it was only two months ago, it feels like a completely different person wore it. Someone younger, with fewer worries and no responsibility. This dress, though, could have only been created by those who craft magic.

"It's amazing," I say, hugging him.

A knock sounds at the door, and Nora pushes in, asking if I need help getting ready. Gaelen excuses himself to get dressed elsewhere. Though he sleeps here with me, and we always eat with Skorri and Nora, he never brings his bags.

Nora's dress is a deep green that looks lovely with the contrast of her hair. She helps me step into mine and laces the back. She insists on pinning the top half of my hair back so it's out of my face, but lets the curls fall around my shoulders. We find the men waiting in the living room; Gaelen is dressed all in black, and Skorri is in a series of dark brown and reds.

"Well, don't you both look handsome!" I say, winking at Skorri.

Gaelen's eyes travel the length of my body before he holds out his hand, waiting for me to place mine inside it, and pulls me into an embrace, kissing my temple.

"You're enchanting," Gaelen whispers in my ear. "Last chance to run, you sure about this?"

"I'm afraid you're stuck with me," I say, leaning up on my toes to kiss his cheek.

"Happily."

No one chooses to end their period of hand-fasting, and five couples, including Gaelen and I, move forward, proclaiming our marriage to the gods. The evening is filled with dancing and drinking. Dwarves apparently take dancing very seriously, and while I dance with a few men, Gaelen is constantly pulled onto the dance floor by dwarven women.

Fen elected to stay back this evening, not being fond of the dwarves, and enjoying sleeping on things not made of rock. But even from here, I can feel his impatience to leave this place.

When we finally retire for the evening, I notice Gaelen is leading me to the visitor's hall, and not back to our room at Skorri and Nora's. I don't say anything, though, content to let him continue his plans. When we finally reach his room, he lights a few lanterns, and I wait by the table.

"I have a present for you," he says, pulling something out of the wardrobe.

"I didn't realize we were doing Yule presents. I didn't get

you anything."

"We aren't, this is something else." He hands me a scabbard containing a dagger.

I pull it free and realize it's almost identical to the one I took from Fen's prison.

"Your balance with a sword is awful, and it seems fate will require you to wield a dagger, so I thought you could at least have a set."

"How did you find one so similar?" I ask, taking in all the details of the hilt, its size and shape, an exact match to the older one I left behind with Fen.

"I made it."

So, this is the project he started with Skorri at the forge when he was upset with me. Of course, he would be thinking of ways to keep me safe, even after thinking I wanted out of our hand-fasting.

"Thank you, it's perfect." I place the dagger on the table and lean up to kiss him. "Is this why we're here, or were you intending for us to sleep here tonight?"

I ask this knowing full well I have no desire to sleep this evening. He moves closer, brushing the hair from my neck.

"I want to fuck my wife, and I don't want her to worry about who might hear," he says, trailing kisses across my collarbone.

"How considerate of you."

Gaelen drops to his knees, running his hand up my leg exposed by the slit in my dress. As he kisses my thigh, I brace myself on the table behind me. He looks up from where he kneels between my legs, heat pooling low in my stomach at the sight of his gaze.

"I was so mad when you walked into that council hall, covered in your own blood, dagger in one hand, and Fenrir behind you. I was terrified at what you had risked, and angry over what I thought your actions meant, but I could also see that something had changed in you. You were so much more confident, commanding. When you stood up to the council, I couldn't have been more proud of you." He lifts my leg at the knee, placing it over his shoulder. "Now, if you'll excuse me, it's been two months, and I haven't spent near enough time tasting you."

His mouth dips to my core, and my head falls back, his tongue knowing where to focus. I run my hand through his hair, feeling my climax building, two of his fingers moving to slide in and out of me. With that final push, my orgasm is pulled out of me.

"So, fucking good," he says, not stopping until my body finishes pulsing.

His eyes lock with mine as I try to catch my breath. Standing slowly, he takes off his jacket, unbuttoning and removing his shirt.

"How do you want to do this?" he asks, repeating my words from the night of our hand-fasting. Only, they have a far different meaning now.

"Do what?" My voice comes out breathy.

"It's official now, and I fully intend to claim every part of you."

A jolt of excitement runs through me at his words.

"Here." My hand falls against the table behind me. "I want to do it here."

His hands move to brush away the hair that's fallen forward into my face, eventually taking all of it in his fist. He kisses me deeply, and I can taste myself on him. Spinning me around, he pushes me down onto the table. One hand stays filled with my hair while I hear the other undoing his pants before he pulls up my dress. His foot slides mine farther apart before he positions himself and slams into me, moving to hold my hip as he continues to thrust.

The speed and force of it, pushing me to the brink quickly. I cry out as my orgasm crashes over me, saying his name. He withdraws, letting go of my hair and standing me up. The look on his face is completely feral as he starts removing my dress. Kissing his way down my chest, he finally takes my nipple into his mouth as my dress hits the ground. He lifts me, and I wrap my legs around him while he carries me to the bed.

Lying me on my back, he slowly kisses his way down my body before filling me with his cock once more. He watches as he thrusts in and out of me before leaning down to kiss me. My hips start moving with him, meeting each of his thrusts. Before I realize it, I'm coming undone once again, him following only seconds behind me.

## Chapter Thrirty-Four

Apparently, the dwarves have tunnels through the mountain range, which makes more sense for meeting trade partners than having them cross a lake that's frozen half of the year.

Melda, the dwarf chosen to accompany us, is currently waiting for us on a platform for the rail system the dwarves use to transport weapons and goods through the mountains. Skorri and Nora have brought us to meet her and say their goodbyes. The tears in Nora's eyes and the squeezing hug that Skorri gives me bring tears to my own eyes, which I wasn't expecting. Gaelen hugs them both as well, and we promise to return when everything is done for an extended visit. I hope it's a promise we get to keep.

We turn to introduce ourselves to Melda, who looks like she has no time for our nonsense. Her hair is cut short, almost to the point of seeing her skin, and each ear is lined with a row of earrings from top to bottom. She explains the cart system, which looks like something you would usually find pulled by a horse, but instead runs on metal rails that snake through the mountain, controlled by levers. She ensures it's safe, but I'm not sure I believe her, and she doesn't seem like the kind of woman who is used to people questioning her.

We don't have many options, and this will cut our trip down drastically, so we climb into the back of the cart. Fen is apprehensive, but his eagerness to leave the mountain wins out. He takes up a great deal of space once he finally lies down. Our bags secured, Melda pulls the first lever, a loud screeching filling the cavern as the cart starts to move forward.

The cart quickly reaches a steady speed, reminding me of a boat sailing through the sea. Between the speed and the lack of struggles that come with traversing mountainous terrain, we should be through the range in no time.

Our only light comes from three enclosed lanterns affixed to the cart, and I worry about seeing the distances ahead. I ask what to do if something damages the rail ahead of us, but Melda doesn't seem concerned, stating that the dwarves use and maintain the tunnels frequently.

Once Melda is comfortable with our understanding of the levers and how they work, we take control of the cart in shifts, Gaelen and I doing ours together. We only stop at designated areas equipped for our needs along the way, and since we don't have to stop for sleep, we make it through the mountains in what I believe is only a week.

We leave our cart behind and exit the mountains through a hidden door, much like the one we entered from. We end up in a forest off the coast, far north of Thurisa. It's mid-morning, the sun having already risen, and the air is chilled, but nowhere near as bad as when we entered the mountain itself. The snow has reached this area, but only in a light sheet.

I watch Fen as he doesn't seem to know where to focus, looking around at the scenery. I can only imagine the smells and sounds he's taking in after being locked away for so long. He looks up at the tops of the trees, where a few winter birds scatter at the sight of him, and then into the depths of the forest, where he is sure to spot small animals in the underbrush. There are so many emotions being pushed at me, but the feeling of wonder is coming through the strongest.

"Why don't you stretch your legs? Might feel nice to run," I suggest.

Fen looks at me gratefully. He walks forward, his fur grazing my skin, and then he's gone. A small pit forms in my stomach when I realize I have no idea where he'll go, or what his plans are, but I promised to get him out, and it feels good to know I was able to keep my word.

"Is he coming back?" Melda asks.

"He's free. That's his choice to make," I say, starting in the direction my heart knows we need to travel.

We make our way through the forest; the ground starting to transform from dirt and leaves to rock and moss. Boulders grow larger the farther we travel.

Where we exited the mountain isn't supposed to be very far from our world's entrance to Yggdrasil, and I wonder how many secret doorways there are. I doubt Melda would tell me if I asked.

It's said that, early on, people would travel to Yggdrasil's entrance for celebrations and to make offerings to the gods. At some point, people stopped traveling out here, and the gods stopped walking our world as often, but that's as far as we know. Maybe they visit us in disguise.

Once we break through the wood line, a large circle formed by standing stones lies in the distance. My body stops moving in its presence. This has to be the entrance. My nerves start to set in when a voice calls out from the brush. Looking over, I catch Bjark and Theorin making their way out of the forest.

"What are you doing here?" I run over, pulling Bjark into a hug.

"We arrived yesterday. We've been hiding out in the northern villages. Soren got word to us that you'd be coming, so we made our way up here hoping to catch you."

Part of me thought I would never see them again, and them being here means more than I can say. I pull Bjark in for another hug, and then Theorin. Gaelen doing the same after me.

"You know this might be dangerous, right?" I ask for good measure.

"Oh, I'm counting on it," Bjark says. "Soren said the king is on the move. I assume he meant here, but we haven't seen another soul, let alone a large group. With luck, we've beaten them, and the job will be done before they arrive."

It would be nice to be so lucky.

"And how have your travels been?" Gaelen asks Theorin.

"Enlightening," he says in response.

Theorin does look changed, though we've all been through

a lot since we first met.

"Sorry, we are being rude. This is Melda, Melda, this is Bjark and Theorin," I say, introducing them to each other.

From the looks on their faces, it's as though they hadn't noticed her yet and are now very confused. Melda looks over the two men, but doesn't say anything.

"So, you didn't find ruins then?" Bjark asks.

"No, we found way more than ruins," I say.

"What about the dagger?" Theorin asks.

"She got it, of course," Gaelen responds for me. "The dwarves weren't thrilled at first, as you can imagine, but Melda was kind enough to volunteer to accompany us for the remainder of our journey."

"It was not kindness that brought me here. The call of fate has echoed through our great halls before. I know to act when I hear it."

The call of fate? I wonder if that's what pulled me to Fen. I wonder just how far he's gotten by now. I almost tell Bjark about him, but if he isn't coming back, maybe it's for the best that no one knows he's free, even if I trust Bjark. If word got out, I don't know how others would respond, and Melda and Gaelen seem to be leaving it up to me.

"Has anyone tried to find you?" Gaelen asks them both.

"Not that we know of. Soren's letters indicated the castle had been locked down until they started preparing to leave.

It's possible Thokkra figured out Thyrvi's plans and hopes to get here in time to stop or use her."

A cold feeling snakes up my spine at Bjark's words. She could know about the dwarves and the dagger. Maybe she figured it out after we left and sent that thing to kill me, thinking it would be the fastest way.

"We haven't stayed in villages for very long. A few taverns, only long enough to send messages letting Soren and Rorik know of our movements, but mostly we made camp deep in the woods, hidden from view. It's possible we missed them."

"What do you know of Rorik and Saoirse?" I ask.

"I know they made it to Thurisa and are safe."

Bjark doesn't elaborate, and I'm tempted to ask after my brother. I don't because if there's something to be known, I don't want to think about it until after everything else.

"Are we ready?" Melda cuts in flatly.

From the look on her face, it's clear she's losing patience with our reunion. I look at everyone and nod.

With every step we take toward the circle, my stomach sinks deeper and deeper. Something inside me is screaming to turn around. Gaelen laces his fingers through mine.

"I think this means you're up, Love," he says as we walk into the circle, now surrounded by the dark stone.

My mouth dries as I take in the stone covering the ground we now stand on, etched with marks of the old language. A howl sounds from the forest, Fen walking out of the trees to our right. My heart leaps at the sight of him and what it means. I hear the surprise coming from Bjark and Theorin as Gaelen shakes his head at them when they grab at their weapons.

Fen steps into the circle with us, covering my fear with his resolve, until it is the only thing I can feel. I take one last look at each of them before reaching down and placing my hand onto the center of the circle, willing it to take us forward. When I look back up, we're inside the world tree.

# Chapter
# Thirty-Five

Standing inside Yggdrasil, it's as though my entire body has been awakened, a strange humming seeming to move through me. At the same time, it feels as though it's in every part of me, like this is the way I was meant to be.

"Does anyone else feel that?" I ask.

Gaelen looks at me, still holding my other hand.

"I don't feel anything," he says as everyone else shakes their head no.

We still stand inside a circle, but now it's much, much larger. And instead of towering stones, we're encircled by twisted archways, formed of branches or roots, filled with vales made of golden shimmers.

Between each archway lies darkness, should we step from the circle. I look around at each of them, ten in total, and I get the sensation that I could walk right through them should I wish, except for the last one.

In that last archway, clearly something is wrong. It's as though it's here, yet not, as though it was split from the rest, from the tree, but couldn't be entirely removed. Where the others are filled with a golden shimmer that moves and breathes, this one is filled with a dark smoke.

It moves within, but it cannot travel far, as if an invisible force is holding it back. I take one step closer, and the screaming that filled me before we entered the tree resumes. The power that was gifted to me, that belongs to me, unfurls, waiting. I know this is where Loki's power is locked, and I know this is going to end badly.

Before I can take another step forward, the sound of boots stomping in unison comes from behind us. Through one of the shimmering pathways, men walk forward wearing the black and red of Thokkra's guards, followed by the king and his witch.

I have grossly underestimated the size of this. I don't know how, but I know Thokkra alone doesn't hold the power to access Yggdrasil or to enter another plane. She has to be working for a god.

"You can do this, but it has to be now!" Gaelen says, grabbing each side of my face and making me look at him.

We should've run. I should've taken him and got on a ship, any ship, going as far away from here as possible. The likelihood we survive this has now dropped to nothing, and while his father may not kill him or Theorin, I know the rest of us won't make it out of here.

With the king here, we risk the chance of the power entering him before I can stab through the vale, destroying it. If that happens, I'll have to reach Gaelen's father and kill him before it takes root and he's able to harness it. The sound of our friends drawing their weapons and forming a line in front of us pulls me from my panicked thoughts. I'm wasting time I don't have.

I look back at the broken archway and notice the runes carved into the wood. I know if I reach out and touch them, I can alter them, their very purpose. Inside this tree, I know it's what I've been doing all along. Whatever is happening inside of me due to my being here is bringing a clarity of mind that I've never felt.

"How long do you intend to toy with the will of gods?" Thokkra yells. "They are vengeful, girl. This will not end well for you!"

I look back at Gaelen, who only nods once.

"Fuck the gods," I say, just before reaching forward and touching the runes, willing the lock to unravel.

I can sense that the magic in place here is old, not wanting to let go easily. When it finally lets go, the smoky power seems to fall forward a bit at first, not recognizing its freedom. I hear the king demand the men part as he pushes through them, coming toward us, lured by the power he craves.

Tendrils of smoke reach out, exploring, and I brace myself for what might happen if they reach him, my hand moving toward the ancient dagger at my waist. But the power isn't rushing away at all.

It's sinking into Gaelen's chest.

# Chapter
# Thirty-Six

What the fuck is happening?

I look up at him and find him staring at me, his face a mixture of sorrow and regret. My mind reels as he puts his arm around my waist, pulling me in. His mouth is against mine in an instant, firm and claiming.

Seconds ago, I felt as though I could've understood anything, my body so alive and in tune with the tree, and the magic. Now I have no idea what's happening. A pained exhale briefly halts our kiss, and then his mouth tries to claim mine again. I pull away to see the cause, and I find my dagger, the dagger I worked so hard for, lodged into his stomach, his left hand still on the hilt.

He used the kiss to distract me. Before I can even think, his weight is crashing into me. Someone yells for the king's soldiers to draw their weapons, and a fierce snarl comes from Fen, holding the king and his men back. There is so much yelling now that I can't keep track of who is saying what. I start to slowly lower us to the ground, trying to stop him from falling.

"What did you do?"

Tears start to stream from my eyes. This isn't good.

"What did you do?" That's all I can say, looking at the blade buried inside of him, the blood seeping into his clothing, and covering my hands.

So much blood, the metallic smell is already filling the air around us. Why this blade? If it were the other, we could've found a way to fix this. I would've made a way.

"What did you do?"

I keep repeating it, but now it comes out as more of a sob, as I'm unable to catch my breath. His eyes roam my face, a slight smile pulling at the corner of his mouth.

"I'm so sorry," he says, weakly caressing my face before his hand falls.

This can't be it. This isn't it. My breath comes too quickly. If one of us was going to die, it was going to be me. I wasn't prepared for this. I didn't allow myself to think of it. I wanted our future. This can't be all there is.

The shouting breaks through my clouded thoughts, everything still happening in front of us, as if there's anything left to fight for. As if he isn't gone.

Theorin is locked in a sword fight with his father. Somehow, Soren is here, dressed as a guard and aiding Bjark and Melda, trying to hold Thokkra's men back; Fen rips the throat out of one that gets too close.

"Move, I have to save the power," Thokkra yells at me, coming forward.

She doesn't know what this dagger means. Nothing can be saved now. However, I have no intention of letting her get close to him again. I'm moving before it even registers, but my mind is sluggish, and my body feels numb until Fen lends me his rage. I pull my other dagger, the one Gaelen made me, reaching Thokkra in just a few steps. She isn't a warrior, just a witch focused only on power, busy thinking she needs to block mine.

She doesn't even think about the physical harm I could do her. Only after I shove my dagger through her stomach, ripping upward as I go, does she look at me, unbelieving. I watch as she falls, waiting only long enough to ensure the light fades from her eyes. I should've killed them all before, never let them come this far. I should've killed her for what she did.

I release the nightmares I had yet to let go of, despite their demand from my emotions. The remaining guards all fall as I return to him, collapsing at his side and watching for the faint movement of breath that I know won't come—so much of his blood pools around us. I want to scream. I want to rip everything apart, but I can't move; the weight of it all holds me down. Fen comes close, letting out a whine, likely from all of my emotions he is being forced to feel.

I look to Gaelen's friends and brother, my friends, not sure how to tell them, but I don't have to say anything. They see it. Theorin has their father on his knees, sword at his throat. The king also looks toward Gaelen's body, and from the expression on his face, only then does the magnitude of all his errors hit him.

Soren stands frozen. Bjark comes to kneel on the other side of Gaelen's body, then his shoulders start to shake. As if Bjark's emotions are the confirmation that Theorin needs, he pulls his blade across their father's throat, and his body falls forward. We stay like this for a moment, silent other than the rasps of breath from the dying guards around us.

From another archway, in walks the Goddess of the Night. If I still harbored any doubt as to who she was when I met her, it fled at the sight. She looks around at the mess, at Fenrir, and then back at me.

"Much has changed since the last time we met," she says in the same melodic voice from before. "You cannot stay here. The gods stir. They will be on their way."

"I don't give a fuck about the gods. Let them come," I sneer back at her.

Anger shoots through her expression, but I know it's not from my disrespect.

"Your blood sings to the roots of the world tree, Child. Do you really think they will be content to let you keep it?" Her eyes are harsh on mine. "I am trying to keep you alive."

"I will not leave him here." Any strength I had remaining draining from my body at the thought.

"I will bring the trickster's vessel, and you will all come with me."

Gaelen, she means Gaelen. It was him the whole time. Shadows reach out from her, toward him.

"Wait!" I say, leaning over.

I grab his hand before kissing his forehead. Then I stand, soaked in his blood, and take a step back. The shadows cover his body before dissipating, and then he's gone.

I feel Fen's recollection before he comes to stand next to me, moving between my arm and body as the Goddess ushers us through one of the shimmering doorways and into her realm.

Chapter
Thirty-Seven

Gaelen

I know I'm dying.

I stabbed the dagger into my own body. But I know for sure, because, as if it were a parting gift, my mind relives the greatest day of my life.

Hagen introduced himself a few minutes ago, and I can't say I like the guy.

There isn't anything personable about him. I don't like the

fact that his sister is marrying some stranger he knows nothing about, and it doesn't seem to bother him, even if I'm the stranger.

There haven't been any new arrivals for some time, but when Saoirse finally walks forward, nodding to Hagen. I assume that's confirmation that Thyrvi's actually coming. I knew she would, but part of me was worried. Saoirse gives me an appraising gaze, like she's trying to decide if I'm good enough for her friend. I could save her the time and tell her I'm not.

Saoirse's parents come forward, and by the number of people present, I think that accounts for everyone from the village, even Erik, unfortunately.

Any thought I might have had leaves my mind at the sight of her. She walks toward me in a dress of the deepest black. The color contrasts with the pale skin of her leg visible through a slit that stops right before reaching her hip, competing for attention with the low cut of her neckline.

I hear Hagen let out an annoyed sigh from the spot next to me as the rest of the village gasps at the sight of her. I haven't been here that long, but I'd never seen Thyrvi dress like this. I don't doubt it was designed to send many messages.

The closer she gets, the more I notice the tiny stones pinned throughout her hair, which she left down, the curls falling around her shoulders. The shiny beads against her dark hair remind me of the night sky. She's the most beautiful woman I've ever seen, standing there like a goddess, and staring daggers into my soul. I know the rest of my life will be spent in worship of her.

The next few moments go by in a blur. I can't take my eyes off her, hoping to commit every bit of this to memory, the rage pouring off her and all, when suddenly her hand is in mine. I savor her touch as we're both wrapped with rope. The shuffling of feet and a throat clearing pull my attention from her skin against mine.

"Gaelen?" Hagen asks.

Thyrvi raises one eyebrow. Oh right.

"I do," I say quickly. If I weren't so focused on every aspect of her, I would've missed the tiniest twitch at the corner of her mouth. She might be angry with me, but she's also enjoying the effect she has on me.

As soon as she says, "I do", I'm leaning down, my free hand coming to tilt her chin up. My lips touch hers briefly before I pull away, and it takes every ounce of self-control I have to do so. From the look on her face, she also wasn't prepared for it to end.

My mind replays the spring, the way she looked in the moonlight, the mornings I woke up next to her, and her laughing with my friends.

Then I am no longer in my body. I stand next to her, looking down as she's bent over me, her tears mixing with my blood.

Her goddess storms in, and even though I can see them, it's as if I'm too far away. I can't hear anything they say. Thyrvi leans down to kiss me, and then it all fades away.

# Acknowledgements

If you have made it this far—thank you!

I started writing this book many years ago, and while the story has reshaped itself many times, the characters have always remained the same. At the time I am writing this acknowledgment, I have known Thyrvi for ten years, so finally seeing her story out in the world feels surreal.

I would like to thank a few people for their support and encouragement while writing this book—my husband, Justin, whom I met when this story was only three chapters in a Scrivener document, and who has always pushed me to write it.

My best friend, Sarah, and my sister, Kennedy, who were the first to read this book.

And finally, a thank you to those who are reviewing and recommending—thank you. The impact this has for indie authors is enormous.

I hope you stay tuned for book two!